PRASE FOR

"*Happily Whatever After* is a charming novel about falling down, getting back up, and chasing that elusive thing called happiness. I adored this book."

— Elin Hilderbrand, *New York Times* bestselling author of *Summer of '69*

"*Happily Whatever After* is a quirky, sweet story about second chances, family, and friendship. Stewart Lewis writes with a perfect blend of humor and wit and delivers a romance that is as hopeful as it is entertaining."

—Jennifer Close, bestselling author of *Girls in White Dresses*

"*Happily Whatever After* is a reminder that our lives can take shape in the most unexpected places. It's a hilarious romp that will make you laugh, cry, and then laugh again."

—Jessica Anya Blau, author of *The Trouble with Lexie*

"A smart, modern look at finding love and figuring out what really matters. Stewart Lewis has created a funny and sometimes poignant story of self-discovery with a moving family relationship at its core."

—Kerry Winfrey, author of *Waiting for Tom Hanks*

happily
whatever
after

happily whatever after

STEWART LEWIS

LAKE UNION
PUBLISHING

Text copyright © 2020 by Stewart Lewis Foehl
All rights reserved.

Published by Lake Union Publishing, Seattle

www.apub.com

Amazon, the Amazon logo, and Lake Union Publishing are trademarks of Amazon.com, Inc., or its affiliates.

ISBN-13: 9781542016407
ISBN-10: 1542016401

Cover design by Liz Casal

Printed in the United States of America

for oliver

If it weren't for second chances we'd all be alone.

—*Gregory and Ilan Isakov*

CHAPTER 1

Single, Broke, and Bitter

It was a well-groomed Scottie dog that first attracted me to what I called the Elite Dog Park, a mound of Astroturf in the shape of an elongated triangle tucked into a trendy section of the city near Dupont Circle. I was walking around aimlessly on an early spring day, and I noticed the dog's owner, dressed in a three-piece suit, cream on cream, right out of *The Great Gatsby*. He pulled out a shiny silver bowl from his leather briefcase and poured the Scottie some Pellegrino from the signature green bottle. The dog took a few licks and then smiled, as if all the other dogs were so beneath him, drinking (gasp) tap water that flowed from a little fountain in the corner of the park. What surprised me the most was that all the other dog owners didn't seem to notice. Perhaps they'd seen it before? I found my mouth agape, and I was magnetically drawn through the double wrought iron gates.

Of course, I didn't know that would be the day that changed everything. After four years of the disaster that was my relationship with Jack, I had also recently lost my job in New York City and moved in with my brother, Brady, in DC, where he was a trending restaurateur. His apartment, which he rarely spent any time in, was a modern penthouse in Logan Circle. It was super chic, with floor-to-ceiling windows, marble bathrooms, and a wraparound terrace. I showed up there jobless, penniless, single, and quickly approaching my midthirties. I would say it was the hands of fate, but they felt more like claws.

After another few licks of the Pellegrino, the Scottie just sat at his owner's feet, blinking slowly and looking around the park at the other dogs, which were mostly in a state of chaotic bliss. This little canine couldn't be bothered, and Gatsby had a similar expression, glancing at the vintage Rolex on his tanned wrist. He was tall and quarterback-handsome, probably in his midforties. I wondered if he was straight. I tried to imagine myself as his educated wife, spending my time throwing parties for charities, procuring art for billionaires, lunching at the club, aging gracefully in our beach house.

That sounded much better than reality, where I had wasted several years stupidly thinking Jack was going to ask me to marry him. We lived above a bakery, so our apartment smelled like butter and hope. It was easy the first year. We slept well together, the sex was tame but meaningful and sweet. The second year was a blur, both of us working too much and in our own orbits. Then the third year we caught some romance back, he kissed me down in the bakery and carried me up the stairs for some afternoon delight. Maybe it was all the cinnamon and sugar we were eating, but I could picture us together for the long haul, even though he had a patch of wiry hair on his upper back and I hated his mother. He could make a red sauce from scratch, had really good teeth, and was easy to be around. But then he withdrew again, and when I tried to talk to him about it, he was an emotional brick wall. The bakery shut down, and it wasn't only the air that went stale. Months went by where it seemed like he didn't even acknowledge that I was alive, that I lived with him, that I left signs-of-existence hairs on the sink, paperbacks on the counter, a scrunchie hanging on the door handle.

Toward the end, he reentered my orbit and started being really nice. We went to see this trendy band in Brooklyn and danced until we were sweating, and on the way home the Uber driver was texting and

Jack cursed him out. I had never seen him do anything like that, and it was kind of sexy. During that car ride, I had a feeling of something shifting between us, and I thought he was finally going to propose. I envisioned rose petals in our apartment, warm candles, one of his old-school Spotify playlists on.

When we got home, I snuck into the bedroom and changed into the sexiest lingerie I owned while he went to the kitchen for a beer. My heart was palpitating. I was reeling with possibility. I tried to sit on the bed casually, but every position seemed staged. When he finally came in, he had this really sad look on his face, like a toddler who had dropped his ice cream cone.

"Babe, I don't think this is working."

I could feel a drop in my chest, but I actually laughed a little at how ridiculous I was being. He was right. Our relationship was basically dinner and sex—we didn't have much in common after that. Marriage seemed to be more about what we were supposed to do, what others wanted us to do, rather than what was right for us.

Still, sitting alone in the dog park, I wondered what he was doing right then.

Probably making red sauce for one.

The benches for humans at the EDP were formed in squares, with cypress trees shooting through their centers, making them very strategic for eavesdropping. In an attempt to distract myself from thoughts of Jack, I listened to Gatsby. Even though I was facing away from him, I could hear every word he was saying, which was how I realized that "Barkley," as he referred to himself, was gay. He was confirming a pedicure for that evening, which some straight guys clearly do, but the clincher was when he called the person on the other end "Doll." As he hung up his phone, the Scottie decided to vaguely sniff the vicinity of my legs. I was wearing a skirt that had shrunk a little on its first wash.

If there was one physical quality of mine that stood out, it was my legs. In my teens, they scored me goals. In my twenties, they got me into clubs. In my thirties, at least for now, they stood the test of time. It was my *life* that needed a makeover.

How did I get to be thirty-four? I had been in DC for two months, and when I first got there, I went out a lot at the insistence of Brady. But then I started to avoid social gatherings, as the first question was, "Are you married?" Then: "Do you have kids?" Then: "Do you have a job?" I felt like saying, *None of the above! I'm a loser, okay? Now tell me about your doctor husband and your honor roll kids and your cottage in Nantucket. Then after that you can complain about your housekeeper.* Honestly, why was everyone so fixated on marriage and kids? Half of the parents Jack and I knew in New York were miserable. Their marriages had deflated after producing offspring. When we first started dating, we bonded over our slight disdain for kids. Cute for an hour, we agreed. Little did I know, Jack basically *was* a kid.

I reached down to pet the Scottie, and he dashed away as if he wouldn't dare be touched by a woman wearing a skirt from JCPenney. Barkley came over to my section of the bench, smiled, and said, "That's Sumner. He's not very social."

"Neither am I," I said. "Being social is overrated."

He looked at me then, *really* looked at me, like I was somebody. Not single, not jobless, not aging, but maybe a person who had something to bring to the table, something worthwhile, and he wanted to find out what that something was.

And then he asked, "So where's your dog?"

CHAPTER 2

HASHTAG GET OVER YOURSELF

I grew up in a WASP-y New England town where Labradors were like furniture—a fixture in everyone's home. Our first Lab puppies were a black and blond pair of cherubic beauties named Ringo and Paul after my dad's favorite Beatles. One Christmas morning he opened the kitchen door and they burst into the room, jumping over the presents, shredding the bows. From that moment on, I was a dog person.

Sumner began barking uncontrollably, which thankfully allowed me to avoid answering the why-the-hell-I-was-at-a-dog-park-without-a-dog question. Barkley snapped on Sumner's collar and apologized, yanking him away toward the exit, waving a quick goodbye. I waved back a little too enthusiastically.

What would I have told him? What would I tell the other people in here if asked? Why was I so nervous about being caught without a dog? I was sick of being an outsider. I just wanted to belong. I looked over at a tall, waiflike woman with an Italian greyhound who wore a wide-brimmed hat that made her look like a human umbrella. Her dog had the same terrified expression that was on her own face. They were both clearly hyperaware of their surroundings. I imagined she was a CIA agent, or a former assassin who was trained to kill within seconds (I obviously had been binging too much Netflix). Or maybe she was an ex-ballerina whose trust fund went to her meth habit. When her greyhound pranced over to sniff my legs (what was it about my legs?), I gently touched her impossibly delicate face. If I had a dog like this, I would always be afraid of snapping it in half. I like big dogs. Ringo, the blond lab I grew up with, was huge—you could literally use his body as a pillow. Jack didn't like dogs, but he kind of took the place of one. I'd spent many nights asleep on that big, booming chest of his, thinking it was all heading somewhere other than nowhere.

After moving from New York to DC, getting a dog was not an option. I needed a job before anything else. I had sent out some résumés, but the market was kind of depressing in terms of what was available, so I started going to the EDP at the ten and two o'clock hour every day, to have a schedule. Sometimes I read, sometimes I drank a cappuccino, and more often than not, the dogs would interact with me, bringing a little brightness to an otherwise bland existence. It was like therapy. Not only could I interact with my favorite animals, I could people watch too. The problem was, I'd have to come clean at some point. There were some folks who were starting to study me, wondering what I was actually doing there.

On the Thursday after I first pseudo-met Barkley, his snooty Scottie was at the dog park again, this time with a young man in a faded pink T-shirt and distressed jeans. It was the sort of outfit that was made to look like it cost $30 but was probably $300. Was he Barkley's son? Boyfriend? Dog walker? He sat down in the same place Barkley had, right near me on the circular bench. Immediately, Sumner trotted up to me, wanting another sniff at my legs.

"Oh, I see how it is, Sumner . . . ," I said. "Now you like me?" Sumner was clearly a snob, but there was no denying he was cute.

"Hey! You two know each other?"

I smiled. "You could say that."

It's amazing how some people thrust a door open when you merely crack it an inch. After that simple sentence, this kid went on a massive tirade about growing up, moving here, meeting Barkley, and the fact that he felt like a "total houseboy." I wanted to say, *It's that or your aunt's house in Ohio. Do the math.*

"And don't get me started on Sumner, who's a full-on hashtag nutjob," he said. "So is Barkley. Do you know he takes him to the dog spa every Friday, where he gets his nails clipped and his coat hand-sheared and, are you ready, a massage! I'm like, hello, I'm the *boyfriend*, where's my fucking massage?"

I laughed, and he rolled his eyes.

"Sumner freaks out every Friday 'cause he *hates* the spa. It's so weird, he totally knows when it's Friday. How in the world does the dog know it's Friday?"

I was a little confused. His train of thought was so tangential, it was difficult to decide which subject to comment on.

"You know he only got Sumner 'cause he saw a Scottie in a Polo ad?"

"Why not?" I offered.

He shook his head and sighed.

"And then there's Barkley and his suits. He wears them in the dead of summer. Even if he's just going to, like, the bank. It's his armor. Anything to hide the major issues underneath."

I nodded, even though I had no idea what he was talking about.

"It's sort of the same with Sumner. Barkley thinks if he just keeps the dog and himself perfect, everything will just turn out fine. Forget about global warming, or the refugee crisis, just make sure life looks glossy like a magazine."

I thought of my brother's apartment, mostly designed by his girlfriend. The bamboo plants in the blown glass pots, the gleaming Italian espresso maker, the thirty-dollar candles. He had done well for himself. In our twenties, Brady was just a dude working odd jobs. He would drag me to indie rock shows where I struggled to hear the lyrics, and I'd drag him to museums where he'd make silly remarks about the paintings. "He looks constipated," he'd say about a Van Gogh self-portrait, or, "I'd smoke a pipe, too, if I had to wear those flowers on my head," about Picasso's *Garçon à la pipe*. Then he got his act together, moved to DC and dabbled in real estate, made some seed money, and now the *Post* just gave his restaurant four stars.

"It's so sad, though," Barkley's boyfriend went on, "because the man has tried everything. You know, I've been dating him for almost two years? Before that, he had four years of Freudian therapy, like major, five days a week. That didn't work, so he became a Buddhist. Yeah, right. Then it was Yoga and Pilates—that lasted maybe a weekend. Now it's juice cleanses. I'm like, honey, look inside yourself! Your internal happiness is not going to come from cashew milk! Didn't you see *Eat Pray Love*? Hashtag get *over* yourself."

I felt a little accosted by his jabbering, but also slightly intrigued. He looked like he had just graduated high school, and the hashtag thing was weird. I considered asking his age, but before I could open my mouth, he started in again.

"Did you know Barkley's father was Bill Clinton's adviser?"

I took my hand away from Sumner and said, "No, that didn't come up."

"Well . . . are you ready? He was closeted! The man had sex with his wife once in his life, to have Barkley. Am I oversharing?"

I let out a noise not unlike a yelp.

"Sorry. Anyway, the guy hung himself when Barkley was thirteen. So his psycho mother just puts away the pictures, and they don't even have a funeral. Total batshit."

He put his hand on my shoulder and looked me right in the eye, as if we'd known each other for years.

"The scary thing is, Barkley never grieved. The man is pushing fifty, and it's like he's still that thirteen-year-old boy. A filthy rich, traumatized, scared-as-hell teenage boy."

He sighed again and pulled out a vape pen. "Super fun times. Anyway, I'm Preston. And I'm dying to know . . . Where's your dog?"

CHAPTER 3

BLANK CANVAS

Post college, I worked in a lot of restaurants in the Boston area, the kind with laminated menus and flat-screen TVs everywhere, just in case you needed five angles of a baseball player from where you were sitting. I dated the bearded bartenders with great smiles, popped Adderall with the skinny hostesses, let the busboys flirt with me. All my friends started getting married, and I was a bridesmaid a few times until I couldn't handle it anymore. Weddings were supposed to be these joyous occasions, but I sometimes felt they were kind of sad, with the gimmicky taco stations, the cupcake towers, the old-school photo booths, the inebriated confessions from random family members, all steeped in a sense of forced merriment. So I just stopped going, which ended up alienating a lot of my former friends. Even then, I was sick of the boyfriend/husband question. Somehow, "I screw bartenders who still wear themed pajamas" didn't seem like good conversation fuel.

In my midtwenties, I moved to New York and got a job as an assistant to a narcissistic TV actress named Sunday. She was really friendly until she could sense the connection between me and Giles, her sweet architect husband, which was not sexual but was significant nonetheless. Giles and I would pretend we were an old couple trying to find something we lost, or talk about how all our friends were dying. We'd imagine we were technophobic, saying stuff like, "Is Siri in the cloud?"

Our repartee was more of a betrayal for Sunday than if I'd been blowing him. I don't think she made him laugh, other than when he was laughing *at* her, like when she would ask if Denmark was a country, or if she looked fat in her pants due to the fact that she ate three peanut M&M'S. When she fired me, I wasn't surprised. I knew I needed to move on. But I did have a hard time saying goodbye to her Great Dane—for me it was always about the dog. He was a big, goofy hunk of love named Larry, and he looked at me with eyes that said, *please, don't leave me with her for the rest of my life, she puts me in kennels half the time, you're the only one who really cares except Giles and he's a workaholic.* It was as if his soul was pouring out of his eyes. I cried, of course, hugging the dog awkwardly in the entryway. "Bye, buddy," I said, and his soft whine literally broke my heart.

When I went back to her apartment a few days after to pick up my umbrella and a pair of shoes I'd left there, I let myself in (I hadn't returned her key, and the doorman knew me) and there she was, mid-screw with the handyman on the kitchen table, Larry curled up on the floor, half watching, half sleeping. It was such a cliché that the guy even had his tool belt on. I felt bad for Giles, but I wasn't going to get involved in that particular mess. I found the umbrella right by the door and sacrificed the shoes, leaving the keys with the doorman on the way out.

After that, I worked at a few art galleries, and eventually I managed one, and that's when I met Jack. He was the contractor who renovated the place. I kept noticing him out of the corner of my eye, and one day he brought me a flower, just one. It was odd, but I found it delightful. If only I could've seen it as a sign.

Managing the Sundaram-Tagore Gallery was not what I had dreamed my life to be, but it wasn't that bad. I loved being in the space, a giant white room flooded with light cast from high, rectangular windows. I found myself anesthetized by the whole vibe. No one spoke loudly, and there was a general hush continually present—the artwork reflected that, too, large canvases with washes of color, dark wooden sculptures of the female form, slightly out-of-focus portraits of the working class. Most of the people involved with the gallery were interesting, if dripping in ego. Those years were very pleasant—getting to know Jack, finding our cute walk-up above Breaking Bread in Greenpoint. I actually felt like I was on some sort of track. My mother was pleased as well, which always made my life more palatable. She was the one who'd taken me to museums when I was a girl. At first I'd hated it, but then I'd started to understand the spell a painting could put me under. The way that light on canvas could recreate life, the feeling that you could almost step into it. It was the way Brady was with music and food. In photographs of us as children, he always had headphones on, eating a fancy grilled cheese, and I was usually looking through an art book bigger than my head. I loved the vibrant colors of Klimt, the beautiful realism of Hopper, the chaos of Pollock. Standing in front of a painting, I would often feel the magnitude of the world beyond myself. That there was so much life and emotion being depicted, I could only begin to understand. It felt limitless, but also powerful, because I knew I was special. I was young, but I could understand it. I could see years of pain in the eyes of an old woman, or unfettered joy in the swinging arms of a boy on a ship. Even in the abstracts, I could just look at them and a mood would overtake me: melancholy, confusion, hopefulness. Later, when I studied art more closely in college, I was secretly thankful my mother had given me the chance to be one step ahead.

Unlike Sunday the actress, when my boss at the gallery, Liv, fired me, I was completely shocked. She told me that I needed to "find color" in my life. It wasn't that I was doing a bad job, but she felt I needed to "branch out" and "evolve." She said the words like they were a taste on her tongue, something she had been longing to describe.

I tried to collect my face, which seemed to have sunk into puddles on the floor. It was strange and sad to feel like you totally knew someone, worked with them for years, only to realize you were utterly disposable, like a gum wrapper or one of those tiny bottles of water. She just threw me away. Of course, this was also the week Jack broke up with me. I excused myself, trying to form a sentence but instead mumbling gibberish, and went into the claustrophobic staff bathroom to ugly-cry. Not because I had lost my job and my boyfriend, but because she was right. At thirty-four, I was a blank canvas.

I immediately called my brother, Brady, and without hesitation he said, "Come to DC. Come here. I have room. I miss you."

I missed him too. I missed his smile, which could melt a glacier. Every time I think back to our childhood, my memory is mostly muted, but I always remember Brady: he was the clarity, the color. Whenever I fell, his arm was automatically there to catch me. If I was sad, he would do this dumb dance where he'd swivel his hips to make me laugh.

"Okay," I said, and two days later I arrived. After I put down my bags in his foyer, Brady hugged me and spun me around, saying, "It's just a bump in the road!"

"More like an endless black hole in the earth," I said.

He laughed, and for a second my whole body felt light, not bogged down by anything. I loved the sound of his laugh.

"You always were dramatic, Page."

He showed me to my room, which was spotless and had the clean-line vibe of a gallery. I knew I'd be comfortable there, but I didn't want to just mooch off him. I'd have to contribute somehow.

"Come on, you must be starving!"

He took me to a Mexican place near U Street, and we ordered jalapeño margaritas. Both the bartender and one of the hostesses seemed to know who Brady was.

"So you're like, kind of a celeb now?"

"It's a small world, at least in the Fourteenth Street corridor. A lot of us know each other."

He looked different. I tried to picture the boy with fear in his eyes after spraining his ankle on the beach. The day I had to carry him even though I was half his size.

"I'm so proud of you," I said.

He waved away the compliment.

"It was good timing, all of it," he said. "I'm just lucky."

He'd always been lucky. In fifth grade, he won a raffle for a private tour of Six Flags. I'll never forget the look on his best friend Billy's face when Brady chose me as his plus-one. Venomous. But this wasn't just luck. Brady had worked hard to get where he was in life, and I was proud of him.

"So have you talked to Mom?" he asked.

"No, but I texted her. Sometimes I wonder if it's worth calling her. It's all about Charlie now."

"Yeah, did you know she asked me last week how the wine bar was? She still thinks I own a wine bar."

"Jesus."

During our second margarita, Brady started to complain about his unpredictable line chef who had been arrested, as if that were more important than my entire life falling apart. To be honest, I didn't mind—it was a much needed distraction. Brady had this way of bringing everything back to him without being rude about it. He was even more strikingly handsome now, with that sunshine smile and a remarkably fit physique despite hardly trying. Naturally, I was the one with love handles having a salad while he filled his six-pack with chips and guacamole. I secretly prayed for the day his metabolism would plummet.

When we got home that night, at the door to the guest room, he said, "It's yours for as long as you need it."

I hugged him, holding on tighter than usual.

"I honestly don't know where I'd be without you," I told him.

"Hey, everything will work out," he said.

I wasn't so sure.

After washing up, I crawled into the bed. The sheets felt like worn T-shirts, and Fiji water bottles lined the side table like a small army. A flat-screen TV was hidden inside a cabinet. It felt like a posh hotel. There were two framed pictures on the wall, both tasteful female nudes. I lay on the bed, staring at the curve of a breast, the soft blonde hair on a forearm.

As I closed my eyes and let my head sink into the luxurious pillows, I briefly wondered if Jack would call and say it was all a mistake. Then I fell into a deep margarita sleep.

CHAPTER 4

HOLY BANANA REPUBLIC

Preston took a long drag from his vape pen and waited for me to answer the dog question.

"I don't have a dog, actually."

There. I said it. And it didn't seem that strange. It was a park for dogs, but it was also a park.

"For real?"

I nodded my head. "For real for real."

"So wait, how do you know Sumner?" he asked.

"I come here a lot. I like dogs."

For Preston, that sufficed. He acted normal, like coming to the dog park without a dog was entirely acceptable. Then he launched right into another tirade.

"I can't stand spoiled dogs. Sumner gets on my last gay nerve. The dog is so entitled and barks nonstop the minute he's not being treated like the only living creature in the universe."

As if Sumner knew exactly what Preston was talking about, he let out a short succession of barks that might have meant, *you're the one who needs all the attention.*

"See?"

"Well, you have to admit he's cute."

Preston looked at me, and his face fell a little.

"But so are you," I added.

He smiled, then his expression turned back to neutral. He had pale-blue eyes and fair brown hair that was clearly highlighted with streaks of surfer-blond. From afar, one could call him an angel. But up close, there was a desperation about him, a need to be adored that was slightly off-putting.

"Thanks, girl. BT Dubs, what's your name?"

Well, that was a first. I hadn't actually properly met anyone (except canines) at the EDP.

"Page. I moved here from New York after I got fired and my boyfriend dumped me."

"What was his name?"

"Jack."

"I thought you were going to say Chad. I don't know about Jacks, but Chads are bad news."

"Good to know."

I flashed to Jack's face the last time I saw him, looking at me like I was just holding him back. Deadweight.

"I'm sorry about Jack, but welcome to DC! It's fun here. Colorful."

"I want colorful."

"We can be colorful together. Taste the rainbow!"

Now the desperation was gone from his eyes, and we were fast friends. Maybe I was the one who was desperate, and Jack was right— I'd dragged him down. I did feel that during my time in New York I was sliding off the surface of things, never really digging in. Before that, my passion in life had always been not having a passion. Although I did act and sing in a short film in college that won an award. But for the most part, I was an alienated art history major with questionable bangs.

"So what do you do here?" I asked. Then I added, "God I hate that question. And now I just asked it."

"It's fine. People think I'm a kept boy or whatever, but I'm not. I mean, I live in Barkley's house, but I'm a designer, working on my own fashion line."

"Wow!"

He saw me notice some grease on his hands and added, "Oh, I'm also an amateur plumber."

"What?"

"I worked with my dad when I was young, learned a lot. So I fixed the sink in the laundry room this morning, and Barkley almost shit a brick."

I laughed. "You never know when you'll need a plumber."

"I'm going to install a new toilet in the powder room too. That should really throw him for a loop."

"A man of many talents."

A lull came over us. Preston looked off into the distance. Then he abruptly turned and put his hand on my thigh. "So are you on the market now?"

"I guess."

"Honey, you're beautiful, and you're funny. We can definitely find you a man."

"A straight one?"

"That would probably be best. Let's see."

We both scanned the park. There was Umbrella Woman with the greyhound, the perpetually smiling woman with the chubby Yorkie-poo, and someone I hadn't seen before on the far side of the park. A tall man in a black windbreaker, his hair a little wild and multicolored, just like his two Bernese mountain dogs.

"Are you thinking what I'm thinking?"

I found myself blushing. A handsomely rugged guy with two big dogs?

"Banana Republic. Three o'clock," Preston said.

"His dogs are gorgeous."

"Honey, forget about the dogs. He's a super snack."

Preston was certainly right about that, although snack wasn't what I was thinking. More like five-course meal.

"What am I supposed to do, walk over to him and go, 'Hi, I'm a loser who has no life and no dog'?"

Preston pursed his lips, calculating. "How about you take Sumner over there? You can pretend he's yours! But don't tell him you're unemployed and undateable."

"What? Who said that I was undateable?"

"Well, why were you dumped?"

It was a good question.

"I'm not even sure, really. A switch went off inside him. And me, I guess. We just didn't fit anymore. But sometimes I think I still love him. Like you can't just stop loving someone."

"Honey, I hear you, but you gotta get into the headspace of being single and raring to mingle." He handed me Sumner's leash. "Now go over there and work those J Law legs of yours."

When one has reached the lowest of lows, things like walking over to a stranger with a borrowed dog from a gay amateur plumber seem actually doable. I literally had nothing to lose.

So off I went, and Sumner seemed happy to follow me. As I got closer, I realized Preston was spot-on. He literally looked like he had just stepped out of a Banana Republic ad. Slightly wrinkled khakis, a royal-blue button-down under the windbreaker, and an assured but not too cocky look on his face. Big hazel eyes and full lips, a whisper of salt-and-pepper stubble.

I walked right up to him and said, "Hello there."

"Oh, hi," he replied. "Wow, he's a winner."

Sumner barked as if in response to the compliment.

"He's kind of moody," I said.

We looked around the park. His two BMDs were bumbling around, their torsos trying to catch up with their limbs, chasing a miniature pinscher.

"What are their names?" I asked, pointing in his dogs' general direction.

"Dumb and Dumber," he said.

"Really?"

He half smiled and shook his head. "Pinot and Cab. The smaller one's Pinot."

"Ah, so you must be a wine person?"

The more this guy appealed to me, the more my IQ seemed to plunge.

"Yeah. I own a small vineyard in Virginia."

I could almost hear Preston saying "OMG." I looked over, and he gave me a not-so-subtle thumbs-up.

"That's great. I love wine." After a short, painful silence, I added, "Especially with painkillers."

He looked at me with wide eyes and grinned. It never failed to surprise me—a flash of a boy coming through a grown man. He was so perfect that I thought he must have cut-up bodies in his basement, or an unhealthy obsession with Jimmy Buffett. Or maybe he wears those shoes with the toes.

"Kidding. Mostly."

He chuckled, and again the boy came through. He looked at me like Barkley and Preston did, like I mattered, and I was starting to get used to it.

"So, umm, do you know that person over there?"

He was referring to Preston, who wasn't doing a good job of acting normal.

"Yeah, that's my nephew. We don't let him out of his cage much."

"Ah. Well, I think he's trying to get your attention . . ."

Nephew? Where had that come from? Now if I actually *did* date him, not only would I have to confess about not owning Sumner, but having only recently met Preston. Upside, it would be a good story for our grandchildren.

He tilted his head a little, as if he was debating giving me his number, or pulling out his phone to take mine, but then he just shrugged and smiled. "Well, it was nice to meet you."

"Thanks!"

I tried to walk slowly back to Preston without appearing like a dog park model, the Astroturf my runway.

Thanks? Why did I say that?

Preston was so impressed he could hardly contain himself. "You slayed it. He watched you the whole way."

"Well, it wasn't half as awkward as I expected it to be. And you're not going to believe this. He owns a winery, and the dogs are named Pinot and Cab."

"Shut up. And, I know he's straight 'cause he hasn't looked at me once."

"Does every gay man look at you?"

"The hot ones, yeah."

Oh, the hubris. Maybe that's what I needed. I'd spent my whole life in the background. I could never be that woman, the one who has her own successful business and dates sexy men who owned wineries. Or could I?

When I returned home after meeting Preston and the god that was Banana Republic, I drew a bath in Brady's master bathroom and grabbed some chardonnay from his sleek wine fridge I could barely open. I played the new Robyn song on my phone, which I set in a glass, and danced a little while I took my clothes off. I knew that BR liking me would be a bit of a stretch, but I did make him laugh. Twice. It was a tiny seed of hope, and right then, I clung to it.

CHAPTER 5

Hot Mess in A Black Dress

The next day, after googling every winery in Virginia and not finding any proprietor that looked like BR, I figured I'd work on real life and not the fantasy one. I started emailing more résumés to the galleries in DC. Unlike before, I felt a small sparkle of possibility every time I hit send and heard the *swoosh* sound.

It was a dry, crisp day, so I celebrated my extensive job searching with a ride on Brady's fancy hybrid bike along the Potomac River. Like any city river, it looked nice from afar, but you wouldn't dare imagine what was beneath the surface. Appliances, the body of an old car, corpses wrapped in plastic and held down by bricks. The scene above the surface was the opposite. Sailboats darted around the shimmering water, and the people I passed, on bikes and otherwise, seemed content and carefree, nothing like the resting New York scowl face I was used to. Washington, DC, in general, seemed more approachable. Tourists fed ducks and joggers smiled, while an old couple sat on a bench sharing a sandwich, watching the world go by. The world was clearly in chaos, but not right there. Looking at the scene, one would never guess our country was at war, kids went to bed hungry, or school shootings were becoming commonplace. I could hear the sounds of birds, the laughter of children, the gentle lapping of the water over the rocks. I wondered, as I had since I arrived, what I was actually doing here. How had I lived so much of my adult life with basically nothing to show for it? Still, I knew I was way better off than a lot of people in the world, and I felt a wave of gratitude as I rode faster, strands of my hair catching the wind.

When I got home, I took a long, hot "rain" shower and created a mantra in my head: *boyfriend, job, dog. Or maybe job, dog, boyfriend. Or boyfriend, dog, job. Whatever.* I put on one of Brady's pale-blue shirts and my favorite pair of jeans and headed back out to grab a coffee at the corner. The guy with the sleeve tattoos washing the windows smiled at me. Could he see my deep desperation or my wellspring of potential?

When I got to the EDP, freshly showered, coffee in hand, I didn't recognize anyone. There were only three people there, so it was blatantly obvious that I came without a dog. A young girl with a pug smirked at me, an old guy with a terrier gave me a quick wave, and a very large man with a golden retriever squinted in my direction. I sat down and opened the paperback I had found on the street for a dollar. I tried to hide the cover—a soft-focused, shirtless man on a horse. The book was so bad it was good. I became so engrossed that I'm not sure how long Barkley and Sumner were there before I noticed them. No Pellegrino this time, but Barkley, dressed in a gray striped suit, carried a container of what looked like homemade dog treats. I walked over to him, and he immediately recognized me, letting a smile slide over his face.

"You really don't have a dog?" he asked.

"No. Did Preston tell you?"

"Yes. You're a mere observer, then?"

He sounded like he was trying to speak old English or something. I hoped it was a one-off and not a regular thing.

"Dogs make me happy. Just being around them."

He seemed to weigh my answer in his head. Then he approved with barely a hint of a nod.

"Plus, they don't talk," he added.

"Yes, there's that."

We sat and watched Sumner avoid the pug who had crazy energy, practically jumping on top of me. I imagined if the whining between the licks were actually diction it would sound something like, *oh my god I can smell everything you just ate and there is too much freedom in this park and why can't I catch any of the squirrels and I can't ever remember being this hungry in my life oh my god I know you're not my owner but DO YOU HAVE ANY TREATS?*

I smiled as the pug finally tired of me and scrambled to the other side of the park.

"That dog reminds me of Preston," Barkley mused.

"Yeah, he's pretty intense, huh?"

"Yes," Barkley said. "Good or bad, he'll always make an impression."

"Mostly good," I said.

"Did you know he's a clothing designer? He could whip something up for you."

"Are you implying I need better clothes?"

He laughed now. "On the contrary. You look great. Office chic."

I would have preferred gallery chic, but coming from Barkley, I couldn't complain. His cuff links had diamonds on them.

"Do you dress like that every day?"

He nodded proudly. "Yes, I do. It's just me. Also, I feel like people respect you more when you're well dressed."

"Is that what you're looking for? Respect?"

"There's a better word. Reverence, maybe."

"Well, let me just bow down in front of your holiness."

He laughed again, a little louder, and it reminded me of Jack. Jack never laughed unless he meant it. That was always a good quality in a person.

"I like you," Barkley said, while Sumner looked at me suspiciously. "You've got a bite. You'd be great at a dinner party."

I didn't know whether that was a compliment or not. I smiled a little, and Sumner let out a quick, sharp bark. Clearly, Barkley was giving me too much attention. He picked Sumner up and put him in his lap, and honestly, the dog looked at me as if to say, *he will never love you like he loves me.* At that moment, I couldn't tell if Sumner was more like Barkley or Preston.

He put Sumner down and fed him an artisanal dog treat that was shaped like a bunny.

"This is going to sound strange, but I like to collect people," he said. "And I'd love you to be part of my collection."

Was he serious?

"Okay, but I'm not a tchotchke."

He handed me one of his embossed cards, which probably cost a hundred dollars each:

BARKLEY McFADDEN
202-867-4533

"Why don't you come over on Saturday night. Seven. Wear an LBD."

What was it with him and Preston and the acronyms?

"I could manage that. Shall I bring anything? Some caviar? A case of Cristal?"

He giggled, and Sumner's whole body shook, and I could almost hear him say, *you think she's funny now, but she's toxic, let's get out of here.*

"Just that smile and a *great* attitude," Barkley said.

"I can manage that."

"Perfect. Bye for now, dear. Say bye-bye, Sumner!"

The dog snorted in disgust and shuffled away.

I stayed for another hour, reading my awesomely horrible book but also looking up whenever I heard the clink of the metal gate to see if it was BR and his varietals. But alas, it was just the usual suspects: Umbrella Woman with the greyhound and the ever-smiling woman with the overweight Yorkie-poo, which I started to refer to (only in my mind) as Porkie-poo. The dog definitely needed a diet. Maybe it should go vegan.

That afternoon, on the way back to Brady's house, I shopped for a little black dress, even though the last thing I should've been doing was spending money (new Page needed a new look). After finding one that properly accentuated my legs at an adorable boutique off 14th Street, I felt a false sense of power, which led to getting my hair and nails done (more debt for my credit card—yay!). The hair "designer," as she called herself, encouraged me to grow out my bangs, and the manicurist upgraded me to the "crystal gel," whatever that means. When I got back to Brady's place, I put on the dress, looked at myself in the mirror, and cried. I was a mess. There were moments, and this was one of them, where I really missed my father. I knew if I could call him, he would somehow make me feel like less of a failure.

Brady came home right then and threw down his keys, running over to me.

"Page. What's wrong?"

He hugged me and I thought, *I have a brother.*

"I just don't know who I am anymore. If I wasn't staying with you, I'd be one of those crazy ladies on the street wearing leopard print on leopard print and lipstick that didn't quite make it to my mouth."

He started to laugh.

"It's not funny."

"But it kind of is. Come on, we're going out. You look great, just pull it together."

And that's what I did.

CHAPTER 6

LOST AT SEA

Brady could get as excited about a turkey sandwich as the latest obscure indie rock record. Tonight it was a pop-up restaurant on a boat that was shipwrecked in a parking lot in Shaw. In the Uber on the way there, Brady was smiling ear to ear, and since his smile was infectious, I joined in.

"You know, you've had the same smile since you were a baby," he said. "My earliest memory is the day you came home from the hospital. You had a pink hat on, and your tiny fingers kept grabbing at the air. And you were smiling."

"I'm pretty sure that was gas, Brady."

He laughed, which was my favorite sound ever. It was more of a *woop* than a *ha*.

We stood in front of the shipwrecked boat, which looked like a movie set. Halogen bulbs hung from ropes, and a DJ dressed like a captain played a track that was slightly cacophonous and dissonant.

"This sounds like Funny Bone!" I said.

"One-hit wonder."

In our early teens, we started a faux band called Funny Bone. We had a logo and everything. Brady could sing, and I was pretty good on backup, but neither of us could really play any instruments. I set up some pots and pans and tried to mouth bass lines while Brady—clearly the front man—would do air guitar on the kitchen counter. Our one song was about catching our principal with his pants down.

"But you were good with the utensils," he said. "Real talent."

The hostess knew exactly who Brady was, seating us at a small table in the bow. I looked at the menu, which had phrases like *farm sourced* and *cage free* and *cucumber air.*

"Air? I think I'd rather have a cheeseburger."

Brady chuckled. "It is a little over the top. But it's comped."

"Good. Because air is expensive."

Brady looked at me, and in a flash I could see a hint of our father, the way his eyes caught the light. It made my insides feel hollow for a second, but then I just felt happy that I was there, lost in the moment, dining with my brother on a boat. We might as well have actually been on the water, nowhere near the land.

"You just reminded me of Dad," I said. It had been ten years since he passed, but "passed" sounded like he was transferred somewhere else, when really, he was just gone.

"Yeah. It might be this," he said, pointing to the little bits of gray prematurely growing at his temples.

A guy who was apparently the chef (I could tell by the Crocs—what was it with chefs and Crocs?) came over and slapped Brady on the back. They started to talk shop, so I excused myself to go to the bathroom.

When I got back to our table, Brady had ordered us a bottle of wine. While he poured me a glass, he said, "Page, I was thinking . . . you should put yourself out there. I'm going to introduce you to someone. He's slightly older, but . . ."

"Wait a second. Why does everyone, including me sometimes, think that a man will solve everything?"

Even though the boyfriend was on my list, I wanted it to be organic. It was exhausting to think about how much of our actions were based on need of approval from others.

"Well, it's either that or focusing on a career."

"I know, I know. Another thing I need. That's actually first on the list."

We each took a bite of our "deconstructed nachos" with cheese that wasn't cheese and sour cream that was made from almond milk.

"Well, I have a lead on a gallery job for you too."

I took a huge gulp of the sulfite-free wine.

"Well, I appreciate it. I binge-sent résumés to all of them, but I'm not even sure I want to work in a gallery again. For someone else, that is."

"Then what would you want to do?"

A young, beautiful beaming couple next to us fed each other bites while laughing.

"Maybe be them?" I suggested.

Brady sighed. "That stuff fades. You need long term satisfaction."

"I'd take a one night stand at this point."

"Seriously, Page, what would your dream job be?"

"I honestly don't know." I looked up at the mast, the sail slightly fluttering. "Can I just be lost at sea?"

He sighed and took a sip from his glass.

"Look, I know you found your calling or whatever . . ."

"Page, running a restaurant is not my calling. A couple years and I'm out. I'll be moving to some wide-open space. I don't know, get chickens."

"Chickens? Okay, if anything, you'll always be able to make me omelets."

"What about sales? You're funny and endearing. You always have been."

"Endearing? That's more like you and Dad."

"Listen, Page, it's not the end of the world. You're thirty-four, not seventy."

The waiter came with "palate cleansers," which he lowered in slow motion. Tiny blue bowls of shaved ice infused with fresh grapefruit and "ghost mint."

"So it's just the ghost of the mint, right?"

"Essence of mint," Brady said, playing along.

"Whatever it is, it's the best thing yet," I said.

"The next course is a bowl of unicorn tears."

I almost thought he was serious, but then he started giggling.

"This is a really good Malbec, though, eh?"

We clinked glasses, and then it was me who sighed.

"I like that dress, by the way," Brady said.

"Well, I actually got invited to a dinner party by a friend from the dog park. Which is why I got it."

"The dog park?"

"Yeah, remember? I told you about it. I've been going there every . . . a lot."

"You don't have a dog . . ."

"I'm aware."

"Hmm. Okay. Well, it's a good way to meet people, as long as they don't think you're stalking them."

"Well, I am, a little, I guess."

"Hey, why don't you start a dog walking company? In the meantime, I mean."

"Yeah, then maybe I'll expand to a lemonade stand!"

"Just saying. Dog walkers can make bank . . ."

The evening continued as such, with Brady trying to be helpful and me getting more and more cynical as each highly manipulated food item was placed in front of us.

On the way home, I made him stop at Five Guys, where I wolfed down a greasy burger under the neon light of the sign. It tasted like heaven.

CHAPTER 7

DAY DRINKING AT THE DOG PARK

The next day, the EDP was packed with a lot of people and dogs I didn't recognize, but the upside was that no one seemed to realize I was dog-less. I got some good squeeze time with a droopy-faced bullmastiff and threw a ball for a graceful Skye terrier.

Still no sign of Banana Republic.

I read more of my trashy novel until I heard someone clear his throat right near me. It was the large man with the golden retriever.

"Excuse me, I was just wondering. Do you have a dog?"

At that point, I didn't really care what people thought. Surely there were weirder things to do than go to a dog park without a dog.

"I just like dogs, really. I don't own one right now."

"I knew it. One day I counted the number of dogs, and there was one extra person." He said this like it was some huge revelation.

"Wow. You must have been on the math team."

He chortled.

"This may sound strange as I don't know you, but I'm looking for someone to walk my dog three times a week. Would you consider that? I could pay you, of course."

I looked at his sad retriever, who was lying down in the dirt part of the park, licking himself in a half-ass way, like his paw was chewing gum that had long lost its flavor.

"Sure, I basically have no life right now, so why not."

I handed him my phone with the notes app opened.

"Oh, excellent. Not about the having no life part!" He typed in his email, then handed me back my phone. We shook hands. "It's Bond. Kevin Bond." He smiled.

"Doesn't really have the same ring to it, I'm afraid," I said.

"I know, but it's fun to say. If you wouldn't mind, email me a reference or two?"

"Will do," I said, unable to keep from smiling. As Kevin sauntered away, I thought, *Maybe Brady was right.* A dog-walking job just *walked* into my lap. Who would I give as a reference, though? I imagined my former boss, Liv, getting a call from Kevin, thinking it might be some sort of prank. I chuckled at the thought.

"Wait a second, you're going to walk that dude's dog?"

It was a young woman, around my age, maybe a little younger, with beautiful sun-kissed skin and a small Louis Vuitton bag, scooting closer on the circular bench. Her eye makeup was intense, and her teeth were perfect. In her lap was a tiny, white, fluffy cotton ball of a dog whose eyes were nowhere to be seen.

"I've done worse things," I said.

"Ha. Me too," she said, letting her dog down on the bench. "Go play, Beanu."

The dog was not having it and just jumped back up on her lap. She grunted.

"Beanu?"

"Yeah. I just made it up. You like it?"

"Interesting."

"She's a teacup poodle. Three pounds."

"Wow. Needs to lay off the carbs."

"Yeah, maybe a juice cleanse?"

She smiled, but her face didn't move that much. I wondered if it was filler. About a dozen silver bracelet bangles rattled as she fixed her hair. "I'm Nadine," she said. "And I know you don't have a dog. I've seen you here before. I'm cool with it. But I seriously think you should reconsider walking that guy's dog."

"He seemed harmless."

"Don't they all."

"Think I can handle him?"

"I guess. But maybe don't go *in* to his apartment."

"That may be a challenge."

She scooted a little closer, placing her manicured hand on my forearm.

"So I'm dating this guy, and my family, who are all kind of snobs, love him. Absolutely love him. Then with me he's like, really emotionally abusive. One time he told me that if I died, no one would miss me, no one would care."

"How touching."

"Right? He's just wicked salty. And he wears turtlenecks."

"So why are you with him?"

"'Cause it's familiar, I guess. My father wasn't the warm and fuzzy type. And he's pretty good in bed. Not my father!"

I laughed, wondering if she knew Preston. I bet they'd hit it off.

Nadine pulled a fancy water bottle out of her Louis Vuitton and took a swig. From her devious smile, I could tell it wasn't water. She handed it to me, and I thought, *Why not.* I took a sip, and it was definitely not H2O. More like a G and T.

"Yum," I said, handing it back.

Beanu licked Nadine's chin, and she cooed to the dog.

"She's adorable," I said.

"Thanks. She's constantly petrified. She peed on my cashmere scarf the day I got her, and I was like, oh, welcome home, bitch."

We each took another long swig, and I could feel my body temperature warming up.

"Those are cool," I said, pointing to her bracelets.

"Thanks. I made them," she said, like it was nothing. It wasn't nothing. They were unusual and beautifully designed.

"Wow."

"I take a class. It's kind of a huge commitment."

"Bigger than Beanu?"

She laughed, and as we continued to sip from her "water" bottle, I told her about how I ended up in DC and my Banana Republic dream.

"So what's your deal, anyway?"

"It's kind of a long story," I said.

"Let me guess, you're looking for your happily ever after?"

"Something like that."

"Yeah, join the club." She sighed. "I think we should just lower the bar. Like, it's okay if we end up with some guy who owns a bowling alley and has a mullet."

I laughed.

"I think I'm just gonna sit here until Banana Republic comes back."

"Sounds like a plan."

So we did. But BR never came. And after drinking more of Nadine's "water," I started feeling a little woozy, so I excused myself.

"Oh hey, here's my card, come take my class sometime!"

I looked at the card. Underneath a flying lotus were the words FREESTYLE FLOW WITH NADINE. On the back it said, FIRST CLASS FREE.

"Wait, you teach yoga?" I said.

"I do. I teach yoga, make bracelets, and shop."

"You forgot day drinking at the dog park."

"When necessary," she said, holding up the now almost empty water bottle.

"Well, thanks for this, and the libation. If he comes, don't steal him," I told her as I headed toward the gates.

"How will I know him?" she called out.

"Oh, trust me, you'll know."

CHAPTER 8

REAL ART

It took four inches of Brady's small batch bourbon, but I wrote a cover letter to Kevin and pressed send, closing my eyes and bracing myself for the sound of the *swoosh*. For references, I put my former boss Liv (what the hell) and Langhorne, an artist we represented at the gallery in New York. In the four years I worked there, Langhorne was the one artist I actually discovered.

I was at a party in Bushwick before it was chic, in a warehouse, where everyone was doing Molly (I declined, not wanting to end up petting strangers all night). I had been invited by my colleague Andrea, who wasn't even there. I drank two warm beers by myself in the corner and then left. On my way down, the elevator stopped on the third floor and opened into an artist's space. Paint and canvases were everywhere, and it smelled of turpentine and coffee grounds. The beers had given me enough confidence to walk in, and I stood right in front of the piece that would eventually go in the window of the gallery. It was a giant canvas with hundreds of photographs adhered to it. Old pictures, of people, all turning away from the camera. From afar it looked like a painting, because of the way he infused the pictures into the canvas with oils. When someone takes a picture of me, I'm usually the one who looks away, which I suppose is what drew me to it. It was one of the most beautiful things I'd ever seen, but I couldn't exactly explain why.

Langhorne came out of the bathroom as if he was expecting me. He had grayish hair and lanky limbs, handsome in a goofy, unkempt way. I apologized for barging in. He waved at me like it was nothing.

"I actually manage a gallery," I added.

"Well, maybe it's my lucky day," he said.

He showed me the rest of the pieces, five total, and they all had the same feeling, but the pictures were different. In one there were pictures of roads, in another, windows. I remember having this sense of something coming alive inside me, like my heart was one of those balloon guys outside of car dealerships that fill with air and swing around. I wanted to raise my arms up and say, "Yes!" I knew it was real art.

I basically forced Liv to go there the next day, and it all unfolded pretty quickly, as these things sometimes do. His first show was put up three weeks later. It sold really well, and of course, Liv took all the credit. Except, during the opening reception, when Langhorne raised his flute of champagne and told the packed crowd, "And most importantly, to Page, who has a keen eye and blind courage, and who is responsible for me being here tonight." Liv shot me a look, but I didn't care. He was right. I was the one who had literally stumbled upon him and recognized his talent. From then on, he always had a soft spot for me. I once dog sat for his pit bull, Boomer. I wondered what he would say if Kevin called him.

That night, I got pulled into sleep easily. Maybe it was Nadine's secret gin and (a little) tonic. I dreamed that I was Liv (glamorous, bilingual, rich) and Liv was me (bored gallery manager, pretty enough, always making coffee). We were playing bocce in some bar, and I (as Liv) was kicking ass.

When I woke up, I thought to myself, that's it. Since forever, the one thing that I was really passionate about (besides dogs, soccer in high school, and Monet in college) was Langhorne's mixed media paintings. Maybe I could start my own gallery. Why should I work for someone else again? All I needed was truckloads of money. I didn't have any myself, but I seemed to be surrounded by rich people, so that was a good start.

CHAPTER 9

Is Anyone Straight?

Barkley's house was one of those old yellow Victorians set back from the street in Georgetown, with impeccable landscaping in front, including fountains and torches. It was the rare occasion where over-the-top seemed just right. I was greeted at the door by a houseman in a bow tie who led me into a sitting room where Preston was curled over an antique table, rolling a joint.

"Page! I'm just having a little smoky treat before the guests arrive. Care to join me?"

I hadn't smoked pot since college. "No thanks, maybe later."

"Ok. Mauricio, could you get this fab woman a cocktail?"

Preston rushed out of the room with his joint, and Mauricio, an extremely good-looking man with perfect olive skin, asked me what I would like to drink.

Even though I felt like I should be ordering a sidecar or a mint julep, I decided on a vodka tonic.

"Of course, Miss . . ."

"Page. You can just call me Page."

"Great. I will be right back."

The room looked like my grandmother's house on Cape Cod, but slightly modernized. Floral patterns on the couches to match the drapes, wicker chairs with ornate legs. Of course, this stuff was most likely "acquired," whereas my grandmother's furniture was simply passed down from previous generations. It was strange how new money sometimes tried so desperately to be old money.

Mauricio came back with my drink, and I sat alone, sipping it while listening to the sounds of a crooner coming out of hidden speakers. I flipped through *Departures* magazine until Preston came back in, a little glassy eyed but still pretty adorable. I wouldn't dare say handsome, as he looked like he belonged in a dorm room rather than at a dinner party.

He started rearranging a silk scarf in different styles in front of a gilded mirror. "What do you think?"

"Honestly? I'm not sure it's working. It's more of what Barkley would wear."

"You know what, you're right. He tries to dress me up sometimes. He told me when I moved in that jeans were not allowed. That lasted like a day. How can I not wear jeans? That's like asking someone not to breathe."

"Jeans are kind of ubiquitous," I agreed.

"Right? So this personal trainer is supposed to come, and a few of Barkley's friends. Of course, they'll probably hit on me. It's so tired, these old queens with wandering hands." He sighed wearily, throwing the scarf in a nearby closet.

"I can only imagine. How did you and Barkley meet?" I asked.

"On SCRUFF," Preston said, as if that was totally normal, which it was, but I just couldn't imagine joining one of those apps myself. "He picked me up in his vintage Rolls, and walked me into Minibar, that place that's like, out of a Bond film. At dinner, he recited Shakespeare by heart. I didn't understand it, but it was super romantic. Barkley can turn it on when he wants to, but as you know, there is baggage. Most of us have carry-ons, but he needs a U-Haul. Where the fuck *is* he by the way?"

"Couldn't tell you."

"Let me go see. Can I get you anything else?"

"A side of Mauricio," I said, but he was already out the door.

A few minutes later, Barkley and Preston came into the room, each carrying what looked like cosmopolitans in chilled martini glasses.

"So," Barkley said, "I see you've met the missus."

"Dream on," Preston said. "I'm not your housewife."

"Well, you do look smashing in an apron. Just an apron, that is." Barkley smiled and sipped, proud of his comeback.

"Besides, you know we met at the dog park. Is your early dementia kicking in?"

I took a big sip of my drink and waited for something to happen.

Thankfully, Barkley suggested we go outside, onto the "lower patio" in the back. Must be nice to have your choice of patios. In New York, I only had one, also known as the "central fire escape."

Not surprisingly, Barkley's patio was right out of *Better Homes & Gardens*. Everything was done in soft, muted colors, all linen and wool—much more understated than the sitting room. I immediately felt more comfortable.

When we got settled, Preston pulled out his vape pen, and Barkley rolled his eyes. "Such an unattractive habit."

"Yeah, well, I'm sure you've popped like ten lorazepams today, so get over it."

I laughed, and Barkley looked a little betrayed. Preston blew out vapor dramatically and said, "Page, I'm dying to know. Have you seen Banana Republic again?"

"No, but you know the big guy with the retriever?"

"Yeah . . ."

"Well, he asked me to be his dog walker."

They both looked at me like I may be certifiable and were considering uninviting me right then and there.

"Isn't that hilarious? Me, a dog walker."

They both laughed to fill the silence. I was trying to be myself, but I guess I didn't know who that was anymore.

"I also met Nadine, with the teacup poodle. Do you know her?"

They both shook their heads.

"She's a trip."

Mauricio led in a fair-skinned, regal-looking man around Barkley's age. He wore a Hawaiian shirt with several platinum (mixed with what looked like diamond) bracelets on his wrists.

"Ah, if it isn't the King of Austria," Barkley said. "Michael, you know Preston, and this is my latest conquest, Page, working the little black dress."

I found myself blushing. Was anyone straight? Mauricio? Highly doubtful.

As if on cue, another man was led in who was, in fact, straight. At least it seemed like he was, but how can you really tell? Joseph, who Barkley introduced as his trainer, got closer and closer to me during the cocktail hour, and it made me a little uncomfortable. His teeth were blinding, and his eyes were huge. By the look of his legs, he could probably hike Kilimanjaro in an hour. He was very interested in me, probably because I was the only woman there. He asked where I lived, and I didn't say with my big brother. Then he told me that I had nice skin, and I told him he did, too, and he smiled like he already knew that.

By the time we were moved into the dining room, I felt a little tipsy. I told myself to go easy on the wine, but it was so good, every sip a special gift. Joseph was next to me, and Michael was on the other side. I could see why Barkley called him "Michael of Austria." He had an imperial tilt to his head and a striking confidence. From what Preston had told me in the hallway, his family owned all the Austrian media outlets, and his brother was running the business since his father had passed.

Michael had been "exiled" to the States because of his "lifestyle."

The dinner was exceptional. Grilled salmon with crispy brussels sprouts and a butter lettuce salad with tangerine and goat cheese.

During dessert (berries, foam, and a tiny cookie), Barkley started talking up his favorite play, *Full Gallop*, about former *Vogue* editor Diana Vreeland.

"I *love* red," he said, doing what seemed to be a pretty spot-on impersonation of Diana. "It's the great clarifier. Curiously, I *loathe* red with any orange in it."

Everyone laughed, even Joseph, who clearly didn't get it.

Mauricio came in with a tray of cappuccinos, and I could hear Sumner barking from whatever room he was confined to. Barkley went on to his impression of some singer who sounded like a baby, and the laughter continued. I popped the last berry into my mouth and thought, *Where the hell am I? I hardly know any of these people, and I'm half-drunk sitting next to the King of Austria.* One of the things I did notice, however, during the course of Barkley's histrionics, was Preston. I could tell how much he idolized him, how his bitchy queen persona had left his face entirely and was replaced with a simple boy in love. It was sweet, until I realized that more likely it was a boy infatuated with cashmere and foam and microcookies.

It felt like school. We were all shifted to a different portion of the house for each part of the evening. We ended up in what was called the parlor, on white leather chairs adorned with silvery-blue pillows shaped like large tubes. Preston and Barkley started talking under their breath, and it was clear there was some sort of disagreement. They left, and so did Joseph the trainer, but not before giving me his card with a hand drawn face on the back, one eye blinking.

So it ended up being just me and the guy who everyone called "Michael of Austria." I know it sounds absurd, but that's how he was referred to and it somehow worked. I didn't dare ask his last name. Mounted on the wall above his head was a sculpture by an artist Liv had represented in New York, Patrick Blaine. It was a face that was partly chewed off, as if a shark had taken a bite of it. Blaine was known for pushing the envelope and meshing genres. Michael of Austria saw that

I was looking at it and said, with a thick accent and a deep voice, "It is a beautiful piece, no?"

"Slightly disturbing as well, but yes. Blaine."

At the mention of the artist's name, a light switched on behind his eyes, and he smiled this wonderful, broad smile. I could feel a shift in the air. It may have been a combination of the Grey Goose, the '91 Bordeaux, and the Italian cappuccino (who knew, the little cookie could've been an edible), but he was clearly impressed that I knew the Blaine. He told me he had three Blaine pieces in his backyard. He also said something about some skulls, very precious ones. It was all blurring a bit for me, but even through the alcohol haze, I could see the recognition in his face, like the look Barkley first had at the EDP, and Banana Republic a little too. I was being *seen*.

Michael of Austria, who had taken his cookie with him, took a bite and froze, his mouth locked in an oval shape. At first I thought he was being dramatic, but then his eyes burned with a palpable fear. I knew right away, even in my inebriated state, that something was terribly wrong. The cookie was caught in his throat. Michael of Austria couldn't breathe. He started to rock his head a little, as if he was about to pass out, and that's when I felt adrenaline rush into my blood. In that instant, I became sober, remembering distinctly the time I learned the Heimlich maneuver in eighth grade. I just jumped up and scooted my body behind him, squeezing my arms around his torso, trying to remember the right spot, and then I pulled in and up at the same time, and it worked exactly as I hoped it would. The cookie, or rather, the almond that was on top of the cookie, probably imported from some special nut farm in Spain, literally shot out of his mouth and across the room, and he said, "Oh, oh, oh God," and his head dipped like he was about to faint. Then Barkley came into the room, and by the look on his face, he was definitely confused as to why I was embracing Michael of Austria from behind.

"He had some trouble with your cookie," I said, catching my breath.

"Your nuts almost killed me," Michael said, and then we all started laughing, and Barkley had Mauricio bring us more wine. The three of us toasted like everything was normal and Michael hadn't almost choked to death. My inebriation came back tenfold, but I was glad to have been useful.

This is what I remember about the rest of the night: Michael of Austria's chauffeur-driven Bentley, how it smelled like cigars and made me dry heave. He kept smiling at me, like it was so natural for us to be together, like I was some kind of angel. We went to a convenience store for bottled water, and I saw my reflection in the window. I was definitely wrecked, but I looked okay. Maybe Brady was right. Thirty-four wasn't the end of the world.

When I got out of the car, Michael just said, "See you tomorrow."

I laughed, fumbling for my set of keys.

CHAPTER 10

HUNGOVER ON A HORSE

I woke at noon to my phone buzzing through the tiny pocket in my LBD, which was clumped in a pile on the floor. My head was throbbing in the same rhythm. I had three texts from Michael of Austria. He must have given me his number, or maybe Preston did.

I have a lunch but how about 2pm

I will send a car for you at 1:15?

What the hell? Did I say something to him last night? That I would meet him? Or does he just assume that whenever he beckons, people will come to him? How does he even know Brady's address? Oh yeah, duh, his driver dropped me off.

Wear jeans and boots.

Huh? I reached for a water bottle next to my bed and chugged the whole thing.

We can take horses out if you like.

I looked at the screen, shaking my head a little. Of course. But where were we going to ride horses? In Dupont Circle? Then I remembered he had said something about a country house.

My phone rang, and it was my mother. I answered right away.

"Hi, Mom. You never call me. What's up?"

"Are you still in bed?"

"No, I just ran a 5k and now I'm painting the kitchen. Are you at Charlie's?"

My mother had been dating a married man for three years, so one could easily deduce where my expertise in men came from.

"Yes, we're at his lake house. Any luck on the job front?"

"Yeah. I'm going to walk this guy's dog."

"What?"

"Nothing. I got here weeks ago, Mom. Can you just tone it down?"

"Well, I worry. You know me, worrywart."

"Well, five chardonnays a night is probably not helping."

I was one to talk. I smelled like a distillery.

"Sorry," I added.

Silence. My mother never admitted the fact that she was an alcoholic. Brady and I called it "the slur" when she called after seven o'clock. When it started happening in the daylight, we knew there was an issue. But what could we expect? Our father had died ten years ago, and her self-medication regime moved from anti-anxiety pills to large amounts of cheap wine. It could be worse. If I had lost my husband of over twenty years, I probably would have chosen crack. It was hard enough being the daughter. Grief changes shape, but it never goes away.

"How is Charlie?"

"Fine," she said, in a tone that meant it was the end of the conversation.

It was admittedly hard to picture her with anyone else. My father was one of my favorite people in my world. He had the power to make me feel like I was the center of the universe. I still have all the letters he wrote me in college, preferring real ones over email. He loved to watch (and gamble on) sports, and I still get emotional when I hear sports announcers on TV.

"Call me when you get a job," she added.

"Is that all you care about?" I asked.

"Well, a boyfriend too."

"Mom!"

Yes, these were both things I wanted, but I didn't need my mother breathing down my neck about it. Especially when she barely called me anymore. Was that why? Because I was somehow broken?

I took a long shower, and it felt really good. I thought about the dinner party, how it was a world completely outside of what I was used to, but still kind of felt like one I belonged in. While I was drying off, my phone buzzed again. Another text from MOA:

car coming

So I was going horseback riding with Austrian royalty. Not exactly what I expected, but better than what I had originally planned for that day, which was nothing.

When I got in the car, a silver SUV this time, I air-kissed Michael. In the rearview, the driver gave me a knowing look.

"How are we feeling today?"

It was all coming back to me. The driver was from Berlin. I had practiced my terrible German on him last night, and he'd laughed at me.

"Tip top," I said, giving him my best smile.

The ride to the Shenandoah foothills was only about an hour, and MOA kept going on tangents, talking about the Olympics, then refugee camps, then his love for Taylor Swift.

"What is it about her that you love?" I asked.

"She is so so so so clever. Her breakups, her insecurities, she turns them into hits!"

"That's true," I agreed.

"And she is like the anti–Barbie doll."

I wasn't sure about that, but Michael seemed so convinced I didn't say anything.

"So what brought you to DC?" I asked.

"Well, I was going to move to California, believe it or not, and my plane got stuck in DC. And one thing led to another, as you Americans say."

"I never say that."

He laughed. "Of course you don't."

"Did you really move to the States because of your family?"

"Well, when my father died, the ground shifted. Everyone thought I was the one that was going to be in charge of the family company. But I don't want that pressure. I am working to raise money for solar energy, and I'm investing in start-ups. I work when I want."

"Sounds ideal," I said. "But do you miss them, your family?"

"My mother, yes. She owns a lot of art. Unusual things. She always consulted me, you see, even when I was a little boy. In some ways, I've been curating her house for my whole life."

"How fascinating."

"My brother I don't miss, because we are always sparring."

"Ah."

"I miss my friends, but I have made a lot here. It has become my home. At first accidentally, now permanently."

The large highway turned into a smaller one with a few strip malls, then we wound up into the hills. I couldn't believe we were suddenly in such a bucolic setting while just having left DC.

The massive white gates of the country estate opened slowly, and we drove the half mile down the long, curvy driveway that led to the main house, which was regal and square—not a palace, more like a fortress. There was, however, a tennis court, stables, and a glistening amoeba-shaped pool. He didn't give me a tour as one would expect, but instead rushed me down a walkway toward the stables.

"You will ride Lila," he said, pointing to a perfectly white mare, saddled and ready, looking calm and super tame. "And I, of course, will ride Sterling."

Sterling was jet-black and shiny, with a soft, sweet look in his eyes. I put my hand on his neck and felt his warmth.

"Wow. They're incredible," I told him.

"Yes, and now we ride!"

Ten minutes later, with the help of his two stable workers, we were mounted and off, trotting along a stream, the angled sun shooting laser-thin lines of light through the trees. I felt like it could have been a commercial for something random, like when you're watching amazing footage of people in nature, and then it turns out to be about toothpaste or laxatives.

We came to a stop to let the horses nibble on the tall grass, and Michael pulled out what looked like a joint, but could have been a rolled cigarette. He was European, after all.

As we started walking the horses farther down the path, I asked him how long he'd known Barkley.

"Two, maybe three years. Barkley is so much about appearances it can be exhausting. And half the time he and Preston aren't talking about what they are talking about, do you know what I mean?"

"Yes. I feel that way about everyone."

He laughed, then coughed a little, offering me the joint. I hadn't been on a horse in years, and I was really hungover, so I thought it might not be a good idea. But even so, I may have been getting a contact high, because I started to feel lightheaded and calm, as if there were nowhere else I'd rather be.

"Thank you, for last night," he said, his eyes glossing over a little. I wasn't sure if it was from pure emotion or if he was just high. Was it one and the same?

"No prob," I said, like it was nothing.

His face turned peaceful and content, and it felt like a door opening.

"Can I tell you a theory I have?"

"Of course."

"Okay. I believe there are five types of people in the world," I began. "One type is what I call 'Airport Bar People.' You know, someone you would meet in an airport bar. An insurance agent, or a midlevel executive. People that are easy, nice, good for a couple one-liners, but basically like extras in the movie of your life."

We crossed the stream and headed up the path on the other side. He seemed intrigued, so I went on.

"Another type is what I call the 'Bright Lights.' People who challenge you, and shift the natural order of things. The curious and super talented. People whose faces you could stare at for hours on end. The ones that are always there for you."

He nodded, showing me that broad smile again.

"Then there's the 'Hangers On,' which Barkley probably has a lot of. These people are parasitic, like they can't exist without having a grip on someone else.

"Then of course there's 'Family,' which in most cases requires a double shot of Patrón and some mild prescription drugs to manage."

"Ha!" he said, and even Sterling gave a little neigh.

We paused to let the horses start in again on some more grass by the edge of the stream.

"What is the last one?"

"Huh?"

"You said there were five."

"Oh, yes, well the last one isn't a type of person really, it's someone that sometimes comes along or doesn't. It's your 'True Love.' Unfortunately, I don't really know about that from experience."

"You are a romantic?"

"Not really. Maybe that's the problem."

"So which type are you?"

"Airport Bar, definitely. I'm in the background. But I feel like that could change, is changing. It's ideally not a static environment."

"And me?"

I ran my hand through Lila's mane.

"Well, I guess I've never met anyone like you. I'd have to create a whole new category."

"Good answer," he said, gently kicking Sterling with his heel, initiating a trot. Lila followed, and both horses locked into a rhythm, then grew into a canter, and for the first time since leaving New York, I felt the weight of Jack lift from me. I didn't need him anymore, because I had what was in front of me—a big scary unknown, but it was mine.

CHAPTER 11

Karma's an Uber-Bitch

Brady was standing in his entryway when I walked in, and it gave me a start. He was never home, and I felt strangely invaded, even though it was his apartment and I was the interloper.

"Hey, Page, what's up?" He looked tired and stressed, which I assumed was related to his job.

"Well, I've just been for a horseback ride in the Shenandoah mountains with the King of Austria."

"What?"

"It's a long story."

"Well, you look good. Windblown."

"You too," I lied. But the truth was, even tired, Brady was good looking. And like our father, he knew how to charm a woman.

I watched him straightening the cuffs on his shirt and sighed.

"What?" he asked.

"Nothing. You just remind me of Dad all the time now."

"Well, I'll take that as a compliment."

His phone dinged, a reminder for an event tomorrow. I was close enough to see the screen. It said, *2pm, Dr. Langley.*

"What is that?" I asked.

"Nothing. Just routine stuff."

"Hmm, okay. Well, it better be."

Every time I saw the name of a doctor or drove by a hospital, I always got a sinking feeling. Even though he left us behind to pay for some of his bad financial choices, my father could do no wrong in our book. He was the glue of our family, and while my mother and I fell apart when he died, Brady ended up turning his life around and taking control. Although, watching him right now, fixing his hair in the hall mirror but getting frustrated, I sensed a tinge of panic behind his cool facade. I made a mental note of the doctor's name so I could google him later.

"I'm off to a soft opening at this place in the Navy Yard. I'd take you with me, but it's only a plus-one and I promised Jane."

"Of course, no problem."

Jane, or "Perfect Jane" as I called her, was Brady's girlfriend. If she wasn't doing Pilates, she was saving the world. Jane was the only person I knew who carried a $10,000 handbag to work at a nonprofit and no one flinched. I had recently been to "girls' night" at her house, a party for three of her girlfriends she threw once a month. That was where they first bombarded me with the husband/kid/job questions. They were all five years younger than me, in sweater sets and pearls, with fiancés and husbands and summer houses on the shore. Perfect Jane and her perfect friends. I remember being insanely jealous, but also somewhat baffled. Yes, Jane actually had a meaningful job, but when the hair was done and the bills were paid and the cars were detailed and the homes were secure, what else was there? Was it just a vacuous sense of happiness? Or were they truly enlightened? They all had blonde highlights and fillers, and they constantly talked about Pilates and dieting. It seemed to me that they were Hangers On, clawing to money and status and outward beauty, but what did I know, really? Would I turn that life away? Probably not.

Brady noticed I was trying to hide a scowl, and he gave me a puppy dog look.

"Are you still bitter about girls' night?" he asked.

"No, I actually like Jane. It's her posse of housewives, who I like to affectionately call the 'Sweater Set,' that can grate on me."

Brady smiled, then checked his teeth and put on his jacket.

"I know you kid about it, but isn't that what you want, Page? Not to be a housewife, but to be in love, get married?"

"Well, I thought I did. Now I'm not really sure. Maybe I'll start with a date."

"Weren't you just on one?"

I thought of Michael bringing me into his bedroom to show me his rare skulls after our horse ride. It was a little creepy, but he still had this gentle, trusting way of looking at me that may have been partly sexual. Or was he just grateful I swooped in for the almond debacle?

"He likes me, but I'm not sure in what capacity. Hard to tell which team he plays on. From what I've heard, I'm guessing he's fluid."

"Wow. How evolved."

"Anyway, we bonded over Blaine, the sculptor. The one Liv represented in New York? He's got three of them in his yard!"

"Aren't those really expensive?"

"Yes, it's about two million. For art in your yard."

"Not exactly the garden gnome variety."

"I think he's lonely. His family is really high profile, and apparently he was banished to the States. Most everyone he knows is still in Austria."

"And how exactly did you meet him?"

"Through Barkley at the dog park."

"Barkley McFadden? That's where you went to dinner? Oh my God. Did he do his impersonations?"

"Yes! How do you know him?"

Brady gave me a look, like he was trying to tell me he knows more than I think he does.

"I actually met him at a charity event we catered, but then he hired Jane's nephew."

"Huh?"

"To mow his lawn. It didn't last. We went to his house, and he was hitting on me, even though I was there with Jane. Did you see his collection of Belgian loafers? He has them in like, thirty colors. The guy's interesting, but a bit of a quack. I see it hasn't taken you long to prey on DC's elite."

"That's the thing. I'm not preying on anybody. I just go to the dog park!"

"Well, I never thought I'd say this, but I think you should keep going. And I want to hear more about Mr. Austria, but I'm late."

"Maybe when I'm Mrs. Austria," I joked.

He kissed me on my hand, something he never did until he started making money in DC.

After he left, my phone buzzed. It was my mother. Twice in a day? I knew something must have been wrong, so I picked it up.

"Hello?"

"Charlie's dying."

I did not become alarmed. My mom was a total drama queen. Every issue was treated like a one-act play. Sometimes I pictured the sound effects, the curtain being raised, her standing in a spotlight.

"Mom, you've been saying that for a year."

"Yeah, but . . . it's not good, honey."

Brady and I were glad she had found someone, but not thrilled that Charlie was married, and that she basically checked out of our lives after meeting him. They were high school sweethearts and hadn't seen each other since they were sixteen, and several years after my father died, Charlie had heard the news and got in touch with my mother. He came over, and after dinner they started dancing, right into the bedroom. Forty years later. Romantic, but the guy was a dick if you asked me, saying how much he loved my mother all the time, but then never leaving his wife. Same old story I guess. Now he had some sort of brain tumor, which actually didn't surprise me. Karma's an uber-bitch.

"I'm sure he'll be fine, Mom."

"I don't know what I was thinking, seeing him all this time. But he's the only other man I've ever loved besides your father."

"Well, maybe it's time to start thinking about someone else. Preferably someone that's available and not . . . dying?"

She laughed a little, then said, "All right, well, I'm going to come see you guys soon, I told the Bradester."

That was my father's nickname for Brady. I felt a pang but shook it off.

"Okay, Mom. We'll have fun, just the three of us." I sounded convincing because I was. Even though she had gotten more fragile and high maintenance in her sixties, and you had to seriously monitor her wine intake, I could use a mother.

Before the sun went down, I took a walk down Q Street and looked up at the scattered clouds. It was another beautiful day, and summer felt imminent, like children in a ballet waiting in the wings, ready to flutter onto the stage. City birds flew in circles around the church, and a young couple stopped to watch. I thought about Brady's question. Would I really have married Jack if he had asked me? If I did, would I just become a part of the Sweater Set? I wanted to be in love, not in a situation. I wanted to be a Bright Light, not an Airport Bar. Everyone always tells you to be yourself, but what if that is something that isn't stagnant and keeps evolving? When do you actually catch up with it?

The EDP was pretty much empty except for a sad-looking woman with a poodle. She asked me where my dog was, and I just shrugged, changing the subject. "Can I ask you something?"

She didn't say yes, but she didn't say no.

"Do you think everyone should get married and have kids?"

She raised her penciled-in eyebrows. "Overrated. I've had two husbands—one's dead and the other's a drunk—and two grown kids that don't even talk to me."

"Wow, you're batting a thousand."

She smiled and touched my arm. "Why don't you start with a dog? They really make great companions."

Unbelievable. How did she even know I was single? Was I that transparent? I did want a dog. Badly. I had even started researching some adoption places online. But that piece didn't fit into the puzzle of my present life.

To avoid any future sympathy from Pencil Eyebrows, I busied myself with my phone, googling the doctor that came up on Brady's screen earlier. *Langley, MD*. As it turned out, it was a woman, with braided blonde hair, breasts that seemed to defy gravity, and bright-blue glasses. She looked like a female doctor in a porn movie. The thought hit me like a slap in the face. Was Brady having an affair? With a gorgeous doctor, probably the only woman in DC who was more perfect than Perfect Jane? Is that why he acted shady when I saw his phone? Did they roleplay, and did she give him "checkups"? I would have to get to the bottom of that possible rabbit hole.

I traded my phone for my cheesy paperback, suddenly desperate to find out if the surfer/cowboy/hunk was going to wake up from the coma. After a while, two dogs barreled up to sniff my legs. My breath actually caught in my throat when I realized who they were—Pinot and Cab.

CHAPTER 12

WHO KNEW?

I tried to breathe normally, scratching behind their irresistible dog ears, then looked up casually, hoping he couldn't hear my rattling heart. But Banana Republic wasn't there. Instead, it was a girl wearing an oversize sweatshirt and skinny jeans. It couldn't be a girlfriend, unless BR was a cradle-robber. I put her at about fourteen. She came over and smiled at me, saying, "Sorry, they're super friendly."

"Not a problem. They're so beautiful. Pinot and Cab, right?"

She looked at me funny, then said, "Yeah. Do you know my dad?"

"Yes, no. I um, just met him briefly, here." *And I just want to spread him on a piece of toast,* I didn't add.

"Oh, cool. Where's your dog?"

"The invisible one!"

"What?"

"Kidding. I just like coming here."

Cab, the larger of the two, seemed suddenly exhausted and plopped down at my feet, crossing his two front paws in a sort of doggy dance pose.

"He didn't eat his food today," the girl said. "Which is weird. Must not be feeling well. So wait, you really don't have a dog?"

"No. But I will soon."

"Oh-kay," she said, half mocking me.

I quickly tried to figure out how to get dirt on BR without her thinking I was more of a freak than she already thought I was.

"Do you take them here a lot?"

"Yeah."

"Cool."

She gave me a skeptical face, like I was too old to use that word. Cab started sniffing my calves.

"He likes you," she said.

"Dogs have a thing for me. Men, that's another story."

She smiled, and I could see a little bit of BR come through her. It was enough to make me blush.

"So I guess you aren't married then?"

There it was again. Even from a teenager! I shook my head, expecting pity, but she seemed to get it.

"Marriage is pretty jacked-up, anyway. My parents split when I was eight, and it happened to three of my friends' parents also, like all in the same summer."

"The great summer of failed marriages."

"Yeah. I'm definitely not getting married. Well, maybe when I'm old . . . like, in my thirties or something."

That stung, so I looked away. Pencil Eyebrows was picking up her poodle, and the last rays of sun had dipped behind the trees. The girl pulled out her phone and started texting furiously. I secretly hoped her text was something like this:

Omg Dad this woman from the dog park is super nice and really pretty—maybe u should date her?

But it was probably more like this:

Dad-I met the dog-less dog park lady. Coming home early.

I attempted to read my book again but realized after a page and a half that I hadn't been taking it in. Instead, I'd been picturing myself as this girl's stepmom. I didn't like small children so much, but taking one on at that age would be perfect. I rested the book on my lap, closed my eyes, and took a deep breath.

The dings and whoops of her texts kept coming and going, until she put her phone back into her pocket and began to slowly pet Cab, who had goop in his eyes. Pinot was at the other end of the park, smelling a particularly interesting part of the fence.

I tried to read again, but stopped midsentence at the sound of her voice. She was singing softly, as if trying to figure out a melody in her head. It was a voice that seemed to be coming from another person entirely. Someone way older, from another time, maybe behind a piano in a smoky bar. I pretended not to listen, but it was like a personal serenade. When she finished, she stood up, smiling again. "Well, I have to bail. Have fun with that classic you're reading."

She was on to me.

"Tell your dad I said hi."

"Sure. What's your name?"

"Page."

"Cool. I'm April. My dad says I was born in winter, but it felt like spring."

I made a noise, as if I was slipping into a hot bath. BR had a daughter who was smart, funny, and had the voice of an old soul. Who knew?

I watched her gather up the dogs and lead them to the exit.

As she waved once more from the sidewalk, I chuckled to myself. To think I could fit into a family with dogs and a winery and a stepchild—was there more than one? I secretly prayed that April would say nice words about me, something that made BR realize I might just be his destiny. Or maybe he had remarried, or worse, had a younger girlfriend. But April didn't mention anyone, which was a good sign.

When I got home that evening and opened my inbox there was an email from Kevin.

From: Bondkevinbond@verizon.net
To: Gallerygirl654@gmail.com

Page—

Thanks for your note and very impressive references! I would love to have you walk Sammy. Not sure what your schedule is, but I'm guessing right now it's wide open? I need someone three times a week, maybe four. I could pay you $25 a walk. I'd love you to come over and hang out with him in his own space first, so text me whenever. I work for myself, so I'm pretty available.

Best,
Kevin
202-569-8576

Wow. How did he know that my schedule was wide open? Was it really that obvious? The words *love* and *come* and *hang out* in the same sentence kind of freaked me out, but $300 a month was a start. I could help pay some of Brady's bills. Or, at the very least, buy my own wine so I could stop drinking all of his. I poured myself the last of the bottle of Riesling from the fridge and texted him.

Hey there it's Page-

Sounds good. How about tomorrow at 3 pm?

I was actually giddy. A dog walker? Maybe I would start an empire. Page's Pooches.

I decided to open another bottle of wine and settle down in front of Brady's mammoth flat-screen TV. I ended up watching three episodes of *Broad City*, courtesy of Hulu on demand. My last thought before falling asleep was, *At least I'm employed.*

CHAPTER 13

RETHINK THE KALE CHIPS

In the morning, as I was cleaning up my room, I came across the card that Joseph, Barkley's trainer, had given me. After some coffee and two bowls of Brady's Kashi Go Lean, I decided to call him. He seemed very Airport Bar, but I was slowly becoming more emboldened by the fact that I had nothing to lose. Besides, I was Airport Bar myself.

He answered on the first ring, which was not a good sign, but I went with it. It took an awkward minute for me to explain who I was, and I realized he must give his card to women all the time. Still, he asked me to lunch, and after an intentional pause, I said yes.

The place was called Sweetgreen, and it only served salad and frozen yogurt. We waited in line for about ten minutes, during which he scrolled Instagram on his phone. Even though I ran the Twitter account for the gallery in New York, I never got into the whole social media thing myself. I am old school. Besides, it's all so "Look at how much better my life is than yours!" Do I really need to see the soup you're about to eat or know that you've "checked in" to Starbucks?

"I bet you get a lot of likes," I told him.

He smiled and then gave me a strange look, which I was completely used to at that point.

We finally got our salads and sat down. Mine had chicken and cheese in it, at least, but his was vegan and sprinkled with kale chips. He talked about the weather (boring) and then started complaining about one of his clients (double boring), and I already wished I didn't let him take me to lunch, because now I had to sit there and pretend he was interesting. He was handsome, for sure, and definitely ripped, but his personality resembled his teeth: white, overpolished, and square. While he talked, I kept my face completely neutral, like I was reading the ingredients on a cracker box: *Whole grain wheat flour. Vegetable oil. Salt.*

"So I never got to ask, what do you do?"

"Mostly I just go to the dog park," I said, smiling. The truth was all I had. Set me free.

"Oh, what kind of dog do you have?"

"I don't have a dog. I just go there because I'm trying to find . . . a life, I guess."

"A life?"

Where would I start with this guy? He had the personality a filing cabinet.

"I'm in sort of a gray area right now. I'm broke, jobless, single, and already heading to the middle of my thirties. My womb is drying and no one's buying."

He laughed, but I stayed deadpan. I took a bite of my organic, marinated chicken, and suddenly the salad tasted amazing. I chewed like I was some kind of ravenous animal saving up for the winter.

"Well, you certainly have a way with words."

"So do you, Joseph!" I exclaimed with my mouth full.

Normally, I would have been mortified by the situation, but I was actually enjoying it. He smiled again, and there was a sodden kale chip covering one of his front teeth, making him look sinister. Instead of subtly giving him a sign it was there, I started giggling uncontrollably.

"What's so funny?" he asked.

I just shook my head and held up my hand.

There were people hovering, trying to get our table, which was good, because we both finished fast. Outside on P Street, he suggested we go back to his place. I couldn't believe that after our obvious lack of chemistry, he still wanted to hook up. Even though he probably would've been a great lay, I feared I would just keep thinking of the kale chip. I told him maybe another time. After we parted, I watched him taking selfies while he walked away. Next.

CHAPTER 14

AVERTING DISASTERS

Kevin Bond lived in a basement apartment of a row house on T Street. Everything seemed walkable from Brady's apartment, which was great because I certainly couldn't afford a gym membership.

On my way, I noticed a couple fighting in the street. The guy was kind of up in the woman's grill, and I knew it was none of my business, but I stopped and watched, positioning myself behind a tree so they couldn't see me. I quickly realized from the bangles and the flowing auburn hair that it was Nadine, from the dog park. Now I could understand why she was day drinking. This guy was accusing her of flirting with some guy at the bank, when she was actually admiring his "fucking shoes," as she put it. Just as it was getting more heated, I walked right up to them and said, "Nadine? Hey!"

"Hi," she said, obviously a little embarrassed.

The guy, who definitely had a resting mean face and seemed fueled by that special kind of anger that comes from lack of sleep, walked right up to me, inches from my face. He smelled of cigar and cheap whiskey. I looked at Nadine, and she actually laughed. Then *he* laughed, and the tension broke, like someone had reached out with scissors and cut the taut string between all of us. We stood there in silence, until Mean Face said, "I gotta bounce," which sounded strange coming out of his mouth.

When he was beyond earshot, Nadine put her hand on my shoulder. "I'm sorry about that . . ."

"It's fine. But wait, he doesn't hit you, does he?"

"No, he's kind of a pussy. I guess he tries to make up for it, like some display. But it's all bark, no bite."

"He wasn't exactly exuding warmth," I said. I didn't tell her I was afraid, but I was for a second. One of the bartenders I'd dated in Boston would sometimes get in my face like that, being all alpha, and it was pathetic but also scary.

"Is there anything, you know, good about him? Besides, you know, the bedroom?"

"I'm still trying to figure that out," she said, laughing.

"Well, be careful."

She sighed, then said she had to go teach yoga, but I didn't think it was true because she seemed a little tipsy. "Thank you," she added, winking at me before walking in the same direction Mean Face had.

As I continued to Kevin's, I thought about the bartender again, how he could be sweet when he wanted to, but how it was all tainted. There was something broken in him that would never be fixed. It was probably the same with Mean Face.

When Kevin opened the door, he seemed even larger in the threshold of his tiny apartment, like he might just implode.

"Hello, welcome, welcome," he said. "How are you?"

"Well, I just had lunch with a narcissistic trainer who had kale in his teeth, so it has to get better from here."

He laughed, but it was more like a wheeze. I reminded myself not to make him laugh too much so he didn't die on me. Hopefully there were no almonds in sight. In his modest living room that smelled of dollar store candles, he brought me a glass of water in a smudged glass. Sammy, who had been half-asleep in the corner, perked up at another presence in his kingdom.

"I spoke to one of your references, the gallery owner? She was very complimentary."

"She better have been. The woman fired me after four years so she could bang a grad student."

He laugh-wheezed again, this time slapping his knee. Sammy got up and sauntered over to us, a worried look in his eyes. Maybe he'd never heard Kevin laugh that much.

After giving me the key to his apartment and showing me the little closet where he stored Sammy's treats, he handed me the leash, and I felt a sense of power and responsibility.

"He always gets two treats after his walk," he said.

"Got it."

A few minutes later, there I was, walking Sammy down T Street, working! When I got to the EDP, I felt proud to actually have a dog with me, and I was thrilled to find Preston, eating a slice of pizza while Sumner drooled at his feet. Nadine, who seemed to have completely sobered up since a half hour ago, was sitting right next to him, now with tiny Beanu shaking in her lap.

"Wait," I said. "You two know each other?"

"We just met!" Preston said.

"Just stay away from her water bottle," I said, sitting on the other side of Preston.

I set Sammy free, and Nadine gave me a look.

"I thought you had a yoga class?"

"I had someone cover for me."

I nodded. It was girl code not to pry further.

"So did you go to his apartment? Was he rapey?" Nadine wanted to know.

"It was fine. I'm employed, so there's that. But more importantly, guess who I met?"

Preston swallowed his bite of pizza and Nadine scooted closer, and they both said, "Who?"

"Banana Republic's daughter!"

"OMG, he's married?" Preston gasped.

"Shut the front door."

"He's not! They split up when she was eight. I tried to get more dirt, but I'm pretty sure he's single."

"Perfect!"

"I need to meet this guy," Nadine said.

"Remember what I told you. Stay away. But you do need to bail on Mean Face."

Preston was confused.

"It's not good," Nadine said. "What I didn't tell you earlier, it wasn't really about the bank teller and his shoes. I may be preggers. He can't deal."

I gasped. I barely knew these people, but it felt like they were old friends. "Really?"

"Well, I'm late."

"Can someone tell me who Mean Face is?"

Nadine filled Preston in as I went to the shady side of the park to check on Sammy. He was playing with a husky, which I thought was sweet, until I got closer and saw Sammy was humping the husky like crazy.

"What the . . ."

A ditzy-looking woman with questionable hygiene grabbed the husky by its collar and yanked the dog back, saying sorry over and over again. I held on to Sammy, who was shaking and panting.

At first, I figured I should be apologizing for Sammy, but then the woman explained to me that she has yet to get her dog spayed, like she forgot to water a plant.

"Seems like not a good situation at a dog park, maybe? Bringing a dog in heat?"

"I know, I know, I'm so sorry."

I coddled Sammy, telling him he was okay. Can you imagine if on my first day with him he got a husky pregnant?

"It's only some dogs she attracts," Ditzy said.

"That's not how it works, lady," said a low voice behind me. It was that older guy I'd seen before, who looked exactly like his beagle. "Dogs can get in fights over dogs in heat. You need to take her out."

He was firm, pointing toward the gate.

"Thank you," I said to him after she left.

"She's got a screw loose," he said.

"Yep, there's clearly no one home," I added, taking Sammy back to the bench, where Preston and Nadine both had their jaws slack.

"The dog was in heat, and she knew!"

"Jesus. What a moron," Nadine said.

Sumner jumped on Preston as if he could tell something shameful had gone down. Dogs had that ninja sixth sense.

Sammy put his head on my lap, and I sighed.

Nadine didn't seem too freaked out about possibly being pregnant and having her boyfriend raise his voice at her on the street. I secretly hoped she was only a little late and just being dramatic. But when she got up to leave, she almost fell over. I helped her up and led her to the gate.

"She is trouble," Preston said when I returned to the bench.

"The good kind," I added.

A few hours later, I ran into Brady in his kitchen, and he insisted on giving me some "spending money" until I got on my feet.

"I'm paying you back with interest," I told him, after he handed me a pretty hefty stack of twenties.

"Well you worked today, so I know you'll eventually pay me back. But don't be pressured about it, please. How'd it go?"

"The dog tried to get another dog pregnant. Humans, too, but that's another story."

"Sounds like a lot going on."

As if on cue, my phone buzzed. It was from Nadine, who I had literally just added to my contacts from the cell number on the card she gave me. The text read:

it's bad. i just wanna get my stuff from his apt.

i'm done. can u back me up?

Brady was looking over my shoulder. "Is this a new friend?"

"Yes. Can I borrow your car?"

"Sure, just drop me off at the restaurant."

Nadine dropped me a pin and the apartment code followed by a THANK U in all caps.

On the way to the restaurant, I felt a surge of energy, and I even sped through a yellow light.

"Whoa," said Brady.

"Sorry. I'm not sure what's gotten into me."

"Well, be careful, sis," Brady said before he got out of the car. "You just got here."

"I will," I said. "Love you."

The drive to Tysons Corner wasn't too bad, and when I got to the apartment door, I took a deep breath. Was I getting myself into something out of my jurisdiction? No, I was helping a friend. God knows us women needed each other, especially in this day and age.

Mean Face opened the door and seemed even more strung out than before. The string was taut again, and I wondered if even he, whom Nadine had called a pussy, had a snapping point.

"So this is it?" he said to Nadine, who stood behind him, surrounded by a bunch of bags with clothes spilling out of them. A lamp was on its side and the rug was ruffled up, like there had been a struggle. "You meet some random chick and then leave me? Are you guys hot for each other?"

"Yeah, we're lesbian lovers," I told him, walking by him and over to Nadine. I stood right next to her. Strength in numbers. Two against one. He walked over to a makeshift bar and grabbed a bottle of Jack by the neck. I could've used a shot myself, but I tried to stay focused, putting Nadine's clothes back into the bags. Mean Face sat with his bottle, seemingly resigned for the moment.

"Hold on, one more thing," Nadine said, and went into the bedroom. Mean Face stared at me, but I wasn't afraid. When we had everything she needed, he didn't try to stop us. At the doorframe, I turned around and said, "Just an FYI, bullying girls is not even a thing anymore. It just makes your dick seem smaller."

Nadine laughed, and we ran toward the elevator.

CHAPTER 15

A Window Opens

"You know when you're putting on jeans and it takes a while for you to straighten the front pockets so it feels right?"

It was Saturday morning, and Brady and I were having toast and apple slices.

"Yeah . . ."

"That's sort of what's happening for me right now. It's like I was walking around all these years with scrunched up pockets."

"The metaphor's a bit of a stretch, but I get it."

Brady was the one person I could free-talk with, and he mostly got me. But that morning he seemed extra distracted by his phone.

"What is it?" I asked. "Jane?"

"No, nothing."

I noticed a shadow cross his face . . . deception? He was my brother, and he couldn't get anything by me, but I could tell he didn't want me to push him, so I didn't. If he was having an affair with Dr. Bang Me, that was his business.

I looked at the picture on his fridge—Jane and him on horses in the Caribbean, the sky behind them looking painted on.

"You know, I never asked you . . . how'd you meet Jane?"

Brady's face softened. "We went on a weekend trip to Rehoboth. There were four couples. Both of our dates got shitfaced and passed out, and we hooked up."

"Wow."

Brady effortlessly popped an apple slice into his mouth.

"So that was it?"

"Actually, we didn't see each other for three months after that. Remember when I broke my wrist?"

"Yeah, you sent me that gross photo."

Brady laughed. "C'mon, you gotta love gnarly injury photos."

"Ugh."

"Anyway, she was there, in Whole Foods, when I pulled the spaz move. She was the one who took me to the ER. She's one of those people who's meant to help other people, you know what I mean? She thrives on it."

"Perfect Jane."

"What?"

"Nothing."

"Oh, I almost forgot, you got this huge package. I put it in the half bathroom."

"Really? What is it?"

"Looks like art. Postmarked Brooklyn."

I immediately went to check it out. It was so big I could barely move it out of the bathroom and into the hallway. In fact, I wasn't even sure how they got it in the door. After peeling the four various layers of protective covering off, there it was. The first piece I ever discovered. It still had the tiny label from the gallery on the back:

LANGHORNE REY
"SOMEWHERE ELSE"
MIXED MEDIA

The tiny photographs blurred into the rich strokes of purples and grays, almost like a galaxy. So many subjects, from all walks of life, looking away from the camera. *Somewhere else.*

He had never sold it?

Brady came up behind me, his jaw loose, eyes wide.

"Wait. He just gave that to you?"

I scrambled for a card or something and found a sticky note stuck to the bottom.

Page-

For safekeeping.

L

"No, but it looks like he's trusting me to keep it."

My fingers were tingling, and I had to blink twice to make sure it was really in front of me. I had looked at it for so many years, but it was like I was seeing it for the first time.

"I wonder how he knew where I was? I guess he could've found your address in the gallery database."

"Yeah," Brady said. "But why?"

"Good question." I looked around for some other note, anything, but it was just more packaging.

"I have to go, I have an appointment," Brady said. "We'll have to figure out somewhere to store that."

Brady hugged me, then took off abruptly, and I sat down on the wood floor in the hallway and stared at it. That was what made great art timeless. Every viewing brought you something else. I wasn't sure exactly what it was bringing me, but I could sense it. It was like someone had opened a window that had long been closed.

CHAPTER 16

DIVERSIONS

The EDP was full of strangers that afternoon, and I realized I had never been there on a weekend. The Saturday crowd was a lot of young fathers who had walking duty. They were all pretty handsome and messily preppy, if a little hungover. My eyes scanned over the dogs, at least a dozen of them, all in an elevated, freak-out state, as if they'd been locked up for decades and had finally been set free. A giant, sour-faced bulldog checked out a sweet, fluffy Pomeranian, and a miniature schnauzer jumped over a lazy mastiff again and again, like a circus act. I noticed the elegantly startled Italian greyhound, but the Umbrella Woman wasn't there. I looked at every human in the park to see if I could locate her. A few minutes later, the greyhound left with a short man with white hair in a black suit with no tie. Her husband? Her next assassination target? Maybe the meth dealer.

I made small talk with some of the fathers about their dogs and the fortunate weather. I felt like a teenager again, hopelessly having eyes for only one person. None of them were BR, or even close. So when I actually did see him, opening the gate to let Pinot and Cab burst through, I tried to act as normal as possible. He was carrying a dog toy that looked like a huge avocado. He waved and walked over, and I had to focus on breathing.

"Hello again!" I said, but it sounded like I was talking to a child. I really had to tone it down. But the man oozed hotness, and his smile was so effortless, how could I just be normal? I pointed at the dog toy he was holding.

"Avocado, huh?" I asked.

"Yeah, Cab is into his good fats."

Of course he was.

"Does he also drink almond milk?"

He chuckled, and Cab came running over, sitting in front of BR, then doing a little spin around.

"That means he wants the avocado," he said.

"He is beyond precious," I said, referring to Cab but also him in my head.

"Where's your little guy?"

"Oh . . . my friend Barkley took him for me last night, 'cause I was helping a friend. He's supposed to meet me here."

They were white lies, but I felt like it was too early in our relationship for me to get into the fact that I didn't have a dog.

BR gave Cab the avocado. The dog whipped it around a little, then just lay down with the toy between his paws, protecting it like a parent would a small child.

Both of our phones dinged at the same time.

"That's my friend I was talking about. Boyfriend troubles."

"Ah, me too," he said.

I felt a plunge in my gut. He had a boyfriend? No!

"My daughter's boyfriend," he clarified, saving me from my panic attack. I almost cried out in rapture, *There is a God!*

"Everything okay?"

"Yeah, it's just, I'd rather she hold off on the boyfriend thing until she's, I don't know, forty?"

"Ha. Good luck with that."

Pinot bumbled over and tried to steal the avocado from Cab, but BR instinctually distracted him by pulling out a small treat from his jacket pocket. It worked, as Pinot ran back into the pack he was playing with before. Cab was clearly wanting to stay right by his owner. That and his avocado was all the dog needed. BR bent down to scratch his head, and Cab nuzzled his snout right into his ear. What I wouldn't give to trade places with Cab. Could I really be jealous of a dog?

"Well, this was a quick one. I've got to take them to their vet checkups."

"City Paws?" It was the vet I always passed near Brady's apartment.

"Yeah, just the once a year thing. A chance for them to charge me a fortune for a few shots."

"Robbery," I confirmed, even though I'd never taken a dog to the vet.

He gave this special whistle, and his two dogs got ready to go in an instant. BR was totally in control. It was sexy. Could he take me with him too?

"Nice to see you," he said, and I could tell he really meant it.

"Thanks!" I said yet again, this time sounding like a twelve-year-old. *Why did I keep thanking him?*

He chuckled again as he walked away, his two beauties on each side of him. I took a mental picture in my brain to file under future family.

Over at my bench, I started reading my paperback. The surfer/cowboy/hunk was out of the coma and being stalked by his baby mama. As riveting as the plot was, my mind was flooded with too many thoughts of BR to concentrate. I felt a familiar tickle on my shins and looked down to see Sumner, actually smiling at me. So my white lie to BR was actually not a lie. Sort of.

"Well, look who's warming up!" Barkley said, taking out his silver doggy bowl and the small Pellegrino bottle.

"You know, the first time I saw you do that, I thought I was hallucinating."

"It's what he likes, what can I say?"

"I take it he drinks regular water too?"

"Yes, but not in the company of other hounds, of course. So I heard you rode Lila."

"Yes, what a beautiful horse."

"Hmm, and worth a fortune I'm told."

The thing about Barkley was he screamed money. There were some people who kept their money private, like a room you would only show some of your guests, but Barkley kept his like a tattoo across his body. It just said money everywhere. Which gave me a thought.

"Hey, do you know Langhorne Rey?"

Barkley put the cap on the Pellegrino bottle and adjusted the cuffs on his heavily starched shirt.

"Heard the name. Conductor?"

"No. Artist. Mixed media."

"Oh yes, the photographs and oil?"

I nodded emphatically.

"So . . . he sent me one of his pieces, called 'Somewhere Else.' I used to work at the gallery that first showed him."

"I see."

You could tell that Barkley was running numbers in his head. Some of Langhorne's work had sold for over $200,000 at the gallery, but surely now they were worth more. It wasn't even mine to sell. But it wouldn't hurt to show it.

I looked up at the sky and saw three birds in a perfect graceful arc disappear into the light of the sun. Maybe that package, that very painting, those birds, it was all a sign telling me to actually do it. Try to start my own gallery. I spoke the words immediately after I thought them.

"So I'm thinking I'd like to have my own gallery here."

Sumner yelped, and Barkley shushed him with a firm swipe of his hands.

"Actually, I'm taking a look at a pawn shop today, believe it or not, over in Columbia Heights. It's for sale for, well, dirt cheap, and I was just going to renovate it for retail and turn it over, but maybe, I don't know, why don't you come look at it with me?"

Sumner yelped again, louder, as if to say, *whoa, daddy, back up. She's nice, but you barely know this woman! Now you're going to buy her a fucking gallery?*

"That would be great."

"We can stop by Room & Board too. I'm in the market for a vase."

As we got up to leave, I said, "Yeah, you really need a vase. Like, pronto."

He laughed and leashed Sumner. I discreetly slipped the paperback into my bag, and off we went.

Barkley in a pawn shop was like a toddler in a strip club. It just didn't work. The display window was super sad, occupied only by a rusted trombone and an amplifier that had ripped meshing in the front. As we walked in, I noticed a lot of gold jewelry under glass, but not much else. The whole place had a look of desperation, a last attempt at survival. It felt strangely familiar.

The owner, an adorable man in a sailor cap who must have been eighty, showed us around. There was a giant basement, and a large bathroom in the back with drip-stained walls. Even the walls looked like they were crying.

Barkley was extremely cordial and told the man we'd be in touch with the Realtor. But when we got back out onto the street, he dusted off his shoulders and said, "Quelle horreur."

"It wasn't that bad. A good space for something. Not an art gallery, but maybe a dry cleaner?"

"Come come," he said, "I think it's best if we get an afternoon martini."

I arrived home at six that night, lightheaded from two martinis at the W rooftop bar with Barkley. At least we ordered french fries to soak it up, and I had a surprisingly tender conversation with him. Like me, he had mother issues, except his mother made mine seem pretty tame. He still had this way of seeing me, and I basked in it. How was I invisible for so long?

The painting was propped in Brady's foyer, not completely out of the elaborate packaging. I still couldn't believe it, like maybe that morning—the whole day—had been a dream. I went into the kitchen, slugged a pint glass of water, and called Langhorne, but both his cell and his studio numbers were disconnected. I would have to call Liv, but not on a martini high—she was usually a buzzkill. I hung up and heard a man's voice I didn't recognize say, "Hello?"

I shuffled back toward the entryway and saw a wiry guy with horn-rimmed glasses, holding a bottle of wine.

"Oh, hi."

"Hi. Your door was open, so I just wanted to . . ."

"Oh, yes. Thanks. Sorry, I'm a little out of it."

His face didn't change. He emanated Airport Bar.

"Are you . . . do you live here?"

I nodded. "Staying here for a while. I'm Brady's sister."

"Oh, I didn't know he had a sister."

"I'm forgettable that way."

He squinted a little, held out his clammy hand, and said, "I'm William."

"Hi, William. Page."

He pointed toward Langhorne's piece. "That sure is something."

Something? It was a lot of things, but not *something*.

"Yes," I said. "Anyway, sorry about the door."

"Oh, no problem. I'm head of the board here, so I worry about these things."

"Ah."

Was I supposed to congratulate him for being head of the condo board? Ask him about the alarm system? I suddenly felt desperately sorry for him. The guy was clearly going to drink that bottle of wine by himself. Which is why, in a complete act of impulse, I said, "Want some help with that?"

His face turned what looked like a dark shade of purple. Could I really do that to people?

"That'd be great. I'm in 602."

"Cool. Twenty minutes?"

His face lightened to a healthy red, and he started bouncing on his heels a little.

"Sounds good!"

He stayed there, bouncing, until I said, "Okay, William," and led him into the hallway. As the door shut behind me, I leaned my back against it and slid down.

I thought of Felicia, my friend from high school who was superstitious and believed in the connection of random events. She would deliberately miss a train, or walk a different way to school every day, just to position herself in unexpected places in the world, to better the odds of some sort of event, the blink of an eye that would change everything. I never really paid her any mind, reminding her she wasn't Gwyneth Paltrow in *Sliding Doors*. Still, sliding down Brady's door right then, I wondered if something about Felicia's philosophy was right.

I got rid of the rest of the wrapping and moved Langhorne's piece into my bedroom. The female nudes would have to go. I took a quick shower and decided to dress down in jeans and a cotton scoop neck top. I splashed a little rosewater on my face and made my way over to apartment 602.

His place was so bland it was like he took a Dull pill to go shopping in Dullsville and buy everything made of Dullness. Lucky for me I had pregamed. The wine was cheap but dry at least. We clinked glasses, and he told me that he worked in insurance (shocker) and loved trivia.

I realized that though he was short and kind of old, his body was very tight, and behind his glasses were a set of light-brown eyes that seemed inviting. I was feeling a little salacious, and even though I was trying to act coy and adjusting my hair and stuff, he put on CNN.

Really?

I ended up dozing to the sound of Wolf Blitzer saying something about another senator accused of sexual harassment. William eventually woke me up and looked at me like I was an alien. Who falls asleep in the house of someone they just met? I felt like saying, *Who puts on CNN on a first date?* It obviously wasn't a date. Was he a serial killer? He totally fit the profile. Anyway, I got the hell out of there. I thanked him for the wine and he said, "Page, just remember to shut your door."

"Will do, Romeo."

CHAPTER 17

YOU COULD BE DIFFERENT

In the morning when I went to pick up Sammy for his walk, Kevin wasn't home. The place smelled like bacon, and my stomach growled with hunger. I opened the refrigerator and saw what looked like tuna salad in a Tupperware bowl. I started to eat it a little with my fingers, with the decadent rush of being in a stranger's home, until Sammy let out a long whine as if to say, *really, you're just going to eat in front of me now? Before our walk?*

On the way out, I noticed a small closet near the entryway with the door slightly open. I'd never been much of a snoop, but this was the new and improved me. The kind who gets sent million-dollar paintings and tries to seduce her random neighbors. Inside were about fifty old-school Super 8 videotapes, lined up perfectly with only dates written in Sharpie on the spines. It looked like they went back about a year. I could immediately tell something wasn't right. I took one out from the bottom right and slipped it into my bag, thinking of Nadine's warning. If Kevin was a psycho of some sort, I would need to know who I was dealing with.

When we got outside, Sammy trotted with vigor, pulling me along, happy to get some air. But when he saw the EDP, he let his head droop, as if he were thinking, *this place again? Whatever.*

As Sammy sniffed his way around without really caring, I furiously finished my paperback. The baby mama stalker tried to kill my cowboy/surfer/hunk, and I almost had a conniption. Luckily, his guardian angel thwarted her plan. When they (literally) rode off into the sunset, I found myself holding back a tear. If someone told me two years ago that a trashy novel would make me cry while babysitting a stranger's dog in DC, I would've told them they were insane. But that was the thing. Life felt infinitely possible. I could almost see Felicia's face smiling at me. Anything could happen. Which is why, when Pinot and Cab came rushing toward me, I hugged them ferociously, like they were my long lost children. Pinot licked my ankle, and Cab did his excited head shake before collapsing again with his legs crossed. They were the most incredible dogs I'd ever seen, much like their owner—who I couldn't see anywhere. Instead, it was his daughter again, this time carrying a can of Coke and a book of her own.

"Hey," April said, in that ambivalent teenage way.

"I have a dog with me today," I told her, so she wouldn't think I was completely out of the running to be her hip stepmom someday.

"Oh, cool. Which one?"

I pointed to Sammy, who was loafing near the doggy water fountain.

"Isn't that . . ."

"The big guy's dog? Yes. I'm helping him out."

"Got it."

She started reading her book, which I could tell from the cover was way more legit than the one I'd just finished. I could feel my heart rate picking up. How was I going to get more dirt on BR without sounding strange?

After a few minutes, Cab coughed and recrossed his paws.

"It's so cute how he does that."

"I know," she said. "Dad points it out to everyone."

"Proud parent."

"Did he eat today?"

"A little."

She put her book on her lap for a minute, and I figured that was my chance.

"So does your dad live here or out at the winery?"

"Both."

She didn't elaborate, and I decided not to pry. At least now I knew he actually had a place here, which sent a surge of delight through me. I tried to suppress my dorky smile.

Her phone buzzed, and I could tell by her groan that it was a parent, though I wasn't sure which. After she was done texting a response, she rolled her eyes and said, "My mother's kind of possessive."

"I hear you. That's why you just have to run as fast as you can in the other direction."

She smirked, and I took it as a small opening. At the gallery in New York, it was all about finding ways into conversations, fishing for just enough info to make your own assessments. Profiling the client. Except BR was hopefully going to be much more than a client.

"Is your dad clingy too?"

"No, he's cool. The only thing he's weird about is my boyfriend. It's like, he doesn't know how to talk to him."

"Hmm. Well, I can imagine that might be awkward. What's your boyfriend like?"

"Jorie? He's a total dichotomy. He looks all tough with his home-made tats, but he writes love poems and cries at the movies."

"Sounds dreamy."

She looked at me a little weird, as if I wanted to steal him from her.

"He's sixteen."

Another subtle reminder that, in her eyes, I was old. I quickly veered the subject away from age.

"So you have dog duty a lot?"

"Lately. My dad is a big sleeper. He likes to just hang out in his pajamas and chill on the weekends."

I felt my face get hot, and a tinge between my legs. BR in pj's? Pinot stopped sniffing around and looked at me as if to say, *all the girls fall for him. But you could be different.* I scratched his back and scanned the park for Sammy. He was still over by the water fountain, half chasing a scrappy rottweiler puppy.

April started in on her book again, and now I could see the cover better, which depicted a hand smashing through glass. Some kind of true crime thing I guessed. Definitely a book that skewed older than she was. But that's what modern kids were all about. Maturity came so much quicker, or at least that's the vibe they gave off.

Sammy came over and looked at me like he was even more bored, which was puzzling. If you're bored at the dog park, what do you have to look forward to? I guessed he wanted his two treats, so I casually said bye to April and took Sammy home. Kevin wasn't there, and I realized I had left the tuna salad on the kitchen counter. I quickly put it away, gave Sammy his treats, and left. It wasn't until I was back at Brady's that I saw the stolen videotape in my bag. I called Brady at work and asked him if he still had our dad's Super 8 video camera.

"What, are you getting into amateur porn now?"

"It's a thought, but no. I just have a tape and want to see what's on it."

He told me Dad's old camera was in the bottom drawer of his home office. I found it and turned it on to see if it worked. The little fold-out screen lit up, and on came some old footage of my father's kind face, smelling the Christmas coffeecake he used to make every year. Then the shot moved to the den, and there was Brady, about five years old, holding me in my unicorn onesie on the couch. My father came in the shot and tickled our toes. Brady squirmed, and I laughed. "Look at you two," my father said, "my peanut butter and jelly." I pressed pause, feeling my face flush, two tears racing down each of my cheeks.

I pressed play again. The shot followed Dad back into the kitchen. He was doing that thing with the spoon on his nose, but it wasn't working. Each time the spoon fell, he just laughed.

The video cut to rolling hills outside the window of a car, and then it went fuzzy again.

I pressed eject and took out the tape, then put in the stolen one from Kevin's closet. I closed my eyes, took a deep breath, and pressed play.

CHAPTER 18

LOSER TO WINNER

Whenever I had been to Elbow, Brady's restaurant named after a British band he loved, it was during peak hours and kind of chaotic, so I never hung out that long. Tonight, he invited me to an early dinner where we could eat mostly uninterrupted.

The manager-slash-bartender Straight Jake made us his signature drink, called Elbow Room, which was bourbon based and had a giant sprig of mint sprouting out of it. They called him Straight Jake because he had a roommate also named Jake who was gay. They didn't have to call his roommate Gay Jake, as it was obvious. But with Straight Jake it helped, because he was a little more polished than your average straight guy. In fact, he was wearing a pale-pink shirt and a gray scarf knotted the European way, and completely pulling it off. It was clear there was a man-crush going on between him and my brother. They called each other "Boo."

Brady brought us plates of the "family meal," which was fried chicken and a salad. We sat at table eleven, the one by the window that looked onto 14th Street. The place was music themed, with old microphones for beer taps, and framed portraits of Bob Dylan and Iggy Pop above the bar. The bathroom walls were covered with old record album covers, mostly from Brady's collection.

After the third sip of my Elbow Room, I told Brady about the tragedy of my pseudo-date with his neighbor, William.

"Page, you gotta be careful. That guy's a whack job. One time when I had a party, he invited himself and then sat in the corner watching everyone like he was at a zoo. So later on, my friend Isabella started talking to him. When I asked her what his deal was, she told me he was a Scientologist."

"Ah, that explains it, I guess."

I ripped off a piece of crispy chicken and popped it in my mouth.

"So what Super 8 tape were you looking at?"

I told him about Kevin's closet, how I snatched one of the tapes but was going to return it.

"Page, this is so not like you."

"Well, I'm on a rampage. I haven't even told you about Banana Republic."

"Who?"

"My future husband. Anyway, the footage was a woman, maybe around our age, going from her house to her car, then her car to work, then work to a restaurant, then back to her car and home again. Like he followed her everywhere with a camera. Do you think he's a private eye?"

Brady laughed. "I don't think they say private eye anymore."

"Well, detective, whatever."

"What if he's planning on killing her?" he asked.

Clearly, I wasn't the only one binging Netflix.

"He doesn't seem like the murderous type."

Brady tossed back a healthy sip of his drink. "Well, it sounds sketchy."

The salad was topped with shaved parmesan. I put a sliver on my tongue. I never used to like parmesan, but it tasted tangy and delicious.

"Tell me something. When did you feel the change? Like, when did you go from loser to winner?"

He gave me a startled look.

"Not that you were a loser, but you know what I mean."

"Well, let's see . . . I was busing tables and smoking too much weed . . . one night, a few weeks after Dad died, I saw Jimmy Shay, you know, from high school? He had this hot . . . sorry, I don't know if I can even say that now . . . he had this beautiful girl on his arm, and he gave me a card with his name embossed under it. Executive vice president, it said. He was making bank. Jimmy Shay! The dude who could barely dress himself in fifth grade. It wasn't that I wanted to be him, per se, but I knew if he could make something of himself, I certainly could. I came to DC, put my life savings on a down payment for a studio, and the rest, as they say, is history."

"Well, I think it's happening to me."

Brady raised up his drink to clink mine. "To going from loser to winner. Although like you said to me, you're not really . . ."

"Brady, I'm living in your guest room and walking a stalker's dog."

"It's just a blip on the radar. Besides, you said something was happening. What is it?"

"Well, I don't know exactly, but it started with the dog park, and then the painting, and now I have this crazy idea of opening my own gallery here."

Brady just stared at me, and then his phone buzzed. He quickly declined the call the minute he saw who it was.

"Page, why don't you try and just get a job first."

"I know, I know. I actually filled out an application at the bookstore, but I'm not sure that's my thing, so I didn't hand it in. Anyway, Langhorne sending me that piece . . . I'm going to sound like Felicia when I say this, but I think it's a sign."

"Speaking of Langhorne, have you tried calling him?"

"Both his phones are disconnected, so I guess I'll have to call Liv. I'm not complaining, but it's not like him to send that to me. Something of that . . . value. Of course, it's just for safekeeping like the note said, but still. I just can't stop thinking about how good it would it look in the window of my new gallery."

"Baby steps."

"What about leaps? Baby leaps."

Brady had barely touched his chicken.

"Not hungry?" I asked.

"Had a late lunch."

"This is our late lunch."

"Whatever. So do you have any ideas for investors?"

"A few . . ."

"Well, maybe you can talk to Peter about spaces. He's the real estate agent I wanted to set you up with."

"The one that's fifty?"

"Forty-six. But he looks forty."

"I love when people say that. No matter how young he looks, he's still going to be fifty when I'm still in my thirties."

"Fifty is the new thirty."

"Yeah, right."

Brady moved some of his salad around his plate and said, "Well, will you at least meet him?"

I thought of Joseph the trainer, and William the neighbor, and Kevin the stalker. Anything had to be better than my current prospects.

"Sure, why not."

"Great, how about brunch tomorrow?" Brady was already texting him.

"Sounds good. Make sure he brings his Depends."

"Page! Be nice."

"Sorry."

Brady got up to deal with some issue the hostess was having at the front. He left his phone, and I couldn't help it. I looked at his latest call, the one he so quickly declined. It was from Dr. Langley, aka Dr. Bang

Me. Hmm. Perfect Jane not quite perfect enough? Or maybe it was just STD results. I slid the phone back where it was just as he returned.

Much later that night I woke to my phone buzzing like crazy, and there were four long texts from Kevin. Apparently he got in a car accident in Virginia and he was fine, but he had been waiting for his car for hours, and now it was too late and he was not going to make it home, and he knew it wasn't my day but could I possibly emergency-walk Sammy?

At first, I hesitated. Was this some lure to get me to his apartment in the middle of the night? But then I thought, *I should help him, it's the right thing to do.*

Walking over to Kevin's at that time of night was a little eerie. I saw a homeless guy peeing on a traffic cone, and a group of young girls stumbling into an Uber. When I got to Kevin's, Sammy was freaking out, his eyes pleading, saying, *tell me nothing happened to him, tell me.*

I comforted him and told him everything was going to be all right. I walked him, and he peed with the force of Niagara Falls. When we got back, I gave him three treats instead of two, and I sat next to his bed until his breathing calmed. When I knew he was asleep, I put the tape back in its place in the closet and crept out without making any noise.

On the way home I texted Kevin saying all was good. He texted back that I was a lifesaver. I thought of the almond debacle with Michael of Austria, and getting Nadine out of Mean Face's apartment. Maybe I was. Which would be good, because then maybe I could save my own.

CHAPTER 19

JESUS, REALLY?

The next morning around eleven o'clock, Brady's friend Peter texted me, asking me to brunch. I texted back yes, maybe a little too quickly, but who cares. If I was going to become a winner, I would have to experience life and show up, right?

I met him at a place on 17th Street that Preston recommended to me over text. Peter seemed unfazed by the glitter tinsel hanging from the cheap chandeliers and the drag queen host. It was "disco brunch," and they were blaring Sister Sledge. I was going to ask Peter if we should find a different place, but he seemed so happy, his face beaming. Brady was right, he looked forty and was well groomed, but there was something artificial going on. Fillers? Medication? Maybe he was just super happy.

"I don't think disco should be celebrated at all, never mind at brunch," I said. "It's just wrong."

Peter gave me a newscaster smile. "At least it's not rap," he said.

I asked the waitress if she wouldn't mind turning the music down a little, and she slowly shook her head.

"I guess we're just going to have to yell at each other," I said, but Peter couldn't hear me.

They served us mimosas even though we didn't order them. I took a sip and winced—the OJ was off.

"Oh, disgusting," I said.

"I don't think," Peter said, but it may have been, "I don't drink." I waved down the busboy, but he just kept smiling and nodding at me, not taking the drinks away. After five minutes of me trying to explain it to him, the drag queen host came to the rescue and took the mimosas.

"It would have been faster to learn Spanish!" Peter yelled.

After the music question and the language barrier, the staff avoided us for over ten minutes. Finally, a sweating middle-aged man walked up with a small pad and a pink pen.

Peter ordered egg whites with fruit and a decaf coffee. I ordered a club sandwich with fries and a Diet Coke. While we waited for the food, we talked about Brady and how they had met (they both did laps at the local pool). Then, somewhat out of the blue, he told me he was getting a vasectomy. Not a particularly strategic piece of information to lead with, but he seemed thrilled about it. In fact, he seemed thrilled about everything. He even said, "These are great forks!" I looked down at mine, wondering what was so special about that particular fork.

"Amazing forks," I yelled, and he looked pained for a brief instant, as if he suddenly realized he'd said a really dumb thing. I changed the subject and asked about the daughter Brady told me he had. That got even creepier, because he actually described her body as "slamming." Luckily the food came fast, and we both started eating voraciously. Then he told me that his daughter was a cocktail waitress in a bar, and he didn't really approve.

"She gets hit on all the time by the pervs who frequent the place."

"Hmm," I said. "You know what I used to do in college? When someone hit on me that I just wanted to immediately get rid of, I'd smile and act like I was really turning on, and they'd say something like, 'How ya doin'?' and I'd say 'Great!' Then I'd pause—the key is to pause—and say, 'Ever since I found Jesus.'"

He smiled, but then he turned bright red. I had obviously hit a nerve.

"Actually," he said, "I *did* find Jesus."

I laughed heartily and started to think this Peter was actually okay, but then I saw his face. He was staring at me with an absolutely blank expression, his former happiness drained. His face was frozen except for his eyes, which were filled with disdain.

"Oh, I have nothing against religion . . . ," I started, but I realized there was no hope. I hadn't touched my fries, so I grabbed the ketchup for something to do. I couldn't believe Brady had failed to mention anything about this.

"I'm born again," he said, like he was telling me his shoe size. "I don't wear it on my sleeve, though."

"Of course not, you wear it in your heart, right?"

This time he winced a little.

"Kidding. I'm sorry. I think it's great."

He smiled and shook his head. He was definitely sexy, and I could see the curve of his pecs underneath his white oxford shirt. Could I get past the Jesus part for a good hookup? On second thought, he probably didn't even do hookups. For me, it had been a while. I didn't want to close the snack bar for good. It was time for a grand reopening. But maybe not with Born Again Peter. I would have to look for a different disciple.

CHAPTER 20

RED FLAGS AND MUSHROOM TEA

"Born again?"

I was standing in Brady's bedroom doorway while he was on his laptop working on a Spotify playlist for the restaurant.

"Honestly"—he was trying not to laugh—"I had no idea. Maybe it was recent."

"I think I totally freaked him out," I said.

"He's good looking, though, right?"

"Yes. But what part of being born again isn't a red flag? Do they even have sex? Or drink?"

Brady finally let out the laugh he was holding in. "Did he just come out and say it?"

I explained the whole disco brunch nightmare, and Brady was clearly delighted by my misfortune. Then he gave me that look, the one that shows that he really was sorry. It reminded me of seventh grade, when my purse got stolen at the mall. I had locked myself in my room, crying those unstoppable thirteen-year-old tears. Brady had gotten one of my mother's old purses, put some of her lipstick in it, along with a lollipop and two scratch lottery cards, and placed it outside my door. When I finally emerged, he was sitting there with that same look he has now.

"I've been on three dates in a week. That's a good average, even though they all pretty much sucked balls."

"Page, you are definitely going to find someone. And let's be honest, Jack was kind of a putz."

"You only met him twice!"

Brady put up his hands. "Just saying."

"Well, sorry I'm not dating Perfect Jane."

"She's not perfect, Page. No one is."

"Still, I have dates with Scientologists and Jesus disciples, and you're banging Mother Teresa Barbie."

"Page, stop. Listen, I actually need to call her. Can you hand me my phone?" I grabbed his phone from his dresser, pretending to see what I saw at the restaurant right then.

"Who's Dr. Langley?"

His face went blank for a second, and he said, "What?"

Clearly he was stalling. I had hit a nerve.

"Forget it," I said.

While he called Perfect Jane, I told myself to let it go. I was living in this palace for free, so why meddle in his personal stuff? Still, I was curious. I googled Dr. Bang Me again and found a Facebook page. She looked even hotter in her normal pictures. Effortlessly dressed, dewy lips, that completely natural blonde hair. There was no husband, only a few shots of her with a few guys at a sports bar. In the picture, the men are all looking at her like, *I can't believe how hot you are.* It was kind of ridiculous.

I retreated to the guest room and texted an old colleague, who gave me Liv's cell number. My finger hesitated slightly before pressing call. She answered on the fifth ring, just before I was about to hang up.

"Page! I was just thinking about you today."

"Really?" I asked, incredulous.

"Yes, we found one of your jackets at the gallery. H&M?"

You stamped me out like a cigarette, and you think I care about my fucking H&M jacket?

"Oh, you can toss it."

"Already did. How can I help?"

"Well, the strangest thing happened. I received that piece from Langhorne, 'Somewhere Else.' Remember?"

She didn't say anything, so I said, "Hello?"

"Langhorne's in a lot of trouble, haven't you heard?"

"No."

"My assistant saw him looking through a garbage can in Hell's Kitchen."

I thought of Langhorne, always ruffled but elegant, only drank scotch, smelled nice.

"No way. Are you serious?"

"I'm afraid I can't really talk about it. He made us a lot of money that one, but he's turning out to be quite the nuisance."

I felt like she was berating me, like I should never have suggested we show his work.

"Langhorne was the best thing to ever happen to you."

"Not anymore, I'm afraid."

"Well, do you know where I can reach him?"

"I'm not sure if there's visiting hours."

"What?"

"Listen, Page, I really have to run. I've got Frances Bean in town, and the gallery's full of dust from the renovations."

"Just . . ."

"I'll speak to you later."

She hung up, and I sank down on my bed.

What had he done? Was he in a mental institution? Or was she just being facetious?

I decided to text Joey, the guy who used to clean the gallery. He worked for Langhorne at one point on the down low, and there was mystery around what that work actually was.

Hi there it's Page.

Do you know what's up w/ Langhorne?

He texted back within minutes, one word:

Jail

I texted back three question marks but got nothing in return. Then I tried calling him, and it went to voice mail.

Jail?

I just couldn't picture Langhorne in jail. In the three years I had known him, we had always hung out in groups, so it's true that I wasn't privy to his personal life. But still, jail? It just didn't seem possible. And what happened to his dog?

In Brady's home office, a search for Langhorne just brought up the usual web articles on him and his art. But on the second page of results there was something about an event cancellation at Art Basel Miami, where he was meant to have been a keynote speaker. They were unclear as to the reason.

My phone buzzed, and I hoped it was Joey with more news, but it was Michael of Austria.

Going to an auction. Care to join?

To maintain a shred of dignity, I waited at least a minute before replying.

Sure

I wondered what one wore to an auction. Definitely not jeans. I would have to get a lot of new clothes for my new fabulous DC life. Dog walker by day, auction bidder by night.

I'll pick you up at five.

Of course, Michael of Austria didn't actually pick me up. His German driver did, but Michael was riding in the back. Before we left, I insisted he come in and look at Langhorne's piece. I loved seeing people's reactions to it, as I had in the gallery so many times. At first they would squint, then they'd move closer, and then they'd step back. Slightly confused, but definitely compelled. That, to me, was the whole point. If you saw someone spreading feces on their body, or a dead horse hanging from the ceiling, you knew exactly what it represented. Blatant metaphors were overrated. This was mysterious and inexplicable, almost a direct reflection of Langhorne himself.

"He sent this to you?" Michael asked. "A gift?"

"No. Just to hold on to it. I'm not sure why, other than he feels a certain loyalty to me . . . I had a strong hand in discovering him. It's my one claim to fame, I guess."

Just like at Barkley's house after that wine-soaked meal, Michael looked at me like I was some kind of vital, important piece in the puzzle of his life.

"How wonderful. I've heard of him, of course, but I thought he was more of a gimmick. This piece is remarkable."

I found myself blushing like a schoolgirl. "I know, right?"

"Indeed."

We went back down to his car, and the driver took us to the auction, which was held in a large glass building in the Penn Quarter. The theme was rare artifacts from Indonesia. Michael was a true gentleman, holding the door and giving me an aisle seat. Since he could tell I was interested, he gave me tidbits about the items: how the pen with letter opener on the top was owned by Indonesia's most famous poet, the mask that they believe eliminates evil, and the marble Buddhas whose prices were based on weight. He seemed proud of all his knowledge and thrilled to share it. Eventually, he bid on an ancient teapot that started at $12,000.

"That better make some kick-ass tea," I whispered to him.

He laughed a little too loud, and some of the other buyers shot us bothersome looks. One of them raised his paddle and his eyebrow at the same time.

"Well, I plan on making mushroom tea," he said.

"Sounds good," I said. "But remember, we are in DC, not at Burning Man."

"Good point," he said, raising his paddle to win the kettle, of course.

We had to wait almost an hour while they wrapped it elaborately and boxed it up. His driver put it into the trunk, and we went to the Tabard Inn for drinks and dinner. Michael ordered a rare scotch, and I had a glass of French burgundy.

I still couldn't tell if he played on my team or not, and if he did, would he be interested in me? Did I even want him to be? He was like a boy-man with dark eyes and a sly smile. The Hawaiian shirts and the heavy silver jewelry somehow suited him. I told him about Kevin's videotapes and Langhorne being in jail. I also told him about my mother's married lover possibly dying and her impending visit. He seemed very interested in my life, which was a refreshing change. In my experience, most men pretended to listen but couldn't care less. Michael was genuinely rapt, and asked sincere questions. While I was in the bathroom, he had them chill the whole bottle of the wine I was drinking in a silver bucket next to the table. It felt wonderfully decadent to have my own bottle, although I told myself I would have to watch my alcohol intake.

I didn't want to turn into my mother, even if she was a happy drunk. Everyone loved her. It was only Brady and I who sometimes cringed when she started to tell the same story or spill sauce on her shirt.

The dinner was amazing: burrata, bacon-wrapped quail (you could wrap a shoe in bacon and it would taste good), and filet mignon with tamarind honey.

The only ruffle was when Michael asked the dreaded question, what did I do for work?

"I'm a dog walker," I said. "It's a promising future."

He smiled, fully assuming it was a joke.

"Actually, I'm thinking about starting a gallery down here. Maybe use Langhorne's piece as my way in the door, so to speak."

"That sounds well intentioned."

"It's true, you know, the only thing I'm passionate about is art, particularly his. And also dogs. Maybe it could be an art gallery with a doggy day care in the basement."

He looked at me like I had a screw loose, but then his face softened. "Maybe not the doggy part."

When he dropped me off, he put his hand on my knee and told me to keep in touch. I almost kissed him, or he almost kissed me, but neither of us wanted to ruin whatever was happening or not.

"It was a fun . . . auction."

He smiled and said, "Listen, I am hosting a cocktail party this weekend. A few, how do you say, art people? You will fit right in."

"Perfect. In the meantime, go easy on the mushroom tea."

CHAPTER 21

THAT'S JUST ME

At the EDP the next day, Sumner had his usual air of condescension, looking at Sammy, then at me, as if to say, *that old thing again? Could someone at least wash him?*

After an air kiss on both cheeks, I sat down and told Preston about my two disaster dates, and the auction with Michael of Austria.

"Wow," he said. "He's taking you to auctions now? Next thing you know, you'll be on Netjets to Vienna for a ball."

"Do they still have balls?"

We giggled like teenagers.

"Actually, I keep meaning to ask you. Does he play on my team?"

Preston raised one eyebrow and said, "With Michael, it's a gray area. We know he dated this film producer woman in Austria for like, ten years, and they were set to have kids, but then there was a big falling-out. I also know, from a close source, that there's a black dancer in London whom he's on and off with. I had a crush on him when we first met, but he showed no response. I'm way too white trash for him anyway. Did you know my mother used to make tuna casserole with sour cream and potato chips on top? How I ended up having a decent sense of style is beyond me."

I thought about BR and how his jacket was worn but fitted, the way his jeans cupped his ass. I told Preston about seeing him again, how cute he was with Cab.

"You really love dogs, huh?" Preston said.

"Duh. But BR could have a pet tarantula and I wouldn't care."

"Ew. Girl, you are spun."

I heard the distinctive clink of the wrought iron gate and turned to look. Before the gate could even close, Pinot and Cab barreled right over, and I almost screamed with delight. I whispered to Preston that it was BR's daughter, April, following behind in the black hoodie.

Sumner trotted off as if he couldn't be bothered with all the commotion. Sammy was lying in the shade of a tree in his favorite corner of the park. Thankfully, there was no sign of the psycho husky owner.

"Hi!" I said.

"Hey," April said. I could tell she was a little self-conscious seeing Preston, maybe because they were closer in age? Anyway, I decided to break the ice.

"April, this is Preston, white-trash hoodlum turned sophisticated power-gay."

Preston blushed, which I'd never seen. "Hey there," he said. Then, pointing at her jeans, he said, "Those are super cute. Are they Rag & Bone?"

"Yes! My friend works there, so I get the family and friends discount."

"For real, we are besties now!"

She smiled, clearly more fascinated with Preston than her future stepmom. Still, I could see BR's face like it was yesterday, how his big eyes brightened when he laughed, how his strong, tanned hands were the perfect mix of masculinity and grace. As I watched the two of them gossip about fashion, I realized that comparatively I really *was* old. I didn't usually feel old, but when you start hanging out with people ten or twenty years younger than you, how can you not? Most of my friends from college were bound by marriages and soccer games and all-inclusive vacations. I'd rather shoot myself than drink sickeningly sweet daiquiris on a man-made beach among doughy insurance agents from Cleveland and their obnoxious offspring, but that's just me.

As April and Preston continued to chat, I subtly tried to blend into their conversation, but it wasn't working. For the next ten minutes, I was chopped liver. I just sat there petting Cab, who looked tired, while Pinot flirted with a gorgeous black Lab.

When April's phone rang, she excused herself and got up to leave, and I noticed the logo on the tote bag she was carrying: EDGEWOOD WINERY. So did Preston, of course. After we waved our goodbyes and she was out of sight, he turned to me and said, "Hopefully you'll be edging *his* wood."

"I'd be happy holding his hand at this point."

He looked at me tenderly. "You really are a romantic, aren't you?"

"No."

"But you're rethinking what love is, right?"

"I guess."

"I do that every day. First, I was convinced love was about money, then I thought it was about power and status, then I thought it was just about caring for one another . . . but let's face it, if Barkley wasn't *Barkley*, I probably wouldn't be with him. There are a million factors, but the most important thing is to be able to love someone and still be yourself. So many people give up themselves for some twisted version of love."

I thought of Jack. *Is that what happened? He just slowly drained my mojo?*

"So you're saying it's not about complacency, it's about compatibility?" I asked.

"Yes!"

As Preston started secretly texting someone that involved lots of emojis, Sumner actually jumped onto my lap. I was stunned. After Preston was done, he said, "Well, you know what our next mission is, right?"

"What?" I asked.

"Site visit! Edgewood Winery!"

I smiled, thinking of the two of us at a winery in Virginia. He had already googled it, showing me the star on the map on his iPhone, which seemed to be pulsating just for me.

"Tomorrow at four. We'll just take a drive out there. I'll pick you up in the Beamer."

I briefly wondered if I had anything planned the next day. I was going to continue the job search, but it was proving to be futile.

"Why not," I said.

"Fab, it's a plan. C'mon, Sumner, let's go make some clothes."

"Oh yeah, how is your collection coming?".

"Well, I'd love to say I'm going to be the next Christian Siriano, but it's kind of not happening at the moment. But that girl, April, she has me inspired."

"Good." I scratched Sumner, and he looked at me as if to say, *don't trust him, he's an emotional roller coaster.*

A few minutes after they left, I got a text from Jack. His grandmother, who was basically his only family, had died. Mimi, as she was called, was a former actress who lived in an old apartment on the Upper West Side. He'd drag me up there once a month to see her, and she'd serve us iced tea with smelly ice cubes. She had framed playbills of the Broadway shows she had been in hanging on the walls. It was impressive, but sad at the same time.

I'm so sorry, I texted back, and he replied with a tear-faced emoji. Then he was typing, and stopping, and typing again, and I waited. I felt bad for him. He really loved her, but I wasn't so sure I was the right person to be consoling him now. We had both agreed it was best that we went our separate ways (well, he suggested and I eventually agreed), so why hold on?

As I walked with Sammy back to Kevin's place, I stopped at my favorite corner near the steeple and looked up at the sky, scattered with wispy clouds. An ambulance went by, and a flock of tiny birds took off from a giant oak tree in a flourish of flapping wings. Maybe it was Mimi. I didn't believe in that sort of thing, but life was continuing to surprise me.

CHAPTER 22

CRAZY LOVE

I opened Kevin's door, and he was standing there with an expression of forgiveness, like I was a child.

"I know you took the tape. You put it back in the wrong space."

"Oh, I just . . . I was . . ."

"It's okay, I have nothing to hide. They're just tapes of Penelope, my ex-girlfriend, and not the kind you'd think."

"I'm so sorry . . ."

I couldn't bear telling him that I'd watched it.

"I was going to make some tea, would you like some? I can write you a check as well."

"Sure, that would be great."

I usually found tea pretty boring, but it was actually decent. Vanilla something, with a lot of honey and milk, which was probably why I could actually drink it.

"Thanks again for the other night. That was a lifesaver."

"No problem. I'm just glad you weren't hurt or anything."

"Just the Toyota."

"Yeah."

After a long silence, I decided to jump on the elephant in the room and ride it. "So I know you don't know me that well, but I'm curious. Are you making some kind of movie, or are you . . ."

"Stalking her?" he offered.

I cleared my throat.

"Neither, really. I mean, I guess you could say I'm stalking her, but I don't wish her any harm, and I'm not trying to get back together. I mean, I would if she wanted to, but that's not likely."

"So why go through all the trouble?"

He took out his checkbook and started writing my check.

"Well, do you believe in true love?"

"I'm not sure. I was just talking about that with a friend of mine. My parents had a version of it, I think. But I haven't. Yet."

He smiled. "Well, I can't really explain it other than saying, I still want to feel like I can see her every day. You know, how she did her hair, what she was wearing, where she was going. And I never want to forget her. So I don't always watch the tapes, but knowing they exist comforts me."

I thought of Kevin, alone in this place with the ex-girlfriend tapes, and felt a wave of unbearable sadness. As if sensing it, Kevin said, "I'm really not crazy, just still in love."

"If you don't mind me asking, why did she leave you?"

He sighed. "She didn't really say why."

"My ex didn't either," I said.

"But I think it was my weight. I have a thyroid problem. Believe it or not, I don't even eat that much."

He gave me a *what are you gonna do* look. Then I remembered something.

"You know, my mother's friend had thyroid issues, too, and she found this Chinese doctor who changed her life."

"Really?"

"I could get you his info if you want."

"Sure. My doctor just talks in circles."

"Yeah," I said, finishing my tea.

As I was leaving, he said, "So do you still want to walk Sammy now that you know my darkest secrets?"

I waved his comment aside like it was nothing.

"Of course. Look, Kevin, it's obvious you're hurting, and I know what that's like. But it's not cool to violate someone's privacy that way, even if your motives are harmless."

"Yeah, I guess."

"Maybe you should get rid of the tapes?"

"I'll think about it."

"Okay, bye, Kevin."

"Bye, Page."

As I walked back to Brady's, I thought of Kevin's ex. Yes, stalking was wrong and invasive, but I still wondered if she knew how much pain he was in over losing her. If she knew it was possible to be needed that much.

CHAPTER 23

IF YOU BUILD IT

I came home to find Brady and Perfect Jane cracking up over a viral YouTube video of a talking cat. I had already seen it, and I didn't have the heart to tell them it wasn't that funny—that four million people can be wrong.

Jane touched my shoulder as if we'd known each other for years. "Hey, ladies' night is tonight! Since I'm renovating, we're doing it at Estadio, this cute tapas place down the street. Will you come?"

"Topless place?"

Jane laughed. "Tapas!"

"Oh."

How could I tell her I'd rather pass a watermelon through my nostril?

"I'd love to. Just need to shower. I smell like dog."

She cringed a little, but then smiled. "Great!"

In the shower, I thought about Kevin, who was probably watching TV with Sammy by his side. How much would it suck to be fat and not even be able to eat your way there? I would at least want to enjoy the process, gorge on ice cream and Doritos and chimichangas. I looked down at my belly, a slight curvature but still pretty flat. I secretly thanked my mother's side of the family for a good metabolism. Although everyone said after forty it would change. My heart sunk a little at the thought, but then I told myself it was okay, everything would change, everything *was* changing. Besides, I had a wonderful evening to look forward to with PJ and the Sweater Set! Barf.

I put on the LBD I wore to Barkley's and some red pumps I used to wear in the gallery. They were a little scuffed, but so was my ego.

When I met her back out in the hallway, Jane made a girly, excited noise.

"Page, you look amazing." This coming from a woman with $200 highlights, blinding teeth, giant blue eyes, a wrinkle-free face, and a Birkin bag.

"Well, I'll let you in on all my beauty secrets. Looks like you really need them."

"You are too funny," she said, which was code for, *I can't really tell if you're a bitch or not.*

We said goodbye to Brady, who said he was going to retire early. He was clearly overworked from restaurant week, or as he called it, "Amateur week in Douchebagistan." And I still wasn't sure about the extra hours he may have been spending with Dr. Bang Me.

As we walked the four blocks to the restaurant, Jane talked the whole time but I wasn't really listening. I just nodded while checking out the dogs that people were walking. There was a Pomeranian that was as white as Jane's teeth, except furry and completely lovable. Also, a pit bull mix with adorable spots being walked by an artsy type guy with thick-framed glasses who held my glance for an extra second.

The restaurant was all reclaimed wood and steel, rustic meets modern. There were TVs above the bar showing old Colombian soccer games.

The place was bustling, and the three girls that completed the Sweater Set were already seated. They all smiled at me in a way that emanated happiness and competition at once. Like, *Great to see you but don't fuck with me.* It was a little Real Housewives of Logan Circle, but after a glass and a half of sangria, I wasn't really bothered.

"That dress is super cute," said SS1. "Is it Dior?"

"No," I said, feeling a rush of heat in my face. "I don't really know actually. I got it at a boutique down the street."

"Oh," she said, like I had just told her I peeled it off a sweaty homeless woman.

"So any luck on the job front?" SS2 asked while touching up her lip gloss.

"I've actually been dog walking."

There it was. The great conversation stopper. They all looked like stunned birds who'd just flown into a glass wall. So I added, "But I am thinking about opening my own gallery here."

That got them out of stunned bird mode, and SS3 said, "That would be so wonderful! Do you know we have an original Rothko in our foyer?"

"No!" I said, trying to imitate them without being facetious.

Jane smiled her most gracious smile and addressed the Sweater Set as a whole. "Page was pivotal in discovering the mixed media artist Langhorne Rey."

The Sweater Set had no clue who Langhorne was, but they all pretended to be completely impressed.

The dishes were small, delicately flavored, and perfectly plated, much like the Sweater Set themselves, although the food actually contained substance.

Halfway into my third sangria, SS1 asked me how the dating was going.

Maybe it was the alcohol, or maybe I just couldn't fathom telling them about the less-than-stellar dates I'd been on, but I started the lie.

"I think I've found someone . . . the one, I mean. He is so hot, and he owns a winery."

Cue the simultaneous Sweater Set *gasp*.

"Oh my . . ."

"No . . ."

"Do tell . . ."

I took a deep breath and pretended I was the most wonderful Sweater Set girl of them all.

"His name is Bruce. Bruce . . . Rodman."

Jane looked at me with what could have been a tinge of incredulity, but I wasn't sure. At least I used the initials BR. And I did know his daughter. So there.

"I'm not really sure where it's going, but he likes my sense of humor."

This was true, right?

"I bet he likes a lot more than that," SS1 said.

"Hmm . . ."

"I'd say . . ."

"So," Jane said, "when can we meet him?"

I swallowed a bite of grilled octopus and said, "Well, he's kind of shy. But soon, I'm sure. I'm just trying to take it slow. It's like, he's almost too perfect, you know?" *To be true*, I didn't say.

"Oh, I know," SS2 offered. "You really have to worry about the pretty ones."

"Well, he's more on the rugged side of pretty."

SS3 made a growling noise.

"Where did you meet him?"

"At Whole Foods actually!"

The thing about lying was, once you were on a roll, why stop?

"He was across from me, checking out the avocados. He showed me the best ones."

"I'm sure he did," said SS3, clearly the horny one. I figured she had a husband who didn't give her enough, and she spent her time binge-reading *Fifty Shades of Lame*.

"Anyway, he gave me this recipe, for his grandmother's crepe batter. He's part French."

Cue another Sweater Set communal *gasp*.

"He grew up in Nice. That's where he learned about wine."

This was sounding so good, I was starting to believe it myself.

"He calls me"—I paused for effect—"*mon petit chou*, which means 'my little cabbage.'" This was Barkley's pet name for Preston, but it transferred well.

"Adorable," Jane said.

As the meal went on, I started to get really tipsy and drifted in and out of the conversation, which was basically more first world problems. SS1 described her "super gross" Lyft driver, SS2 complained about her Pilates studio moving four blocks farther from their place in Bethesda, and SS3 claimed her old Victorian house was so drafty, she was heating the outside. Jane paid the check, which had to have been a fortune.

On the way back to Brady's, I told Jane to keep the news about my new beau on the down low.

"You do realize anything said on girls' night is free game, right?"

"Well, just with Brady. He gets really protective of who I date sometimes."

Jane raised an eyebrow. "I see. My lips are sealed. But don't think you're not handing over that crepe batter recipe."

Out of the entire Sweater Set, Jane really wasn't that bad. Underneath the perfection, there was a real person in there. Someone you could actually picture stubbing her toe, or spilling sauce on her skirt.

When we got inside, I poured us some water and we awkwardly clinked glasses. Brady's phone, which he'd left on the counter, started to buzz. Jane didn't look at it, but I did. It was a notification from earlier. Dr. Langley again.

"Jane, do you know why his doctor is calling?" *The completely hot one that I Facebook-stalked*, I didn't add.

"Oh"—she waved it off—"I noticed that too. He said it was something about low platelets, just needed to do some tests. Standard stuff."

"Gotcha," I replied, but really I was thinking that I was going to have to help Brady come up with a better excuse than low platelets. I mean, how long did he think he'd get away with Dr. Bang Me *texting* him over low platelets at all hours anyway?

"I was going to stay over tonight, but I have Pilates at seven a.m. . . . can you tell Brady if you see him first?"

"Of course. I have Pilates too. Then it's off to CrossFit."

Jane laughed and hugged me goodbye.

As I got ready for bed, I chuckled, recalling my Bruce Rodman story. The truth was, I always wanted to be that successful and smart girl, telling the other girls about her full life with her dream boyfriend. And I was that girl, for a hot minute, even if it was all a ruse.

CHAPTER 24

Namaste (Have a Nice Day)

Since the Sweater Set constantly talked about exercise, I felt like I really needed to step up. I pulled out Nadine's card, went online, and saw she was teaching that morning. I fished my yoga pants out of the bottom of my suitcase in Brady's closet and headed out. On the way, I texted my mother for the info on the miracle Chinese doctor and then forwarded it to Kevin. He texted back a thumbs-up.

Nadine was in total professional mode. I was sure the water bottle she had in the studio was actually holding water. She looked different somehow, but I couldn't place it. The people in the class were mostly middle-aged women and a few guys with man buns.

"So remember, you came here today, which means you're taking care of yourself. I'd like you all to set an intention for class . . ."

My "intention" was for the doctor to help Kevin. He really was a nice guy, who made a bad choice to stalk his ex. Still, he deserved to be happier. No one is perfect, and everyone deserves someone, right?

". . . and remember, your breath is your friend."

Was she serious?

". . . and all those doors that have been closed to you? Now it's time to open them . . ."

Easier said than done, I thought, but went with it.

"Now let's start on all fours . . ."

I tried to not let my mind go to a sexual place, but it was hard when everyone was wearing tight clothing and basically showing off their genitals as we stretched.

"Try to connect your breath with your body and your mind, so it's all one thing . . ."

I always found it hard to "connect" with your breathing when you're in some impossible balancing pose. But for the most part, the class was great, and I ended up getting really into the flow. The key thing about yoga, for me, is having an instructor with a pleasant, calming voice—someone who can articulate well but also knows when to stop talking. Too much talking kills my groove. Nadine was perfect, aside from the noise of her silver bracelets, which I would normally describe as mellifluous but in this situation found slightly annoying.

During Savasana, my favorite pose where you basically do nothing, I thought about Jack, who was probably speaking at his grandmother's funeral at that very moment. I realized I never really saw him cry, and for some reason that made *me* start to cry. Maybe it was all the toxins from the Sweater Set dinner being released, but I was an emotional wreck.

Nadine came around to each of us and pressed on our shoulders. It was then that I peeked out of one eye and noticed her cleavage. That was it. Her breasts were like, two cup sizes larger than the last time I saw her. I closed my eyes and held my breath. When she went on to the next person, I mouthed the words *Oh my God* to myself. If she was pregnant, they wouldn't have grown that fast. She must have had the girls done!

We ended in a sitting position to breathe some more, and I secretly wiped my face with my sleeve. Nadine thanked us for coming and said, "Namaste," which I always thought sounded like "Have a nice day." So that's what I said instead.

I wanted to personally thank Nadine after class, but she was being cornered by someone, so I just waved goodbye.

On my way down the stairs, I got an email from one of the galleries I'd reached out to. They were asking if I could come by for an interview at two o'clock. I booked it back to Brady's, changed into my LBD and red pumps (again), and made it to Dupont with five minutes to spare. I walked into the space with confidence, ready to kill it. Then my hope balloon deflated when I saw, lined up outside an office in the back of the gallery, five girls—all of them hotter, younger, and probably smarter than me. And they all wore suits. I looked like a hooker in comparison. I thought of those pictures they used to show kids, *Which one is different and does not belong?*

I sat on a plastic chair next to the Suits and pretended there was something absorbing on my phone, even though it was another story about the president hate-tweeting again.

After about forty minutes someone called my name, and I was finally led into the office. The man behind the desk was bald with a white beard, wearing (and pulling off) a silk scarf. He introduced himself as Spencer and asked me some general questions, but I wasn't sure he was even listening to my answers. His eyes were fixated on the wall right above me. Was there a spider?

"Art is the thing that moves me," I said, after a short lull in the conversation.

"What went wrong at the last gallery?"

"I got bored of New York," I said.

He raised an eyebrow, like maybe he was impressed by that answer.

"And what do you think of DC?" he asked.

"Not as boring," I said.

He asked me about Langhorne, who I noted as a reference on my CV I had sent him.

"I brought him in, so to speak. For his first show."

"Now look where he is!"

He smiled, but I gave him a blank stare.

"I'm guessing the scandal will only help . . ."

"Well," he stood up. "Thanks for coming in."

"My pleasure," I said. "Didn't get the memo about the suit."

He tilted his head a little and said, "You look fine. But I'm sure you know that. Have a nice day."

"Namaste," I said under my breath.

On my way out, I got a look at some of the art. It was overthought, pretentious, and just plain bad. I'm not sure I could've worked there, and that interview was awkward, but at least I was trying. It never hurt to try.

CHAPTER 25

THE CORK DORKS

Preston was curbside in a silver Honda Civic.

"What happened to the Beamer idea?" I asked as I got in the front seat.

"Keeping it real," he said.

I looked at his designer jeans, his nine-dollar coffee, and the watch gleaming on his wrist.

"Yeah, and the TAG Heuer really helps."

"Well, it was a present from Barkley, and he told me I could never take it off."

"That seems a little dramatic."

"Welcome to my world." As we pulled out, he held out his vape pen.

"Preston, I think I'm a little old to be riding around in Hondas with millennials smoking pot."

"Girl, it's basically legal now. And great for road trips."

We got onto the beltway, and he plugged in his phone. The first song on his playlist was Radiohead.

He took a long drag off the pen and passed it to me. *What the hell,* I thought, taking a small hit.

We got quiet for a while, zoning out to Thom Yorke's desperate but calming wail over a slightly industrial beat and fuzzy guitars. Then, Preston turned the music down and turned to me.

"Do you know who turned me on to Radiohead?"

"Who?"

"This kid Joe Hailey. He was a total jock. I was emo at the time, and I barely knew the guy. He was the freaking prom king! Anyway, he had a crush on me."

"Obviously," I said.

"So there was this huge party at some girl's parents' lake house, and I found myself in the pantry with him, draining the last of the keg. He pointed at my skull earring and my thumb ring and said, 'Press, you don't need all that.' It was the first time anyone had ever called me Press, and it felt so intimate, you know? Then he put his hand on my face, like he was cradling it."

"Wow. Then what?"

"He just smiled and walked away. It was the first time I had felt affection from another boy. I just stood there like a dork, smiling, until some couple came in, giggling and ripping off each other's clothes. After that, Joe never paid any attention to me.

"Until the last day of school, when he took me for a ride in his F-150, parked it down by the reservoir, and let me give him a blow job. I had no idea what I was doing, but he seemed to like it. Am I oversharing?"

"Slightly, but go on."

"So it was the weirdest thing. Before he came, he pulled my head up, opened the door, and finished outside the car."

Preston glanced at me with caution. I tried to seem less riveted than I was.

"Then what happened?"

"Nothing, really. He drove me home, and that was the last I've seen him. Or even thought about him."

"Hmm."

"Here's the thing. Most guys would just come in someone's mouth without asking, right?"

I thought of my own experiences in that regard. "Yes."

"Well, he didn't. He was polite about it. I'll never forget that. Sometimes, it's the little things."

I thought of Jack tickling my back in the middle of the night, waiting for my martini to arrive before sipping his own craft beer.

"Yes, it is. I don't know if that story was really touching, or if I'm just stoned out of my mind."

Preston laughed, and I could see so much innocence in him, even after the blow job story. Perhaps more. It was like watching a slow sunrise. His future hinted at so much more life and color. He was just getting started.

"So is that when you knew you were gay?"

"Ha! Girl, I had a breakfast nook in my tree house."

I laughed until my stomach hurt.

"I think I'm high," I finally said.

We exited onto a smaller, windy, country road, following the GPS woman who spoke in a British accent. After a few more miles, we had "reached our destination." A rustic sign at the bottom of a long driveway read **EDGEWOOD WINERY Est. 2004.** Underneath, there was a smaller homemade sign flapping in the wind that said: TASTING, FRIDAYS AT 4PM.

"Shit, it's Thursday," Preston said.

We drove very slowly up the driveway and saw a lithe woman getting out of a Jeep, her hair pulled back in a tight blonde ponytail. She looked like someone who could train a horse, bake a pie, and do a cover shoot for *Country Woman* magazine. Of course, the perfect match for BR. I started to tell Preston to turn around, but she came right up to my side of the car, saying, "Can I help you?"

"We were just wondering about the tasting, but we're obviously a day early," Preston said.

"Yes, but the store is open."

"Oh, great."

She gave a little wave and pointed us toward a parking space next to the store, which was more like a small barn. I was probably still stoned and slightly paranoid, as I found myself looking around to see if BR was going to pop out and bust us right then and there. But the only person in the store was a small, mousy lady with fair skin and a bad wig.

"Her hair is apricot," Preston whispered. "No one's hair is actually that color."

I tried to make my face normal and not judge her, but I did give Preston a *let's make this quick* look. There was a picture of Pinot and Cab by the register that almost made me faint. Several amateur brochures for nearby activities sat collecting dust.

Preston bought two bottles of cabernet with Barkley's black card, and I found myself touching the photo of the dogs. On our way out of the store, an older Land Rover pulled in, and I just knew it was BR—of course he had an old Land Rover. He parked in front of the house, which was about fifty yards away. The driver's door opened, and out came Pinot, galloping toward us.

I grabbed Preston and dragged him back into the store. The clerk woman had gone into the back, so we crouched by the window wine display and peeked out between the bottles.

"OMG, what if he comes over here?" Preston gasped.

"I am so screwed right now. I am ruining my chances!"

"Oh, you're back." Apricot Wig had returned. "Can I help you find anything else?"

We just stood there, frozen, as BR walked toward the store. He looked so hot I almost melted, and Preston turned to the woman and said, "Um. This is going to sound crazy, but do you have a back door?"

Before she could point toward the rear of the store, the two of us were sprinting back to it. We got outside and ran around to the side and had to bushwhack a little to get back to the front. Some bramble scraped my arm.

"Ow!" I yelled.

"Shh!" Preston said.

At the front we peeked around, and it seemed like the coast was clear. No sign of BR or Pinot.

"Ok, you get the car started and back up a little, then I'll jump in—that way if he comes out, I'll be blocked."

Preston did as he was told and sure enough, right when it was my cue, I heard the creaky door of the barn open again. To be sure I wasn't seen, I crawled across the driveway and then slid in, putting my head on Preston's lap. Preston covered me with his sweatshirt. Then came the sound of BR's smooth and deep voice.

"Everything okay?"

It sounded like he was inside the car.

Preston said, "Fine!" a little too enthusiastically, and then he added, "She's just not feeling well. Indigestion. Anyway, thanks, love the place!"

Preston peeled out, and we just started giggling hysterically.

When we got onto the main road, he said, "You can sit up now."

"Did he see me?"

"No. I'm sure he didn't."

"Do you think he recognized you from the dog park?"

"No!"

"What if they have security cameras? I can't believe I just totally blew it."

"Honey, the place was a barn. It didn't have security cameras. And that cougar woman, when he walked by her, they waved to each other. You know, like she was an employee or something. I still think he's single. I really do!"

"Or maybe that was the ex, April's mom."

"Could be. You looked hilarious crawling in the gravel."

"Shut up."

We turned onto the main highway, agreeing that the woman was either the ex-wife or someone who worked there. I said a secret prayer that she wasn't a current squeeze.

"I was wondering, though . . . where was Cab?"

"What?" Preston asked.

"Cab, the other dog. It was just Pinot."

"How am I supposed to know?"

"He hasn't been feeling well, I do know that."

"Girl, let's worry about the man before the dogs."

"Oh, c'mon, it's always about the dogs."

As we sped toward DC, I told Preston about the Sweater Set, and how I made up his name and French backstory.

"Page, we're going to have to work on the plausibility a little bit. I don't think Rodman is a very French name."

"Well, the Sweater Set aren't exactly the brightest crayons in the box. But Perfect Jane, I think she may be on to me."

"Oh well, all the power to you. Like Oprah says, put it out into the universe!"

"It's out there. Just not sure if the universe will hear little old me."

"You're not old, and you're not little. You are a force."

I laughed.

"Say it. Go on, say it."

"I am a force," said softly.

"Like you mean it . . ."

"I am a force!" I said, this time almost believing it.

CHAPTER 26

An Ultimate Low

I don't know if it was the winery shit show, the epic fail of a job interview, or the pathetic attempts at dating, but I didn't feel like a force that night. I tried to lift myself up by pouring some scotch, taking a bath, lighting some candles, and listening to my favorite Spotify playlist.

Brady was not at the restaurant or at home, and I happened to know Jane was at a work event. Where was he? Was he off having an affair with Dr. Bang Me? How come he was he getting it from two sides and I was batting zero?

After my bath, I dried off and put on one of Brady's dress shirts. I started reading a listicle online to get my mind off it, but it was about how to find a man, and it was completely unrealistic. Photoshopped girls with negative body fat graced the ads on the site, and I felt tears burn the backs of my eyes. Then I heard that catchy jingle, the one that happens when someone is FaceTiming you. It was Jack. In a moment of weakness, I pressed accept.

He was sitting on his couch, and he looked older, but still handsome.

"I'm sorry about Mimi," I said.

"Me too."

I found myself wanting to be there next to him, which was stupid, because I could've sworn I was over him.

"How's DC?" he said.

"Up and down, I guess."

"Yeah. You'll figure it out, though. You always do."

"Not sure about that."

Why was he FaceTiming me? Was he just vulnerable because Mimi died?

He started talking about his work, and I was half listening, until he said, "You know what day it is?"

"Thursday," I said.

He smiled, and I couldn't help but smile back. We had agreed, on one of our first dates, that Thursday was always a good day for sex. It was our thing. We had sex on other days, but a lot on Thursdays.

He took off his shirt, and I could see that broad, familiar chest of his.

"We aren't doing this," I said.

"Why not?"

Screw it, I thought, downing the rest of my scotch and unbuttoning my shirt. I wasn't wearing a bra, and Jack's face lit up on the screen.

"You have the most beautiful breasts. Can you touch them?"

"If you touch yours."

So there we were, touching our nipples on FaceTime. I thought it couldn't get any worse, but it did. I got on top of the bed and gave him a show, like I was some kind of amateur burlesque performer, and then I got dirtier. He kept saying *yes, yes*, and I was getting really turned on, until I was close to having an orgasm, but when I looked at the screen, it had frozen on a shot of Jack's hairy balls. I let out a sound that was part laugh and part cry. Then I sighed and closed my laptop, put on a robe, and went to the kitchen to get gelato. One pint of salted caramel and two more glasses of scotch later, I opened my laptop again, and the FaceTime screen was still there, frozen on his balls.

I tried to force quit but it wasn't working, and I actually started laughing. When one was this miserable, laughter was completely

126

necessary. But eventually it turned to tears, and I called my mother. It went to voice mail, and I started blabbering.

"I feel like we never talked after the whole Charlie thing happened. I get it, you need him or whatever, but I'm your daughter, don't forget that. I know I'm not as successful as Brady but . . ." A voice came on asking whether I'd like to continue to record, or erase and rerecord. I chose the latter and simply said, "Hi, Mom, it's me, Page," and hung up. I thought of who else I could call, and scrolled through my contacts, most of whom were people in New York I barely knew. I started deleting them, one by one.

Before I fell asleep, a text came in from Jack.

sorry my wifi is broken.

So are we, I thought, turning my phone off. *So are we.*

CHAPTER 27

BLASTS FROM THE PAST

At the EDP, Sammy gave me his *this place again?* look, and I said, "C'mon, it's better than that depressing apartment you live in."

As I was entering, Nadine and her tiny dog Beanu were leaving, and we hugged by the gates.

"I loved your class!" I told her.

"Thanks, you have to come back," she said. "Yoga is everything."

"I don't know about that, but it was definitely relaxing."

She was hiding her cleavage under a thin cashmere sweater so I didn't bring it up, but she must have sensed me looking.

"It's okay, you can touch them if you want."

I laughed.

"My dad's a plastic surgeon, so it was on the house."

"No way!"

"But don't worry, I know it's a slippery slope. That's all I'm doing. Well, maybe my nose. Anyway, it's unbelievable. When I had no tits, I didn't even register with guys. Now it's like I have to fight them off."

"Yeah, me too," I joked.

"You're fine in that department," she said. "Anyway, thanks again for coming to my class. And for helping me last week. I'm so done with him."

"Good. Are you . . . you know . . ."

"Still late? Yes."

"Oh."

"I think it's just stress. And getting new tits."

I laughed.

"Anyway, I'll keep you posted."

Beanu licked her face, and she waved goodbye, her bracelets jingling.

I sat down at my usual bench and told Sammy to go play with some of the new dogs I hadn't seen before. I was thinking, even between the winery debacle and the FaceTime nightmare, it could be worse: I could be pregnant with Mean Face's baby.

A woman about my height in a business casual suit looked at me a little strangely, but then we realized, in an instant, that we knew each other. The recognition in our eyes was like a current of electricity. It was Felicia's aunt. Back in the day, we used to steal her boxes of chardonnay. She was the very chill aunt, always lounging by the pool reading, half in the bag on those suburban Massachusetts afternoons that seemed to go on forever. She had, however, aged quite well.

"Page!"

"Fancy meeting you here," I said.

She gave me a hug and squealed, "You look great!" The thing about this statement is that it's so obligatory. You're never going to hear, "You look like a cow!" or "Have you ever heard of sunblock?" so essentially, you can never tell if the person is lying or not. My father told me people look down and to the left after they lie, and she didn't do that. She just wore an earnest expression, which gave me hope that she was actually being honest.

We sat down, and I introduced her to Sammy.

"Is he yours?"

"No, he's . . . a friend's."

I didn't want to go into the dog-walking job, and it wasn't a complete lie. Since we'd been talking more, Kevin was actually becoming a friend anyway.

"Wait, I'm going to call Felicia. I can't believe this. You know she's been trying to get a hold of you? This is crazy, just finding you here."

As we waited for Felicia to pick up, she told me she was in town on business, and house sitting over the weekend, which came with two Boston terriers, Baby and Sweets, who were currently ruling the EDP at the top of the Astroturf mound.

When Felicia answered, she thrust the phone at me as if it were a check for a million dollars.

"Hello?"

"Page, I have been trying to reach you forever! When did your cell change? I knew you weren't at the gallery, but did they give you my messages?"

"Yes, I'm so sorry, I was meaning to call you."

I walked to the corner of the park, almost tripping over a feisty Jack Russell.

"What's going on?"

"Well, it's kind of a nightmare. Jack and I broke up, then I got fired, now I'm living with Brady here in DC, and walking some guy's dog. Aren't you jealous?"

She laughed and said, "Well, you're not going to believe this. You remember Greg Henley from high school?"

I braced myself against the fence and said, "Yes, he was like, the quarterback Ken Doll from hell."

"Well, we're engaged! And I'm having an engagement party next Friday! And you HAVE to come . . ."

Just not on FaceTime, I thought. *But really?*

I could feel my hands starting to sweat and my throat tighten. Every friend from college, and now Felicia. All getting married except me.

"I am so happy for you," I said, desperately trying to sound genuine.

"We have to catch up. Listen, why don't you come up Thursday night, a bunch of us are just going to chill at my parents' place."

"I'll see what I can do. I may have a job interview."

"Well, the party's Friday at five. Please, please say you'll be there and I'll know it's fate, that Aunt Rita was in the right place in DC and . . ."

She was starting to get hysterical, which was so unlike her. It freaked me out, so I just said, "Yes, yes, I'll come."

I could hear her yelling through the phone as I passed it back to Rita.

"So you're coming?" she asked after hanging up.

"Of course," I said, and she squealed again.

Sammy ran up to me and tilted his head as if to say, *who's this chick now?*

"Great! See you Friday!" Rita gathered up the terriers and went on her way.

I sat there, slightly baffled. Felicia was marrying Greg Henley? I looked at my arm, still a little scraped from my fantasy husband's bushes.

Sammy wagged his tail and snorted, his way of telling me he wanted to go as well. While walking him home, I thought about Felicia. How did I lose touch with her? It seemed that being in my thirties was a way of slowly disconnecting with my former life. The random people I knew, and even some close friends, just fell away, like shedding skin. The information age seemed to isolate people even more, texting replacing conversation, everyone obsessed with their screens.

As I approached Kevin's door, I noticed one of his neighbors, a hipster dude, sizing me up. What was it about me now? Was there a possible upside to having nothing to lose? Did failure have a certain allure?

Things had to get better. They just had to. *Press on*, I could almost hear my father saying. *Press on.*

CHAPTER 28

DOODLES AND DITTIES

Sammy inhaled his two treats, then plopped down on his doggy bed in a slump of defeat. As I was leaving, I noticed Kevin's bedroom door was slightly ajar. It squeaked a little as I opened it farther, and I turned back to see Sammy looking at me from the living room, his expression saying, *who's the stalker now?*

Everything looked normal in the room, except one thing I couldn't miss. There was a giant tapestry on the wall, and I could see it was covering something behind it. I peeled it back slowly, expecting to see childish artwork, or maybe just stains, but it was a massive, intricate doodle drawing, right on the wall. A million tiny twists of line. It was mesmerizing. I stepped back and took it all in. I could see giraffes and swans, spider webs and fern leaves, open hands and screaming faces. I'm not sure how long I stared at it, but eventually Sammy barked from the hallway, as if to say, *that's enough, get out of his room now.* I took a picture of it on my phone, quickly tacked the tapestry back up, and shuffled out the door, but not before ruffling Sammy's ears, saying, "You're a good boy. If you know what's best for you, don't you dare tell Kevin I was in his room."

I applied for two more jobs that afternoon, both of which seemed implausible. One was at a bakery, and under "baking experience" I wrote that I knew my way around a rolling pin (even though I'd never baked anything in my life). The other was at a coffee shop, and the woman who took my application, who had a tattoo of a snake around her neck, didn't even look me in the eye. The job situation was not so promising.

I went back to the EDP on my own. Several of the dog owners were used to me now, and they didn't ask the *Where's your dog?* question that I always heard as *Where's your life?* I was still figuring that one out.

I watched a couple of Weimaraners spin around like maniacs, and it reminded me of Jack. All those years I was just chasing my own tail, thinking it would get me somewhere other than dizzy and confused. As if he heard my thoughts, I got a text from him. Everything okay? it said. Yeah, just peachy, Jack. Easy to answer in a text. I immediately deleted it. Brady was right. What a putz. But so was I for giving in to him last night. I shunned the thought from my mind.

Sipping my to-go cappuccino, I scrolled to the pic of Kevin's doodle wall on my phone. It really was beautiful. My reaction when I first saw it was not unlike the feeling I got when looking at Langhorne's work for the first time—it just took me to another place. Which is where I was when BR walked up, seemingly glad to see me.

"Hey there."

"Hi," I said, snapping out of my daze.

As Pinot sniffed out the Weimaraners, he asked me how my week was going.

"Oh, you know, stalked your winery," I said under my breath.

"What?"

"I guess I'm just not really good at adulting."

"Ha. Is anyone?"

"I applied for a job at a bakery, and the only thing I can bake is potatoes."

He laughed, and I noticed how nice his teeth were. I tried not to stare at his hair, which was mostly dark brown but had some red and a few grays. He had it de-styled into a casual, just-rode-my-horse look.

I had to resist the urge to run my hands through it. And don't get me started on those beautiful eyes. I couldn't look into them for too long or I'd faint.

BR checked his phone and sighed.

"Something wrong?" I asked.

"Well, my other dog, Cab . . ."

"I've missed him!"

"He's just not himself, and I'm kind of in denial about it. The vet doesn't really know what it is."

"Oh."

The edge of his leg was touching mine ever so slightly. I don't think he noticed, but for me it felt like my leg had lasers running through it.

"I just can't imagine anything ever happening to him."

"I hear you. We had two Labs when I was younger, Paul and Ringo. When Paul died, I didn't go to school for a week. When Ringo died, I cried until there were no more tears left in my body."

He turned and smiled, like he'd glimpsed another layer of me.

"By the way, I must confess, I don't have a dog."

"I eventually picked up on that," he said, still smiling. "But are you going to get one? I mean, now?"

"Well, I've been researching, and I have my eye on this one adoption agency. But there's a lot of loose ends in my life that need to be tied up before I can . . ."

"Ah, those. There's always going to be loose ends."

Maybe you can tie one for me, I wanted to say.

He took out a tin of Altoids and offered me one. I hated Altoids, but I took it like it was a dollop of youth serum. Maybe it meant he was going to kiss me.

He got another notification on his phone and then turned to face me, putting his hand on my shoulder.

"So I'm not really a helicopter parent, but I am trying out this app that tracks my daughter's phone. Basically everything that comes through her phone goes through mine."

"That sounds super helicopter."

He slid his hand from my shoulder, even though I was secretly willing him to keep it there.

"Really?"

"Does she know this?"

His expression turned sheepish as he slowly shook his head.

"This is not okay," I said.

A silence followed during which I was internally punching myself. Why was I berating the man of my dreams? How was I going to get out of this?

"Of course, I don't have a child, so I don't know what it's like."

Now I sounded like I wouldn't be a good stepmom.

"But your daughter, I've met her a few times. You can tell how smart she is by just looking at her. And I heard her sing a little, what a voice . . ."

"Yeah, well, that's what this is about. She sent a demo to LA, and this guy who's the uncle of her friend at school runs this really hip label, the one that has Phoenix and Mumford & Sons."

I was secretly pleased that I got the musical references. Maybe I wasn't that old!

"So what's the problem?"

Pinot came up and put his face on my leg, and I rubbed behind his ears.

"This is going to sound . . . I don't know . . . I guess I still picture her with her blankie and her juice boxes. It's hard to, you know . . ."

"I get it, it's like watching something you love leave you. Not leave you physically, but you know what I mean."

"Yeah."

I wanted to hug him so bad, and my arms actually started to move in his direction, but then I chickened out.

"And I don't want to sound like an American Idol judge," I said, "but she has a really unique tone."

He smiled. "So they want her to come to LA and do this showcase, for the whole label."

"That's amazing!"

"Right? But I have to convince her mother. She's the one that's helicopter. It drives April crazy."

Pinot looked up at me, and I could've sworn he was saying, *please marry my dad. Please?*

"Speak of the devil," BR said, and up walked April, who had apparently been on her phone outside of the park.

"I'm gonna go home and get Cab, take him back to the vet. Can you take it from here?"

"Yeah, Dad, it's cool."

"Okay, see you around . . . ," he said to me as we locked eyes. Then he turned and kissed April on her forehead. I realized I still didn't know his name! After he left, April turned to me and said, "He doesn't show it, but my dad is kind of freaking out. He loves Pinot, but he's always been obsessed with Cab. From when he was a baby, Cab has slept in his bed. Pinot sleeps in the kitchen."

"Aw. Well, I hope he's okay."

"I'm sure he will be."

April took out an iPod Shuffle and started scrolling through it.

"Wow, haven't seen one of those in a while," I said.

"I know, it's ancient, but my dad gave it me when I was seven, and he put all these songs on it. Some of them are super dorky, but a lot of them influenced my songwriting."

"That is so great."

"Yeah, and he also recorded these messages and put them on here, told me they were secret. Little things about life, I guess. Some of them are cheesy, but I still like to listen to them."

I was so happy she was comfortable enough to tell me about this. I tried not to oversmile like an idiot. Her phone buzzed, and she put the iPod down on the bench. I stared at it in awe.

After a bunch of frantic texting, she whistled for Pinot and said, "I have to go meet Jorie. I swear he has more drama than my girlfriends do."

I smiled and said, "No prob, nice seeing you."

"You too, so long," she said, but it almost sounded like, "You too, Mom." Or maybe I was officially losing it. How was I going to land BR? Was he really just going to fall for my ballsy charm? For the fact that I won over his daughter and his dogs?

I watched a cute Frenchie strut around, and then I gave some love to what looked like a pit bull–Lab mix that was clearly craving attention. As I got up to leave, I noticed something glinting from the corner of my eye. A ray of sun was reflecting off the silver iPod on the bench. April had left it there. I grabbed it quickly and stuck it into my bag.

I must have looked silly run-walking back to Brady's place, where I immediately found earphones, lay on my bed, and put the iPod on play. The first song I heard was Joni Mitchell's "A Case of You." A dark choice for a seven-year-old, but poignant nonetheless.

As I got up and walked through Brady's place, "How Sweet It Is" by James Taylor came on. Again, an odd choice, but at least it wasn't "Sexual Healing." I barely knew the guy, but BR just wasn't creepy . . . he was the opposite of creepy. With those kind eyes and that chiseled jawline, he looked like he could give your car an oil change and then pick you a bouquet of wildflowers.

As I walked onto the terrace, a warm breeze hit my face, and on came the sound of BR's voice:

When you were born, I had this feeling that all was right in the world. Your little pink face and your chubby fingers. I knew you were going to be special, from the very first moment. I hope that whatever you do in life, you do it from your heart. Eat life, as my mother used to say. Eat life.

I felt a trembling sensation in my core. What the hell was going on? I was listening to sweet messages by this guy whose name I didn't know but was obsessed with, and they were for his daughter. I went back inside and sat on Brady's couch. The next song, "Yellow" by Coldplay, brought me back to middle school, when I had a crush on Adam Ellis. He was a transfer student, and only at my school for a semester. He wore big black boots even in summer, and he had a fake tattoo of a dragonfly on his hand. One day at a soccer game, I noticed him watching in the crowd. At the eighth grade dance, we danced to "Yellow." At the end of the song, he kissed me on the lips, gently, and that was the last I'd ever seen of him. But the song has always transported me back to that gymnasium with its cheap decorations, how Adam smelled like chocolate and smoke, and that feeling that maybe I, too, could get swept into love. I felt that with BR at the park. I realized then, as the song came to an end, that I'd never felt that with Jack, meaning obviously it wasn't love. Yes, I was on the cusp of thirty-five, but there was no reason why I shouldn't find it now.

CHAPTER 29

Inroads

On the way to the party, Michael of Austria seemed distracted.

"Is everything good?"

"Well, it's just my mother. She broke her hip."

"Oh no! Are you going to see her? I mean, go back to Austria?"

"That's the problem. I want to, but my brother doesn't want me to. He's, well, I think he's somehow ashamed of me."

"That's ridiculous. Because you're eccentric? That's something to be celebrated."

He smiled, and the darkness seemed to wash out of his face.

"I spoke to her this morning, but she was on the drugs, you know, kind of, how do you say, mushy?"

"Yeah."

"The thing is, she is not ashamed of me. She never has been. It's just the men in my family that are so twisted up."

I took his hand and said, "Men are definitely twisted."

"I will call her tomorrow, and if she still wants me to come, I will."

He snickered, and I said, "What?"

"I insisted they get an elevator in their house, and my father didn't want to. Now she is thanking her stars."

"She's thanking you, her brightest star," I said, and he smiled again.

We were dropped off at the Jefferson hotel bar, where a man with a bow tie was playing a grand piano for a private party of about thirty people. The space was all leather and wood, you could almost feel the ghosts of presidents and senators past.

They were serving flutes of Moet and salmon croquettes on shiny silver trays. Michael took me around almost as if I were his date, and a lot of people gave me looks that said, *We know, he's an odd bird.* Whatever my relationship with him was, I was all over it, especially because half of the crowd were art dealers and collectors. Spencer, the man from my gallery interview, still rocking the white beard and silk scarf, was now on the other side of the coin, blushing in the presence of Michael. I gave him my best *you have no idea what you're missing* eyes.

Most of the crowd were older white men shaped like pears, but with handsome faces and real pedigrees. After talking with a woman who had written a screenplay about Picasso, I found myself abandoned in the corner, but it was okay.

A round-faced, smiling woman brought me some ice water, and right away I recognized her. Without thinking, I blurted out, "Porkie-poo!"

"What?"

I laughed like I just cracked myself up.

"The Yorkie-poo! You have the Yorkie-poo?"

"Oh, yes, and you have the big golden."

"Some of the time," I said, and she winked.

A skinny man with wire-rimmed glasses and shoulder-length salt-and-pepper hair came over and sat down next to me. With his long nose and his air of femininity, he seemed like a cross between Steven Tyler and Woody Allen, if that were even possible.

His name was Rex, and we started talking about David Choe, the graffiti artist who painted the offices of a then unknown Facebook, and passed up the sixty grand in cash for stock instead, which was now worth hundreds of millions.

"Crazy, right?" he said.

"Yeah. Good instincts he has in business. Not so much in painting."

He looked taken aback. "You don't like his work?"

"Well, from what I've seen, it doesn't slay me, no."

Apparently Rex found my honesty inviting.

"Hmm," he said, smiling in a slightly peculiar way. "Are you on Facebook?"

"God no," I said. "It just seems like such a waste of time. Internet crack."

He chuckled.

"So don't tell me you own David Choe," I said.

"I do, in fact. One piece. I bought it at a show in London, before the Facebook thing broke. I daresay it was a good investment."

Now I was impressed.

"Okay. I'll just take my foot out of my mouth now."

A young waitress poured us more champagne, and I learned that Rex was not only an art collector, but also a songwriter, and he had penned two songs with Dolly Parton that were what he described as "the gift that keeps on giving." I found it a little tacky to bring up, but at least he didn't mention any numbers.

Before we left, Rex gave me his card and said he and his wife would love to show me their collection in their Navy Yard loft. I told him I'd be honored. At this rate, I'd be hobnobbing with every power couple in DC by summer.

On the way back to Brady's apartment, I told Michael that my gallery plans were starting to take shape.

"I know it's a long shot, but I'd love work for myself. I have good instincts about art, so why not try?"

"That is the right attitude!" he said, beaming like a middle-aged boy. "We will talk further on this subject, yes, yes."

"Thank you, Michael, for everything."

"Of course, of course. Sleep well, my dear."

He kissed me on both cheeks as usual, and I let myself into Brady's place, which was empty. Brady must have been working late again, or getting another "checkup."

Before bed, I tried my mother again, but it went to voice mail. I remember she used to make sure we talked every Sunday. Then after she met Charlie, it became once a month. Now it was just sporadically. Still, I really could use a parental figure. Hearing BR, the way his voice went a little softer when talking about April, I instantly knew the girl had nothing to worry about. But that's what I thought too. I thought I could call my father at a time like this. He could diffuse a situation for me like no one else, and he always cared. And he would never be the one to end the conversation, because he was all in. I got that from Brady, too, though not as intensely.

As I curled into a fetal position, I made a wish. I didn't believe in that stuff, but I had already set an intention for Kevin, so I was on a roll.

Please, let Brady not be having an affair. It's not fair to Jane.

Maybe I was just being silly, but either way, the time had come. I would ask him flat out, and be *his* listening ear for once.

CHAPTER 30

CATCHING UP

Sitting on my bench at the EDP, I heard the familiar rattle of Sumner's Gucci collar, and of course, he went right to my legs. Behind him, Barkley was in his usual three-piece suit, but he had a slight scowl on his face.

"Barkley, I never see you in the mornings."

"Exactly, mornings are for commerce," he said, wiping the bench with his handkerchief and sitting down next to me.

Since he looked like he could use some distracting, I filled him in on everything: the gallery plans, Kevin's doodle, April's iPod, and my further endearment to BR.

"I know I've only met him a few times, but he's apparently beautiful on the inside too."

"Well," Barkley said, "there are two things that attract beauty."

"What?" I asked.

"Money, and beauty."

"Well, I better be beautiful then."

Sumner barked as if to say, *not BR beautiful.*

Barkley put his hand on my shoulder. "You have no problems in that department, dear."

"Speaking of beauty, how is Preston?"

Barkley sighed. "He's at the gym right now, doing free weights but hopefully not his trainer."

"How's his collection coming along?"

"It's actually quite remarkable. You must come over and see it."

"I want to. I have to book a train up north, to go to a friend's engagement party in my hometown. She's marrying the pretty boy jock with no brain."

"Sounds promising."

"Yeah, we'll see. I feel weird about it, but maybe I'm just jealous. Like, I just wanna marry BR, live on his winery, and fuck like rabbits."

Barkley belly-laughed. "You know, normally I don't care for a lady who curses, but it suits you."

"The trick is to limit your curses, so that when you actually do curse, it carries more weight."

Sammy came over and Sumner sniffed him, then looked up at Barkley as if to say, *this goofball again? He obviously has never seen the inside of a dog spa. Please.*

Sammy was ready for his treats. It was the only time of the day the dog actually smiled. Barkley's phone rang, but before he answered it he said, "You must come over immediately upon your return."

"Who says that? Upon your return."

"Gentlemen of a certain class level," Barkley said.

"Well, class or no class, I'll be there. Especially if you're serving more of that '91 Bordeaux."

"That can be arranged."

Barkley finally answered his phone. I scratched behind Sumner's ears and made my way out of the park with Sammy.

On Q Street, I saw the dog before the person. A little white puffball. "Beanu!" I said, looking up to see Nadine on her phone, giving me the *hold on* gesture. Sammy couldn't be bothered with Beanu and plopped down on the sidewalk. Nadine was smiling into the phone, and I wondered if I should be listening or not. After she hung up, she grabbed Beanu, and I noticed her eyes were damp.

"Are you okay?" I asked, knowing she obviously wasn't.

"I'm not pregnant."

"This is good, right? No Mean Face baby?"

We hugged.

"I'm so relieved," she said. "It's like I can finally breathe."

"Yeah," I said.

"Thanks again for helping me. How can I return the favor?"

"Let's go out for drinks some time?"

"Yes. On me!"

She kissed me on the cheek and was off, leaving me in a cloud of her Chanel No. 5.

Walking back to Kevin's, I turned to Sammy and said, "Crisis averted, huh?"

Sammy just tilted his head a little, like it was nothing, just humans doing those crazy things they do.

CHAPTER 31

SOMETHING STRONGER

Kevin was there when we got to his apartment, watching CNN and eating carrots from a ceramic bowl. As I went to reach for Sammy's treats, Kevin stood up and intercepted me so he could do the honors.

"Would you like some tea?"

I really didn't want tea again, so I said, "Do you have something stronger?"

A few minutes later he came back from the kitchen with two tumblers filled with a few inches of vodka. We clinked glasses and I said, "I have to go to an engagement party in my hometown. I'm not sure there's enough vodka in Massachusetts for me to deal with it."

He did his little snort laugh, and maybe it was the initial rush from my first big gulp of the cold, bitter liquid, but I said, "I saw your masterpiece. Your bedroom door was open. I couldn't resist, I'm so sorry. I didn't snoop at all except for pulling back the tapestry."

His face became a study in reds. I tried to say something, but there was a disconnect between my brain and my mouth. Kevin covered his face with his hands.

I had to fill the silence.

"It's . . . completely fresh and unique. Like this giant work of lines that you can find a million things in."

He lowered his hands and looked right at me, all the colors now drained from his face.

"It's nothing."

"Are you kidding me? Have you always drawn?"

"Since I was a kid, I guess. Then after Penelope . . ." He looked off into space.

"Well, I'd say that is one good thing that came out of that breakup. You know, I'm trying to open a gallery, and if I do, I'd love to have it in my opening show. That is, if we can actually take your wall out of here."

His eyes brightened a little, but he didn't say anything. I told him we could talk about it later. Sammy came over and put his snout on Kevin's thigh. A simple gesture, but one that never got old. Dogs were eternally sweet.

"So who's getting married?" Kevin asked, changing the subject.

"Oh, my friend Felicia."

He seemed to be waiting for me to elaborate, so I told him about Greg Henley, and how the last time I remember seeing him was at Julia Hurst's house, where a bunch of us went after an early release day in high school. Someone's brother had just gotten back from a Phish tour with a sheet of LSD, and each of us took a half dose.

"Wow," Kevin said. "I was playing Dungeons & Dragons in high school, and you were having acid trips."

"Just one, actually. It was me, Felicia, Julia, and Greg. We ended up going for a ride on her horses. It was crazy beautiful, the sun on the tall grass, and we were just smiling until our faces hurt. Then, like everything too magical to be real, it turned ugly. Julia's horse that she'd had since she was ten collapsed, and the three other horses stopped short, as if they knew something was terribly wrong.

"And the horse died, right there, with Julia crying, slumped over its body. It created a whole new meaning to the words 'bad trip.'"

Kevin sipped his vodka and said, "Holy shit."

"But the thing that I remember most is Greg. He just like, ran away. We all stayed and dealt with the situation, but he bailed. Felicia is one of my only friends left, and she's marrying a coward."

"I hate it when that happens," Kevin said, and for the first time I laughed at something he said.

We sat in silence, finishing our drinks with Sammy curled at our feet, until Kevin cleared his throat and said, "Now that you've seen my wall and know about Penelope, you must think I'm a nutjob."

"No! I mean, the stalking thing was bad. You should probably stop that. But you . . . you're good."

When the vodka was gone, I gathered my bag and jacket to leave, and he walked me to the door.

I was feeling fortitude, but it was most likely the alcohol talking. "Can I ask you something?"

"Sure."

"Do you think I'm girlfriend material?"

Kevin smiled but then got serious when he knew I was.

"Everyone is someone's true love," he said, his eyes flashing warmth.

"Yeah, I guess you're right."

"My brother says Penelope was way too hot for me, that I need to lower my bar."

"Screw that."

"That's what I said."

"But you do need to move on from her . . ."

"Yeah. That's why you're walking Sammy. I'm in therapy."

"Great, great."

"Page. About the gallery thing. That would be . . . yeah, that would be amazing."

Tell me about it, I thought. It was the perfect thing. And now I had two really strong pieces. An excellent start.

"Oh! And your mother texted me. That doctor from Boston, he's going to be here in DC at a convention this weekend, and he agreed to see me."

"Excellent!"

Funny that my mother was texting Kevin but not answering my calls. At least she was helping, though.

We stood there, beaming at each other, until I said, "Okay, well, have a good one."

"You too."

On my way home, I couldn't help but to wonder if the intention I set in Nadine's yoga class meant something. I hoped so. Kevin wasn't perfect, but he deserved a break.

CHAPTER 32

Strange Behavior

When I got home, Brady was gone again.

I went into his room just as Jane texted me, asking where he was. I called him on his cell, and it went straight to voice mail.

I sat on his bed, looking around the room, wondering what was going on. I couldn't see it, but I could feel it.

Back in the guest room, the painting still leaned against the wall. As it turned out, it was too big even if I replaced the female nudes. I wondered about the third floor, maybe there would be space to put it up there for now. I decided to check it out. I knew Brady used it for storage.

As I ascended the stairs, I could hear the muffled sound of drums. There was a thin hallway with a small room at the end. I opened the door and stood there, motionless.

Brady, in only his boxer briefs and a pair of huge headphones, was nodding slowly to the beat. The walls were lined with records, and a turntable sat precariously on a repurposed box serving as a table.

It was like looking at a different person. I knew Brady had a record collection, but not this big. He never mentioned it.

When the song ended, he noticed me standing there, and a flash of embarrassment passed over him, like a child caught with his hand in the cookie jar.

"What the . . ."

"Welcome to the music cave," he said.

I walked in, running my fingers across the stacks of records.

"You never had this many."

"I thought I told you, about a year ago I bought this collection from a church. A church! And they had like, Led Zeppelin and Johnny Cash!"

Something was off. Brady seemed manic.

"This is awesome," I said. "But what's going on with you?"

It was like he didn't hear the question. He was on a whole different thought.

"Do you remember the time you carried me down the beach?"

"Of course," I told him. "I remember it vividly."

We were kids, running fast and howling, our bare feet splattering the shallow surf. Brady was in front of me, his wavy brown hair catching the orange rays of the fading sun. Our parents were far away, probably inside by then, Dad with his scotch and the crossword on the couch, Mom with her wine at the kitchen table, reading. A cluster of birds dipped down near our heads, hovering a bit before flying away. Brady stepped on a slippery rock and I heard a clicking sound, like turning a key in a lock, and he twisted, collapsing into himself, falling on his face.

"I must have passed out, because I don't remember anything right after I sprained it," Brady said. "When I woke up, you were carrying me, my baby sister!"

"You had snot all over you," I said. "You were scared. You had a brave face, but there was something underneath it. Fear."

I realized he had the same expression right then.

"Brady, how long have you been up here?"

"A couple of hours."

"Don't you have to go to the restaurant?"

He started giggling a little.

"Are you high?"

That made him giggle more. Then he pulled himself together and stood up.

"I'm so proud of you, Page."

"What . . . for having no life?"

He started laughing again, but it sounded off and made me a little queasy. Maybe he was drunk?

"Page, you have the world ahead of you."

"It's actually starting to feel like that."

He hugged me, and I could feel him take a really deep breath. When we separated, he looked more normal. Still, asking him about Dr. Bang Me seemed out of the question timing wise.

"You know what? You're right. I have to go to Elbow and close. We had two hundred and fourteen guests on the books tonight. I hope they didn't burn the place down or something."

"Okay. You may want to put some clothes on."

Off he went, leaving me in the music cave. There was a musky smell, and a sandwich on a plate with only one bite taken out of it. Next to the turntable was a small, pocket-size picture of our dad in the navy. There were shiny thumbprints on it, like it had been recently held. I missed him too.

As I got ready for bed, I put on April's iPod, and there it was, the sound of BR's voice:

The day you came into my life, I couldn't stop singing.

I looked into the mirror and smiled, but then I felt a drop in my stomach. Was I committing a terrible crime listening to something so intimate between a father and a daughter?

In bed, I thought again of Brady spraining his ankle when we were kids. How just moments before it happened, we had been so free, splashing around in some kind of childhood oblivion. Having no idea how fragile, how vulnerable we were.

CHAPTER 33

THE HEADBUTT

When I went to get Sammy for his walk, I was startled by Kevin, who usually wasn't there at that time. It looked like he'd been crying.

"What's wrong?" I asked.

"I lost my bread and butter client this morning. I'm sorry, I meant to text you. I won't need you to walk Sammy anymore."

"Wait, what about your therapy?"

"I don't think I'll be able to afford it now . . ."

He looked so sad, I couldn't take it. I had to think of something to cheer him up.

"Look," I said. "Why don't you keep up the therapy. And I can still walk Sammy, free of charge. It's not like I'm doing anything else."

"Really?"

"Absolutely. Besides, I've become attached to the big guy."

Sammy whined, knowing we were talking about him. He looked at Kevin as if to say, *she did save me from boinking the husky bitch.*

"Okay, thanks. That would be great. Also, I'm meeting with that doctor, but I'm not sure I can afford . . ."

"It's just a consultation, and he owes my mother, so you're good."

Kevin sighed. "Why are you being so nice to me?"

"Because you're a nice person," I said.

"You are too. Thank you."

"It's nothing. Come on, buddy!"

I took Sammy out into the bright world, and he actually seemed to be smiling. Maybe he knew his father was going to be around more. When it came down to it, dogs just wanted to be near their people. It was about proximity.

The EDP was pretty empty, but Sammy seemed to have extra energy, trying to wake the old Lab who just liked to sleep, his owner in a foldout chair reading a World War II biography.

"A little light reading for the dog park?" I said to him.

He never spoke, but at least it got a smile out of him.

I sat on my bench, which wasn't the same without the peanut gallery of Preston and Nadine. A few minutes later, I heard the clank of the gates, and up ran Pinot. I felt like I was reuniting with my lost child who'd been kidnapped.

"Pinot!" I yelled. When he got to me, I leaned down just as he jumped up, and our heads collided. There was ringing in my ears, and my nose was numb. I tried to shake it off, as BR was fast approaching, his hair perfectly windblown, his face slightly tan and weathered. It was hard to ignore the fact that my nose was throbbing, but I smiled, twirling my hair a little. It wasn't until I finally looked at him that I realized something was terribly wrong. Then it was like a dam breaking. Blood, pouring out of my left nostril and running onto my white top. *Really?* I thought. *This is what's happening?*

"Do you want some help?" he asked.

"Um, sure," I said, slightly mortified.

"Okay, okay, lean forward a little." BR took charge, placing one hand firmly on the small of my back while pinching the top of my nose with the other. Mr. World War II came over with some napkins and handed them to BR like they were a paramedic team.

"Just relax," BR said. "You'll be fine."

"Pinot and I, we butted heads."

He laughed. "I think Pinot won."

BR was right. Pinot was running around the park like nothing happened. Dogs were so incredibly resilient.

He moved some of my hair out of the way, and I could see a close-up of the stubble on his chin. For a second I thought he was going to kiss me, but that was the last thing he was going to do, obviously.

"I must look super cute right now. The whole bloodied face look is really in in Paris."

BR laughed. "My daughter used to get these all the time. I've got a stomach for it."

So there I was, literally in BR's arms, except I looked like a murder victim. Still, I gazed into his eyes, which were such a beautiful shade of hazel, and said, "Thank you."

"No problem."

Once the flow stopped, I wiped my face, and he offered me his sweatshirt.

"No, I'll just get blood on it."

"It's fine, take it."

"No, no. I'll just run home and hope that no one thinks they're suddenly in an episode of *The Walking Dead.*"

He laughed again.

"Let me drive you. We can take your . . . wait . . ."

"Sammy. He's my friend's dog I'm walking."

"Okay. Well, let's take Sammy back and then get you home."

"You're a lifesaver," I said.

We put Sammy and Pinot in the back of his Land Rover, and I got into the front. His car even smelled like a Banana Republic ad, or what one might imagine it smelled like. Cedar, with a hint of citrus. The seats were worn, and there were pictures taped to the dash, one of April and one of Pinot and Cab as puppies.

"How is Cab doing?" I asked, still holding a napkin to my nose just in case.

"Oh, you know, not great. I'm kind of a wreck about it."

"Yeah."

"His whole life the dog's never left my side. The vets are still trying to figure out what's really wrong, but I have this feeling they might not. And I just can't . . ."

"I get it."

I wanted desperately to make him feel better, even though I was the bloody mess. I pulled down the visor and glanced in the little mirror. I had dried blood between my nose and lips, and a little on my chin.

"Wow, I'm really killing it today."

He smiled.

"You should see the other guy," I added. "So is April gonna do the showcase?"

"Yes, actually. I talked to the label guys more, and they seem pretty legit."

"Mom okay with it?"

"She'll have to be. She projects a lot on her; we both do. I think being a parent is a process of accepting they're going to be who they are. You just have to love them for who they are, not who you want them to be. God, I sound like a self-help manual."

"No!" *You sound like the sweetest human being ever*, I wanted to say. Not only on April's iPod, but in real life.

We dropped off Sammy, and luckily Kevin was out. I was still so bloody, it was probably best he didn't see me like that.

When we got to Brady's apartment, I told him that I would think good thoughts for Cab. I almost gave him April's iPod, but I thought it best to give it directly back to April.

"Get yourself cleaned up and drink a lot of water."

"Yes, sir." If he had told me to jump off a balcony, I would've.

"Bye, then."

"Bye."

We didn't touch or kiss, but the look that we shared seemed like something even more intimate. Or at least that's what it felt like to me.

CHAPTER 34

HOMETOWN BLUES

The Acela train was packed with business travelers in wrinkled suits barely looking up from their phones. I thought about Felicia. She was having her moment; someone was going to pledge to love her forever. She was getting her Happily Ever After. Even if it was with Greg Henley. I sighed and rested my eyes on the Connecticut coastline out the window.

The rumbling of the train put me to sleep, and I woke up in New Haven. I went to the café car and got myself a sandwich and a beer, and when I returned to my seat, I took out April's iPod. The first song that came on was Carole King's "Will You Still Love Me Tomorrow," and it was all I could do not to start bawling all over my ham sandwich. Not only was this guy adorable and sexy, he was obviously a romantic at heart. After living in New York for so long, my own heart had hardened, but somewhere deep down maybe Preston was right. Maybe I was a romantic too.

When Felicia picked me up at the train station, I barely recognized her. It'd only been a couple of years, but everything about her had changed. For as long as I could remember she had this edgy, tomboy look, and now there was not a trace. Her normally cropped brown hair was longer and dyed black, and she was wearing a ruffled top and skinny jeans. Her keychain had plastic sunflowers and a mini high-heeled shoe hanging off it. It was all a bit girly. I must have given something away in my expression, because she flipped her hair and said, "Too much?"

"No!" I lied.

She jumped up and down a little, holding my shoulders while I just stood there in awe. "It's so good to see you!"

We got into her SUV, and she started talking about the party, the catering, the band. I was drowning her out, looking at the houses in our town, which now appeared bigger and closer together. Sometimes prosperity was depressing.

When we pulled into her driveway, she looked over at me and said, "You look great, Page. You seem . . . I don't know, grounded."

"Well, if by grounded you mean being completely lost, that's exactly what I am."

She laughed in that quick, high-pitched way that I remembered. No matter how much people changed, their laughter remained the same.

When we got inside her house, a bunch of people were already there, and some of them I hadn't seen since high school. I got cornered by Holly Dixon, who we used to call Homely Dixon. She was no longer homely, but she was super boring, talking about her husband's logistics job and how he hated the commute to Providence. I wondered when I was going to be offered a drink—everyone had one but me. I thought about subtly walking toward the kitchen when finally, an older woman brought me a glass of wine, which I downed. Sometimes alcohol was completely necessary.

Felicia seemed really happy in her new persona, the girly girl about to get married, but something was unsettling about the whole night, everyone trying to feed into her moment, following her around like puppy dogs.

There was one person who, like me, was on the emotional periphery. Julia Hurst. Toward the end of the night, I noticed her sneaking off to the back porch. I followed her, and though I hadn't smoked in over five years, it just felt like the right time. She smiled and handed me a

Marlboro Light. As the smoke curled above our heads into the flood-light above the garage, I thought about Julia's horse, and that terrible, terrible afternoon. It replayed in my head, in slow motion, crumbling limbs and the sound, like a giant sigh. "You loved that horse, didn't you?" I asked Julia now, like it was yesterday. She knew exactly what I was talking about. It was a dark moment in our past that would always glue us together.

"Yes. More than any person, that's for sure."

"It wasn't your fault. It would've . . ."

"It's cool, Page. I've moved on by now. But remember Greg? He acted like the opposite of what everyone thought he was."

"I know. What is Felicia thinking?" I asked.

"Beats me. I'd rather eat bush than marry him."

I laughed. Julia always had this dichotomy about her. She wore pearls and cashmere but cursed like a sailor.

"It's just so hard. I'm happy for her, but I'm also . . ."

"Mortified? Everyone is. They're just acting like it's super normal, which makes it worse. No one even likes him!"

I took the last drag and said, "Well, maybe he's changed. We have to give her the benefit of the doubt . . . don't you think?"

She looked at me acutely and said, "What about you, Page? I heard you had this cute boyfriend and ran some gallery in the city."

"That all went to shit."

"Welcome to my world. I had a billionaire fiancé and a book deal, both of which also, as you put it, went to shit."

"Well, you look great, Julia. I mean it."

"Thanks. You do too."

She stamped out her cigarette with her black pumps. "Well, we better go in there and continue the charade."

About an hour later, after eating some flatbread pizza and listening to more meaningless jabber from Not So Homely Dixon, I excused myself and took a Lyft back to my childhood home. I was secretly relieved that my mother was already asleep when I got there. I wanted to see her, but not at that moment. She had left me a note scribbled on an old piece of mail that said:

Hi Sweetheart!

Chicken salad in fridge.

Luv Mom

I was incredibly worn out from the long train ride, three chardonnays, and a lot of fake smiling. Underneath Mom's note, I wrote:

Mom—

Exhausted, please don't wake me early.

P

My old room was now a two-toned guest room right out of Pottery Barn. The bed was turned down, like in a hotel, and I fell asleep the minute I lay down, before I could even undress.

In the morning, as my mother poured my coffee, I could tell the minute I saw her face that something was up.

"Is Charlie okay?"

"Yes. They were able to remove the tumor. He's free and clear. But now he's not returning my calls!"

"What? How long?"

"Two weeks. It makes me sick knowing his wife may have read our emails, can you imagine? Every time the doorbell rings I think it's her, or when I'm at the grocery store, I keep waiting for her to walk up and slap me in the face with an eggplant or something."

"Mom, she lives in Vermont."

"Still."

"Well, look at it this way. Maybe now you can find a man who's available."

"At my age?"

My mother was sixty-three, and it was starting to show. She still had bright eyes, but the skin on her face had begun its descent.

"You look fine, Mom."

"Well, I don't feel it. How is DC? How's the Bradester? He left me a message, but I couldn't understand him. He sounded weird. Is something going on?"

"He's just working a lot." I didn't want to worry her, even though it clearly wasn't just his demanding job. I still hadn't asked him about Dr. Bang Me, but I did leave him a note ordering him to text me twice a day.

My mother's eyes brimmed with tears. "What do you say, Charlie's my ghost?"

"He's ghosting you, Mom. You're being ghosted."

That made her actually cry. I walked over and hugged her.

"Look, the best thing you can do now is move on. That's what I'm trying to do with Jack."

She calmed down a little and grabbed a tissue. Then she shook it off and started to butter some toast for us.

"Do you remember Julia Hurst?" I asked.

"Yes. Her parents are megabucks."

"I saw her last night. She seemed, well, a little disillusioned by the whole Felicia and Greg thing, as am I."

"Well, people get married for many reasons. It's best to let it run its course."

"By that you mean divorce?"

"Well, your father and I used to go to weddings and he'd whisper a time frame in my ear, how long he thought the marriage would last. But he had a sick sense of humor, like you."

"I give Felicia and Greg two years."

"That's generous."

I took a bite of the toast. It tasted simple and good, but it also made me a little sad.

"Do you remember Julia's horse dying?"

"Of course. I think I shut it out of my mind, though."

"Well, last night, it seemed like she really never got over it. She mentioned loving the horse more than she'd ever loved any human."

"Girls are like that with animals. What about you and our dogs? You were obsessed."

"Yeah, I was. I may adopt one in DC, if I can get my act together. But with Julia, it was her escape. Her parents had all that money but never gave her much love."

She looked at me, then reached to move a piece of hair out of my eyes. It felt weirdly intimate. I knew she loved me, but my mother and I were never that close. She always resented the deep connection I had with my father. It looked like she was going to cry again, but then she just laughed a little and said, "We always had more love than money."

She was right. We were never as rich as my friends. We somehow squeezed into the tax bracket.

"So did Felicia seem happy?"

"You know what? The whole thing was kind of sad. It was like this fake happiness, and everyone seemed to be playing along."

"Hmm, well, maybe it's not fake. Ever since you went to New York, you judge everything too much. If people change, or seem happy in a situation you'd never put yourself in, just be happy for them."

I felt a sting in my chest. Maybe she was right. No matter how annoying mothers could be, they were usually right. Really, who was I to judge?

"I *am* happy for her. I guess I'm just a little skeptical about love. After the whole Jack thing."

"Well, any prospects in DC?"

"Yes. But I'm not going to jinx it." As if bleeding all over him hadn't already.

Mom seemed happy enough that there was something.

"Page, you're a smart, pretty, and funny young woman. There's no reason . . ."

"I should be single? Yeah, I'm working on it."

CHAPTER 35

OH NO HE DIDN'T

The party was at the same country club we went to as kids, where Felicia and I used to peek through the tiny hole in the women's locker room that looked into the men's, laughing at some fat guy's hairy ass, or screaming when our favorite lifeguard would drop his suit. It was the first time I ever saw a penis in real life, and I remember thinking it was the scariest, strangest thing, but I had to get my hands on one.

The food was served in those long silver trays, buffet style. I mostly sat in the corner with Julia Hurst, mainlining pinot noir.

I watched Felicia, laughing with Greg, and realized they actually seemed good together, in some messed up way. Weren't we all messed up? I certainly was, because I found myself stepping outside to call Jack. He'd texted again since the FaceTime nightmare, but I still hadn't responded. From the porch, the hills of the manicured golf course rolled into the distance underneath a slight fog. It rang and rang until he finally picked up, even though he clearly was in a loud bar. *It's me*, I kept saying, *it's me*, but it was a lost cause. Either he couldn't hear me, or he was ignoring me. I hung up.

Back inside, the band—whose members were some guys from our high school class—started playing. They were called the Tomato Dodgers.

"It's Friend Rock," Julia said.

"What?"

"You know, when you go see a band, but they kind of aren't that great, but you go anyway, 'cause they're your friends. Friend Rock."

Felicia was dancing with Greg's father, which was a little creepy. The keyboardist was pretty buzzed, wearing his sunglasses inside. Someone threw a bra onstage, which seemed like a really adolescent move.

When they started playing Nirvana, the dance floor filled up, and then they played even more songs we grew up with. It was nostalgic in a good way. Julia and I even danced during most of "Wonderwall."

As the evening wound down, I went to find the bathroom, and I ran into Greg for the first time. He looked like a handsome, drunk guy in a suit, his tie askew, his eyes a little wild. I wondered if he was partaking in something other than alcohol. We smiled at each other, and then his face collapsed a little, and out of the blue, he said, "Page. I used to watch your soccer practices."

I thought of Adam Ellis. Him too? I became dizzy, so I leaned against the wall.

"What?"

"I used to . . . forget it," he said, and walked past me.

I went into the ladies' room and looked at myself in the mirror. Even semidrunk, I looked okay. Actually, better than most of the girls from our graduating class. So there. Then the door opened, and it was Greg again, obviously in the wrong bathroom.

"Greg, what are you doing?"

"So you're like some city girl, huh? All mighty and powerful?"

He walked closer to me, and I backed up farther. I knew he was all bark and no bite, he always had been, but I still felt uneasy.

"No, actually. I got fired and . . ."

He went on without hearing me.

"You know, I always felt that you thought you were better than all of us. You look like that right now. You look like you can't wait to get the hell out of here. So tell me, Page, why did you come? Why did you grace us with your presence?"

A woman who was part of the staff walked in, got the vibe, then immediately turned around and left.

"To be here for Felicia, I guess."

"So what about you? Do you want to fall in love? Get married?"

"I do, I think. Hey, I always meant to ask you, why did you bail when Julia's horse died?"

"Seriously? You're asking me this right now?"

"Yeah."

He rubbed his eyes and coughed.

"Dunno."

"I know we were high and everything, but it was a pussy move, Greg."

He looked as if my words maimed him, and he could've just fallen to the floor. But instead he wiped his brow, looked in the mirror, straightened his tie, and said, "Well Page, you've always been kind of judgmental. You should try and have more empathy."

Did he even know what that word meant?

"I'll get on that. In the meantime, why don't you go to the correct bathroom."

He shrugged and left, and I said to myself, "Jesus. First my mother, now Greg Henley."

Julia came in and asked me if everything was all right, and I said, "Do you think I judge people too much?"

"Yes. But we all do. Let's get the fuck out of here."

On our way home, we stopped at Dunkin' Donuts and ate crullers in our dresses under the fluorescent lights of the parking lot, and I told Julia about Brady's weirdness and possible affair, and the whole mess of my situation. She seemed engrossed, like I was describing some exotic life she could never have dreamed of.

When I got home, my mother was waiting up for me. She could tell I was buzzed and brought me decaf. After a few minutes, she tucked a piece of hair behind my ear and said, "Page, I want us to be close. Closer."

"Okay, Mom. Okay."

"You know what? You never know when you're going to be alone. I just wanted to make the decision myself. It hurts to give up that power."

"I know, Mom."

"But you have the chance to do it right."

"What is even right?"

"I don't know, as long as in your heart you're happy. You know, with your father there were some hiccups, but I always had this feeling . . ."

"That everything was going to be all right?"

"Yes."

"Me, too, with Jack."

"Here we are, down on our luck."

I felt a wave of tiredness, or maybe it was gratitude.

"Mom?"

"Yes, honey?"

"I do love you. Even though we've braided in and out of each other's lives. I carry you with me. Every day."

She wiped at her eyes, and I started to head upstairs. At the top of the landing I turned around and saw her standing there, gazing toward me with a hopeful expression.

"You know what? You and Greg Henley are right. I judge people too much. Maybe Felicia and him will have a happy life. But I really don't think so."

"Go to bed, honey."

"Okay, good night."

I jumped out of my dress and got into bed, pulling April's iPod from the drawer and clicking the little arrow until I heard BR's voice again:

Music should be heard in every house. I hope you like these songs, and that maybe they'll strike a chord with you.

I immediately thought of Brady and all his records. I texted him, and thankfully he responded that he was fine, just closing the restaurant. I typed that I'd be home tomorrow, and he started to respond like three times, but then the dots just disappeared.

CHAPTER 36

MOM TIME

My mother woke me up by shoving the cordless landline phone in my face. I groggily said hello.

"Page? It's Langhorne. I'm sorry, I didn't know who else to call. I couldn't get ahold of your brother. I knew your last name and the town you grew up in, but I had no idea you'd actually be there. This is incredible."

"I went to a friend's engagement party last night." He was breathing heavily, and I could hear the click of a lighter. "What's going on?"

He sighed and told me he'd been in jail. He'd gotten out on bail, but was currently well past his court date and hiding in a friend's basement in Boston, someone he went to art school with.

"I need to see you," he said. "As soon as possible."

"Well, it's not like my life is super important or anything. I'm a dog walker. But wait, did you, you know, do anything . . ."

"Did I kill someone? No! It's tax evasion, and another little thing."

I knew that was code for kind of a big thing, but I trusted him. And I could sense the desperation in his voice. He really needed me, and I'm not going to lie, that felt good.

"I'll come there before I go back to DC. What's the address?"

I wrote it down, and he thanked me profusely. After showering, my phone buzzed as I was drying off. It was a text from a number I didn't recognize.

Hey it's April . . . I got ur number from Preston at the park. Do u have my iPod?

My heart twitched as I thought of a response. I needed it to sound casual, like I hadn't listened to every second of it.

Oh yeah it's in my bag! Text me when u r back at the dog park?

k thanx

During breakfast, my mother seemed to be studying me. I started to eat faster, so I could pack my bag and take off. It's not that I had anything against her. In fact, I was starting to forgive her. But being in my childhood home was only great in small doses.

Before I left, at my mother's request, we went through her wardrobe and I told her what to keep and what to toss.

"Page, I want you to know something."

"Yes?"

My mother can get watery eyed in a flash, and right then tears started rolling down her cheeks. When I was little, it was embarrassing—she would cry when the commercials said cotton was the fabric of our lives.

"I miss him too, you know," she said.

I threw a hideous Christmas sweater in the toss pile, then looked at her. I knew that, but for the first time I realized we actually had more in common than not. We both were in love with the same man, but of course mine was a daughter-father love and hers was a wife-husband love. Tears formed in my own eyes, and I said, "I know, Mom. It's okay. It's going to be okay."

I felt a sweep of nausea in my belly. Whenever I said or heard those words, I had the opposite reaction, a sense that it's never really going to be okay. It's just something people say. So I finished it off with, "He's gone. There's nothing we can do about it," which made her cry more. I walked over to her and hugged her again, twice in two days. More than I can ever remember hugging her. But she needed me. I wished that I could stay. I just knew there was a life out there waiting for me, and it wasn't anywhere near this town. Still, it felt good to briefly get out of my own drama, and try to put myself in her shoes. I always thought it was me who suffered from Dad's death the most, but nothing could compare to her pain. She was just good at numbing it with cheap wine and a bald married guy. Now it would just be the wine.

I told her about Kevin seeing the doctor in DC.

"If there's a bill, can you pay it and I'll pay you back?" I asked her.

"Since when are we paying this guy's bill?"

"Just helping him out. I also might represent some of his work. He draws."

"Well, he better make *you* some money then."

"That's the idea."

There was a long silence, and I said, "Mom, are you really going to be okay?"

"I guess so. I'm just happy I have you and Brady."

I wasn't about to get into Brady's behavior, not now.

"We are glad to have you too," I told her. "And don't worry, you can still find someone to share your life with. Just put yourself out there."

Yeah, that's really working for me, I didn't add.

When we said goodbye, I had to pry myself from the vise grip of her arms. I didn't remind her it was going to be okay. In fact, I would never say that again. Until I really believed it.

CHAPTER 37

ILLICIT ARTIST

I took the T to Brookline Village and found the warehouse basement where Langhorne was hiding. He came to the door in disguise, which struck me as ridiculous. A ski hat and sunglasses?

"Lang, you're not a terrorist. Are you?"

"No! Page, I'm so happy to see you. You look well."

"Well. If you mean, hungover from my friend's engagement to the pretty boy quarterback who called me out in the girl's bathroom, then yes. If you mean my boyfriend kicked me out and my boss fired me in the same week, and now I'm dog walking and staying with my brother, pushing into my midthirties with no husband or kids, then fuck yeah. I am fantastic!"

He laughed, as most people do at my misery, and offered me coffee from an old pot on a Bunsen burner. The place was littered with bad art. As if he sensed my reaction, Langhorne said, "Nice guy, not much talent. Hardly uses the place, so it's been a lifesaver for me."

I took a sip of the bitter, lukewarm coffee and said, "Lang, how the hell did you go from art-world luminary to fugitive?"

He sighed.

"Everyone turned on me, Page. Once the money started coming in. I mean, really coming in. It's funny, I just saw this guy on a morning show, talking about how winning the lottery ruined his life, and I was like, that's me! How many people get to say that?"

"Probably more than you think. Did you really have an uncle in the Cayman Islands? I read something in a blog."

"You can't write that shit. The man took me to my first baseball game. Bought me my first set of brushes. He basically raised me. I hadn't seen him in like, ten years, and he came to New York, gave me this whole spiel, like if I gave him a million I'd save a quarter million in taxes. I fell for it. The guy is probably in Bora Bora right now. Unbelievable. My own flesh and blood."

"How heartwarming."

"That's not the half of it. I got involved with this girl, a beautiful girl, of course, who ended up being tied to this drug ring. Get this, they wanted to smuggle meth in my paintings."

"That sounds like a solid business plan."

"It gets worse, but I can't even get into it. Listen, thank you so much for coming. I need your help. I had one backup. A safe-deposit box. Did you get the piece I sent to your brother's?"

"Yes."

"Great. Well, there's a key on the back of it. To a safe-deposit box in both of our names. There's a fifty-thousand-dollar bond inside it. It won't save me, but it will help me get a proper lawyer and buy me time. All I need you to do is get the money, put it in your account, then wire it here." He handed me some account information, apparently the second-rate artist guy's whose space we were in. I looked around, taking in the sadness of the situation. Langhorne had been on the top of his game. Now he had toilet paper stuck to his shoe, some dried egg on his scraggly beard, and rabid, animal eyes I couldn't look at for too long. I told him I would help him, but that I had to make the train.

As I was leaving, he spun me around and kissed me, and it happened so fast I didn't have a chance to resist. When I looked at his eyes, they had briefly gone soft, the old Langhorne peeking through. I had a sudden urge to get the hell out of there.

"Lang, you can't just kiss people."

"When this is all over," he said, "I want to take you somewhere, just the two of us."

I thought of all the girls who were usually on Langhorne's arm. Ten years younger than me, slightly anorexic, fuck-me eyes glaring at him, kill-you eyes glaring at everyone else.

"Lang, I'm happy to help you. But I'm not, we're not . . ."

"Page, I know, I know, but you're literally the only person I can trust."

"That doesn't mean we should fuck."

He looked shocked.

"Listen, just do me a favor. Meet me, a year from today. At noon under the arch in Washington Square. You don't have to go into some sunset with me, just show up. Okay?"

I looked at the calendar on my phone: April 12.

"Okay," I said, even though it seemed like a crazy idea. I would be a year older, hopefully getting regularly eaten out by BR on our four-poster bed overlooking the vineyards, and Lang would probably be in further trouble with the law, possibly even in prison.

I started to walk away, and he called after me. There was vulnerability in his voice I'd never heard before. "Page. The painting . . ."

"It's in good hands. But I may use it if I open a gallery. Not sell it, of course."

"Absolutely. You have my blessing. Thank you."

"Thank *you*, Lang. Hang in there."

CHAPTER 38

I Can't Even

On the train south, I replayed the kiss in my mind. Was he just desperate, or was it real? It was such an impulsive, awkward gesture that it just felt wrong.

Even though I slept for most of the ride, when I finally got back to Brady's, I felt like I could sleep more, for days even. As I stepped inside, I could smell Jane's perfume, and I saw her kitten heels lined up under the foyer table. But it was quiet. The door to Brady's room was slightly ajar, and I walked up cautiously just in case they were asleep.

When I looked in, I could see Jane, smoothing the hair off Brady's face, which was sunken and ghost-pale. As I leaned closer, I saw that he was asleep. Jane noticed me out of the corner of her eye and quickly came out into the hallway, shutting the door behind her. She didn't even need to say anything. My mind flashed to the doctor texting, Brady listening to his records, holding a picture of my father. How stupid was I to think it was an affair? How was I in such denial?

I almost fainted, but Jane grabbed me and led me to the kitchen, where prescription bottles were lined up like an army, next to a stack of instructions. I looked at them and then looked at Jane, who was trying to hold back her tears. We hugged, and I really held her, like she was all I had in the world. At that moment, she was.

I said the word out loud, not really believing it.

"Cancer."

She nodded. "The same as your father's."

"Prostate?"

She nodded again.

"He already had his first chemo treatment today, that's why he looks so . . ."

I broke from her embrace, suddenly enraged.

"Why didn't you tell me! I would have come home!"

"He didn't want to. Page, we only found out yesterday. He didn't want to tell you until he really knew what was going on. The doctor wanted to be aggressive . . ."

"*Shh*. Just, be quiet for a second." I tried to find more capacity in my lungs for air. "I can't even . . ." I closed my eyes, and a slideshow ran on the inside of my eyelids. Brady as a dragon for Halloween, the big tail that made him trip the whole night. Brady on the trampoline, arced like a dolphin in the air, mid backflip. Carrying him after he sprained his ankle on the beach, his breath hot on my neck. My father tickling us, calling us Peanut Butter and Jelly.

"They caught it early," Jane said, her face now completely composed. "And the doctor said he has youth on his side."

"I need to see him. Am I allowed to wake him up?"

"I wouldn't. Just remember, it's the night of the first treatment. He'll look better tomorrow. He has to do it twice a week, and after three weeks . . ."

"Okay, okay. I'm just going to go in there and wait until he wakes up."

"Okay."

"Jane?"

"Yes?"

"Thank you."

We hugged again, and I went into Brady's room and sat next to his bed. As he slept, his face crinkled with every other breath, like he'd eaten something sour. I hoped he wasn't having bad dreams. But I knew he was, because after a little while he bolted upright, yelling the word "No!"

"Brady, I'm right here."

"Page . . ." He smiled and sank back onto the pillow. "How was your trip?"

"Seriously? Brady, we're not talking about me right now. How are you?"

"I've been poisoned."

"What the hell?"

"I knew something was wrong, Page, because I couldn't get it up!"

He was clearly looped on something other than the cancer meds.

"Brady . . ."

"That's never been a problem for me! And then. Well, I'm not going to overshare."

"But they caught it early."

"Yes. Hereditary. But I'm half Dad's age when he got it!"

"You'll beat it—you have to."

"Doc says sixty percent chance, but she's hopeful."

I gave him his water, which he sipped through a straw.

"Do you have someone to cover at Elbow?"

"Only Straight Jake knows how to close. He's handling it."

"Good."

I took his clammy hand.

"I just want to go to Montana. You know about my Montana thing, right?"

"No."

"It's kind of a pipe dream. But I want to end up somewhere with open space and big sky, you know?"

"Oh yeah, chickens."

"Chickens! Out of the city. I'd open a place, but it would be small, like wine and tapas."

"Yeah, Montana is known for its tapas."

"Shut up."

Jane came to the door and asked if everything was okay.

"Living the dream," Brady said, then started coughing. I put my hand on his sweaty forehead. He looked terrible.

Jane walked over and took a lozenge from the side table and slipped it in Brady's mouth.

"I got my girls, that's all I need."

Jane and I looked at each other, trying to hold it together.

Then we waited in silence. It was obvious what all of us were thinking: this is mortality, that thing we shove into the recesses of our mind. And here it was, right in front of our faces.

After a few minutes, Brady fell back asleep and started snoring again.

"You should get some rest," Jane told me.

"Are you . . ."

"I'm going to stay right here."

I looked at her, so focused and calm. Strong.

"Please wake me if anything happens."

"I will."

We hugged again, and I was beginning to get used to her perfume. At first it was heady and disorienting, but now it was starting to feel like home.

In bed, I stared at the ceiling, thoughts swirling in my mind. Brady? He was the one everyone loved. The guy with the sunshine smile. A PB&J without the PB just wouldn't work. I refused to walk through this world as a Jelly sandwich.

I thought of my mother. This news would put her over the edge. Who was going to tell her? I would need to go see Dr. Langley, to get the 411 firsthand. But for now, I would have to sleep. It was hard to fathom, knowing my big brother was sleeping off poison that was trying to kill other poison that was in his otherwise perfectly healthy body. But pure exhaustion overcame me like a wave.

I didn't believe in God, really, but I prayed to anyone or anything that would hear me. *Please don't take him away from me. Don't you dare take him away.*

CHAPTER 39

When it Rains . . .

The next morning, Brady was up and in the kitchen, making a smoothie. For a second, it was as if last night never happened, but then I felt a sinking feeling all the way down to my toes.

"What are you doing? Where's Jane?"

"Running. I'm fine, just a little queasy."

"Aren't you supposed to be resting? Here, sit down at least."

I put him on a stool and took over the smoothie making.

"Doc said it's different for everyone. Also, the first treatment is milder, so it's going to get worse."

He looked pretty good considering he'd had chemo yesterday. But when I passed him the smoothie, he immediately dropped it, the green, sludgy liquid spraying all over the tile floor.

"Dammit!" he yelled.

We both looked at the mess, then Brady's face just crumbled, and he lost it. I hadn't seen him cry like this since he was five. I grabbed him and held him as tight as I could, not caring that I was stepping right in the smoothie.

"What the fuck?" he said, his eyes pleading into mine. "This is not supposed to . . . there's so much I want to do."

"You will, you will," I said, trying to hold back my own tears. "But for now, just calm down, and I'm going to clean this up and make you another one."

As I cleaned up the spill, I told myself to be strong. When people around you were falling apart, you had to keep it together. I did it with my father, and I'd do it with Brady.

After I finished the cleanup, I made another one and put it in front of him. He took one sip, sighed, and went back to his bedroom. I followed him, suggesting I get his turntable and some of his records. He gave me a list, and I was happy to be doing something that would help him, albeit temporarily.

When I returned with the records and the turntable, I set them up in the corner of his room. He was dozing off, and I just sat by him quietly until Jane came back from her run and told me I could go.

"Where?" I asked.

"Don't you walk the dog?"

"Oh my God, Sammy. I forgot. How did you know?"

"I put a sticky note on the fridge."

Jane was always writing sticky notes, mostly to Brady in loopy handwriting with hearts above the *i*'s.

"Ah, okay. Thank you. I'll only be gone an hour or so. You'll text me immediately if you need anything, though, right?"

"Yes. Of course."

Then it occurred to me. Jane had a job too. A real one.

"What about your nonprofit?"

"It's a well-oiled machine. It can run without me."

"I doubt that," I said, and she smiled. "Bye, guys."

"Bye, Page," Brady said. "Sorry about the smoothie."

"I think I can forgive you."

I looked at Jane for reassurance.

"Don't worry, I'll be here," she said.

As I walked over to Kevin's house, I tried to picture a world without Brady. It was too much to even contemplate. I felt humbled and downright silly for even complaining about my life and my problems, which were infinitesimal compared to what Brady was facing. I couldn't even imagine.

Sammy was happy to see me, and I was glad for the distraction, although Brady's pale face lingered like a ghost in the back of my thoughts.

He'll get through it. He has to.

On our way to the park, Sammy knew something was up and kept looking at me with a question in his face. There was no way I could even begin to answer him.

When we got through the gates, Sammy stayed close to me and didn't run to his corner, knowing that whatever I was dealing with, he needed to stay close. Dogs just knew.

I glanced around to see if there was anyone I knew, even Umbrella Woman or the Sad Poodle Lady. No one. I was about to start crying when I saw Pinot rush through the gates. This time I didn't lean down and just scratched his ears from a sitting position. It was BR again, looking fresh faced and relaxed, wearing jeans and a slightly ruffled polo shirt—urban preppy chic. He still had that silvery scruff on his face, and he gave me a wide grin before he said, "Hey! How's the nose?"

"All better. No running hugs for Pinot, though."

He smiled, and I remembered that I still had his daughter's iPod in my bag. It felt like a shameful secret.

"How's it going?"

"Oh, pretty good." What was I saying? I was a wreck. But I couldn't tell him about Brady. Not right then. "I just got back from an engagement party up north."

"Oh yeah? Who's the lucky girl?"

"A friend from high school. It was kind of depressing, actually."

Why did I say that? He's going to think I'm judgmental like everyone else.

"Depressing how?" BR asked.

"Well, I've always hated how desperate everyone is to get married,
like if you don't there's something wrong with you."

He looked at me, nodding slowly.

"Wait, are you married?" I asked.

"No. I was, though. We did it way too young."

"A lot of people do," I said, trying to play down my excitement
about his marital status. "I mean I'd still like to be, you know, together
with someone, but I've turned off the whole idea of marriage lately. At
least conventional marriage."

I was talking to BR about my marriage theory, and I still didn't
know his name. I wanted to yell, *You, though! I'd marry you!*

"Tell me about it. But we're friends, my ex and I. Which is good."

"Of course you are."

I don't know why I said that. He started to pet Pinot, which seemed
to be both of our go-to moves when we were at a loss.

"I meant, you seem like someone who'd be friends with his ex," I
added.

"I'll take that as a compliment."

"I have more. Compliments, that is."

He smiled, and his eyes seemed to shine.

"So how is Cab?"

He slowly shook his head. "It's not looking good."

"Oh no."

"He's on three different medications now. It's weird, when the vet
talks to me I feel like he may as well be a car mechanic. I have no idea
what he's saying."

I smiled, forgetting for a brief second that I had a brother at home,
recovering from his first round of chemo. But then the sinking feeling
returned. I took a deep breath.

"What's wrong?" he asked, and seeing his pure expression, I just couldn't hold it back any longer. The words came out.

"My brother, we just found out he has prostate cancer, same as my dad had. He just started chemo."

"Oh. I'm so sorry . . ."

"It's okay. I mean it's not okay, but he's young. They say that he can beat it. I still have to talk to the doctor, though."

He put his arm on my shoulder, and it was like flicking a switch. Water instantly pooled in my eyes as we sat there in silence, dogs running around us, all oblivious to the thin line between life and death.

A loud crackle of thunder startled me, and it immediately began to rain. Everyone ran out of the park, except BR and me, who ran under the only tree big enough to shelter us. Our faces were inches from each other. If we were in a movie, this would be the moment we had our first kiss, but in real life, we just locked eyes. It wasn't the time. We both had impending death in our families.

He hugged me, and I tried not to cry, but it wasn't working.

"Don't cry. You got this. I'll be wishing the best for you and your brother . . ." He was talking into my hair.

"Me too, for Cab," I offered, and we just stood there, huddled together, as the rain pounded down all around us. It was as if Mother Nature was scolding us, or telling us to wake up.

"You never think about dying until it shows its face," I said.

"True."

I thought about finally asking what his name was, but it just seemed wrong in that moment.

After the rain died down, his phone buzzed, and he said, "Gotta take off. Hang in there, okay?"

I nodded.

He grabbed Pinot and headed toward the gates. "See you soon?" he asked.

"I guess," I answered, my heart in my throat.

Then he was gone.

Sammy was still under the bench, and I went back to get him, but he didn't seem like he wanted to go anywhere. So I sat on the damp bench, pulled out my phone, and texted Felicia to congratulate her again and thank her for inviting me. She sent back emojis. Hearts and a butterfly. Then a text came in from my mother, saying hope all is well with two hearts. This is what it had come to. Not even words, just symbols. I couldn't fathom telling her about Brady. I shuddered at the thought. Brady could do no wrong in her eyes. Parents are not supposed to play favorites, but let's be honest, he was her favorite child. How long could we keep it from her? We couldn't, could we?

I took Sammy back to Kevin's, wiped him down with a towel, gave him his treats, and headed back to Brady's apartment.

I was happy to see him propped up in his bed, playing one of his obscure indie rock records. There was a little more color in his face. I kissed him on his forehead, and he smiled.

"I was thinking," I told him. "What about Mom? Have you . . ."

"No. I just don't . . . I can't deal. Can we hold off on telling her?"

"Not for long," I said. "She will freak out knowing we kept it from her. But I'm talking to Dr. Langley tomorrow. I want to make sure I'm on the same . . ."

"Page! Same page! Ha."

"Brady, are you taking painkillers?"

"Just a smidge. I'm actually going to work tonight."

"What?"

"Just for like ten minutes to go over the seasonal menu change. I'm feeling okay, I just . . ."

Brady looked at the ceiling as if there might be something beyond it, some unknown that was scary as hell.

"I get sinking spells."

"Me too."

"So yeah, I think going to work, listening to music, talking to Jane, and having you here, these are all good things, because when I'm alone and my thoughts start swirling, it's like, too dark."

"I know. I know."

I squeezed his hand. He closed his eyes and started dozing off. I took the headphones out of his other hand. I noticed the picture of our father on his nightstand. He must have asked Jane to bring it down.

In the kitchen, Jane was cooking lasagna and chicken and individually wrapping portions to freeze, so there would always be easy meals for Brady.

"You really are amazing," I said.

"It's nothing, just some preparation. None of us want to be cooking, right?"

"Not me. I can barely boil water."

She smiled, handing me a piece of celery. I took it, even though celery was maybe the most boring food ever.

"You know, one of my colleagues came over to help with the groceries. Her father works at Sotheby's. She had heard of the guy that painted that, painting or whatever you call it. Is it insured?"

"I doubt it, because it's not physically in the gallery anymore. Plus, Langhorne is super scattered. Even if he had his own policy, I'm sure it's lapsed."

"Well, she said you need to get it insured."

"I know. That's on my list. But to be honest, all lists are out the window now."

"Yeah," she said, stopping what she was doing for a second to look at me.

"I'm so glad you're here," I told her.

"Right back at you. Some things you can't do alone."

"Like live without my brother," I said.

She nodded, and I started helping her, because when your heart is breaking, it feels good to do something with your hands.

In bed that night, I checked my phone. There was a text from Nadine, one from Rex inviting me to see his collection, and three from Michael of Austria asking about my gallery plans. I turned it off. I knew I was still in denial a little, like I would maybe wake up tomorrow and it would all be a dream. Brady, the person who as a kid would want to sit with people who were dining alone. The guy who's never been unkind, always listens, and has a smile that warms the world.

Before I went to sleep, I turned on the iPod again. A weird female voice said *low battery*, then BR's voice came on again.

You are my everything.

There was a dwindling noise, and the iPod shut down. *Please, please, Brady*, I thought, *don't die.*

CHAPTER 40

FIX BRADY MODE

For the next few days, I didn't leave the house. Brady wasn't well enough to work, even though he wanted to. To fill in for his nights off, Straight Jake taught me how to close the restaurant and deposit the cash. Jane did most of the cooking, and the days were long. Brady was in and out of consciousness with the meds, but mostly it was just about being in the same room with him. We talked, listened to music, played cards if he was feeling like it. On nights that Jane didn't sleep over, I slept on the comfy chair in his room.

While driving to the hospital for Brady's second treatment, I told him about Langhorne and the money, and the fact that I still had April's iPod. Then I felt stupid for even talking about my life when his was on the line. Luckily, he wasn't really listening, just staring out the window in a contemplative daze.

The treatment room was actually really nice—like a hotel. There were four soft and inviting chairs, the other three occupied by people who looked far worse off than Brady.

"Jesus, it's *Night of the Living Dead* in here," Brady said under his breath.

"*Shh,*" I told him, suppressing a smile.

There was a library down the hall, and I found him a coffee-table book on Montana. When I brought it back, he said, "If I can't go there, at least I can look at the pictures."

"Positive thinking, remember?"

"Okay, Oprah."

I finally got to meet the infamous Dr. Langley, who was just as gorgeous as her picture, if not more. I had to quickly erase the thoughts in my mind as she showed me Brady's charts.

"After this treatment, we'll do some blood work and be able to tell how well it's working." She dropped her pen, and when she bent over, the whole porn star thing resurfaced. I imagined her adding, *Then I'll do a really thorough physical, if you know what I mean.*

When she stood back up, she gave me a strange look. "Everything okay?"

Her professional ease and kindness just made her even hotter.

"Fine."

If I was a lesbian, I'd totally sleep with you, I didn't add. Why did I have to have such an active imagination? Especially right then? My brother was . . .

"So . . . do you think he's going to die?"

She put on a pleasant, empathetic face and slowly removed her glasses. "Like I told him and Jane, I think he's got a great chance of beating this. But I can't promise anything."

Doctor speak. I'd heard it all before with my father. I remember one of them using the words "Cautiously optimistic." I wanted to punch the dude. But I just thanked Dr. Langley, and she put her hand on my shoulder before she left. She smelled like fresh baked bread, which she'd probably never eaten in her life.

"So," I told Brady as he was finishing up, "I finally got to meet Dr. Bang Me."

He started laughing, which was not good, because it turned into coughing.

"You're killing me," Brady said between laugh-coughs, "literally."

When I led him back out to the car, I could feel his weight leaning against me. We would fight this. I was here for a reason.

When we got back into the car, I suggested we get ice cream.

"Yeah, chemo goes really well with ice cream," he said.

"Remember when you were a kid, you'd mix all the flavors? It was so gross."

"I just have a more advanced palate."

"Whatever."

As I drove us home, Brady put his hand on my arm and said, "This is going to sound weird, but do you think, you know, if this doesn't work, I'll be able to see Dad?"

I was at a stoplight, frozen. I'm not sure how many minutes passed, but it turned green and someone behind me honked, which jolted me out of my daze. I could barely see with the tears filling my eyes. I pulled over onto the shoulder and shut off the engine.

"I don't know, Brady. I guess that's the greatest part. Nobody knows."

He looked over at me, his mouth open, trying to form the words. "I'm not ready . . . to leave yet." He wasn't crying, but the fear in his voice was palpable. I grabbed his hand, squeezed, and took a deep breath.

"I'm not ready for you to leave either."

Cars sped by. One woman slowed down and shot us a dirty look. I didn't care.

"It should've been me," I said, unable to contain myself.

"Stop that."

He started rubbing my shoulder, which was not the right scenario. He wasn't supposed to be the consoling one. I had to be strong now. Stronger than ever. I wiped my tears with my sleeve and quieted my breath.

"I'm sorry," I said, feeling pathetic.

"Don't be. I'm really glad you're here."

I took a second deep breath as another car sped by.

"You know," Brady said. "I keep thinking about the time you carried me at the beach."

"Me too," I said. "I'll remember it forever."

"But there is no forever. There might be just this, for me . . ."

I hugged him the best I could across the seat, and he let out the slightest whimper.

A car slowed down and honked at us, and I honked back. Brady sat up straight and sighed. "We should go before we both die of road rage."

He was right. I started the car and continued back.

Brady was so weak when we got home, I thought I couldn't handle him, but I did. By the time we got from the garage to the elevator, I was sweating.

I led him right to his bed, and he was asleep within minutes. I watched him for a while, like I had been doing a lot. I remembered someone telling me that there were only so many people you can outlive in your lifetime. I already lost my father. I wasn't sure if I could handle losing Brady as well.

CHAPTER 41

This Could Get Ugly

There was no more delaying. I had to call my mother.

I lied a little about when Brady's diagnosis was, but she was still furious.

"I could have been there all this time!" She was yelling into the phone, which I was holding a foot from my ear.

"He didn't want to worry you."

"Oh, that's great, Page. Don't tell me that my own son has cancer, take away time I could have spent with him when we don't know how much he has left, so I *don't worry*."

"I'm telling you now!"

She started crying hysterically.

"Mom, please, we have everything under control, just calm down."

"Don't tell me to calm down!"

So I let her cry, thinking of all the tears I watched her shed when we went through this with my father. Could she do it again? Are we even built to be that resilient? Finally she blew her nose, and I could hear her breathing deeply, getting herself together.

"Okay, okay. Well, I'm coming there. Right after I pack a bag."

"Why don't you just come in the morning?"

"Page!"

She didn't have to say anything else. It was all in her voice. Right then I felt terrible for holding the information from her. But it was what Brady had wanted.

I warmed him up some soup for lunch that day, but he barely touched it. He looked ten years older, like his face had shrunken into itself. It was hard to pretend everything was going to be okay.

That afternoon I told him that Mom was coming and she knew everything.

"I know, she's been texting me nonstop," Brady said. "Page, I was thinking, you should ask Mom for your marriage money to help start your gallery."

"Brady, the only thing I want right now is for you to get better. What the hell is that, anyway, marriage money? What if I don't want to get married?"

"Exactly, the thinking is a little old fashioned. So why not use it to start your dream?"

"*Shh.*"

He was right, but I couldn't think about that then. Spencer, who had changed his mind when he saw me with Michael of Austria, had emailed asking if I wanted to cover weekends at his gallery. I also had made an appointment to see a space, but it was all on hold. Right then it was hard to even see that far in the future. It was a daily effort to fix Brady, and everything else became insignificant.

Jane arrived to take over duty, and before I left to walk Sammy, Brady said, "Come here," and kissed me on my hand. It was something he'd done a lot, but now it felt precious, knowing that there might not be an infinite supply.

I decided to change it up and took Sammy on a long walk instead of to the EDP. I wasn't feeling social anyway. It felt good to just move, getting lost in Spotify on my phone.

When I returned to Brady's, I knew my mother had arrived because there was a distinct smell of disinfectant. Her go-to reaction to grief and potential loss was cleanliness. Right then she was washing the base-boards in the living room, with a bucket of steaming water and some rags. Her hair was up, which made her look younger, and her cheeks were flushed from crying. When she saw me, she dropped the rag she was holding and ran over to me, giving me a bear hug.

"Is he sleeping?" I asked.

"Yes. I brought the cowbell we used for your father, so he can ring it when he needs anything."

"Okay. I usually just hang out in his room until he wakes up."

She nodded.

"Why are you cleaning?"

"Just doing some of the stuff the housekeepers miss."

"Have you heard from Charlie yet?"

"No. I've given up on him."

"Good. I mean, not good, but you deserve someone who isn't married, Mom."

"Do I deserve to lose my only son?"

She broke down, and I just stroked her back, like she had done with me as a child. When she was finished sobbing, I grabbed a tissue and dabbed at her face.

"I know it's hard, but we have to keep it together for him. He hates it when we cry."

"Okay, okay, I know."

"I'll set up the blow-up mattress in Brady's office, so you can take my room."

"Don't be silly."

"Mom, just do as I say, okay?"

"Okay."

"We have to take him to another treatment this afternoon. They are doing them in succession at first. You can meet the doctor."

She nodded, looking at her watch. "I'm just going to finish . . ."

"Clean all you want, but we are leaving at one thirty."

Brady's office, which was now my room, had just enough space on the floor for the blow-up mattress. I sat at his desktop computer and checked my email. There were some out-of-office replies from galleries that I pitched, and another from that friend of Langhorne's, asking about the money transfer. I couldn't put that off much longer.

Through the browser history, I found the pet adoption agency's website I had been researching and clicked on the profile of the dog I wanted. His name was Happy, and he was a one-year-old vizsla. He reminded me of a dog version of Frank Sinatra: cool and graceful, an old soul. He had a small scar below his left eye, which I thought of as a perfect imperfection. I knew it was silly to even think of getting a dog at that point, but it helped to know one was out there, one that was a perfect match for me. Though I also knew he'd most likely be adopted by someone else any day now.

After Brady's last treatment, I had ordered a wheelchair, which was much easier than taking his weight. At one thirty Mom and I loaded Brady into the car, and we got to the hospital with ten minutes to spare. The nurses were always so nice, and I thought about how fulfilling that job must be for them. Sad, but fulfilling.

While Brady got his treatment, he streamed his favorite show, *Ray Donovan*, on the iPad we brought for him. He claimed that the characters were so messed up, it seemed like beating prostate cancer was nothing. I admired his attitude. He wanted company, but he didn't want sympathy.

My mother met with Dr. Langley and seemed to be more appeased hearing it from her rather than me. When we got him home, he immediately threw up all over the baseboards my mother had just cleaned. He kept apologizing, and I shushed him, leading him into the bathtub where I ran the water right over his clothes.

Taking off the wet clothes was a chore, and again, I was sweating by the time I got him into his robe and into bed.

"This is not what you signed up for, Page," Brady said. "This could get ugly."

"Some things we don't sign up for, we just do. You're lucky I'm not squeamish."

"Is Mom cleaning it up?" he asked.

"Yes. It's actually good, we'll have some quiet time."

He smiled and took my hand, and I tried my best not to cry, but a few tears leaked out. I wiped them away without him noticing.

CHAPTER 42

SERENADE

The next day Brady was doing a little better, and we all worked as a team: Jane on food patrol, Mom doing laundry, and me hanging out in his room keeping him company. It actually felt good to be a part of something, to make myself useful, even if it was showing Brady pictures from the old albums Mom brought, or listening to him tell me his philosophy behind each track on Dylan's *Blood on the Tracks*.

Jane and I pretty much kept it together, but my mother went through a few long crying jags, which was expected. I cried, too, but only in the shower.

That Friday, I took Sammy to the EDP and tried to clear my head. The only person I knew was the Sad Poodle Lady, whose scowl was extra bold. I thought about Brady thinking about me and my future, when his own was in jeopardy. I looked at the poodle lady again, and I decided to try and cheer her up.

"Hi there," I said.

"Oh, hi," she replied, a little surprised that I was talking to her. "What's going on?"

"Well, I'm actually thinking about opening an art gallery, here in DC."

She looked at me like I had told her I was opening a Subway sandwich shop.

"You enjoy art at all?" I asked.

"Art?" She just stared at me. I actually started to giggle a little, and then I saw Pinot run toward me, hopping around, saying, *look! I'm a dog!* April was right behind him, with a ukulele case dangling from her right hand. The Sad Poodle Lady got up and walked away without saying anything.

April sat down next to me.

"Isn't she a ray of sunshine . . . ," I said.

"Lighting up the world," April added wearily.

"Oh!" I reached into my bag. "Your iPod! I'm so sorry I've had it so long." I handed it to her. "The battery died. I think it turned itself on in my bag or something."

I couldn't tell her that I'd listened to the whole thing.

"Thanks for grabbing it and keeping it for me," she said.

I could keep it longer if you like. I could keep your father in my pocket for the rest of eternity.

"No prob," I said. "I've just had to take care of my brother, who's been sick. Anyway, how's it going? Your dad told me about some showcase?"

"Yeah. In the end, Mom didn't let me go to LA, but I've been working on a demo with this New York guy who works for the same label. At first I thought he just, you know, *liked* me, but he's not like that. He really gets my songs."

"Wow. That is so neat." I had never said the word *neat* in my entire life. I felt like the biggest dork.

Pinot sat down at our feet, his earlier energy now diminished.

"How is Cab?"

"He's with my dad at the winery. He's having surgery next week."

"Oh no!"

"Yeah, my dad's still a mess."

I scratched behind Pinot's ears and told him, "Don't you worry, buddy, Cab will be back in no time."

April took out her ukulele.

"So you gonna serenade me?"

"You really want to hear something?"

"Absolutely," I said.

She started playing this lilting progression, and her silky retro voice rose elegantly over the chords.

> Used to get me high
> Now it gets me by

As she was playing, my mind started scheming. If I opened a gallery, I could have her play at the opening, and then BR would have to come and fall in love with me in all my chic art-world glory.

> Look into my eyes
> It's so easy to lie

I slowly shook my head in awe. How does a girl that age sound like someone who's been through everything? She was barely out of puberty!

When she finished I just said, "Wow."

"You like it?"

"Beautiful. Did you write that?"

"Yeah, I don't usually do covers."

Pinot got up and sniffed April's knees.

"Looks like he liked it too."

She started plucking again, and I wished she would sing more, but she stopped abruptly and put it away.

"Hey, this is a hypothetical, but if I ever open a gallery here, would you maybe play a couple songs at the launch?"

"Hmm," she said. Then her face got all serious. "You'd have to talk to my agent."

I smiled. She was sharp, just like her father.

"Well, could you pencil me in?" I asked, taking her lead.

"Consider it penciled."

We sat there, her song still lingering in the air. I looked up and closed my eyes, letting the sun kiss my face, feeling long-needed perspective, thinking good thoughts for Brady, for Cab, for Kevin, for anyone who was suffering. I felt lucky to just be there, in that light.

CHAPTER 43

STEP ONE

I hadn't been doing anything about the prospect of a gallery, but I felt like I should at least insure the painting now that Brady had both Mom and Jane around to help out. I called Rex and reached his assistant, and even though Rex was apparently in the middle of a meeting, he took my call, giving me the phone number of his wife's insurance company.

Electra, as she was called, was awestruck by the Langhorne piece the minute she arrived. She looked like a female version of Rex. Someone who spent a lot of time doing mushrooms, but now prefers champagne. Ex-hippy socialite art collector's wife. Somewhere along the line, she started to shave her legs, and the patchouli became Chanel No. 5. But you can't fully take the hippy out of the girl. You could see it in her eyes: kind, wise, and a little loopy.

"This is unbelievable. He just gave this to you?"

I thought of the awkward kiss, and the safe-deposit box key I had found taped to the back of the painting, now sitting in my pocket.

"Just to hold on to."

She looked at me skeptically.

"How do you mean?" she pried.

"Well, he's in a little trouble at the moment."

"Hmm, I heard."

She walked around the painting as if it were her prey. I knew Electra wasn't her real name. It was probably Eleanor.

"Well," she said, "I would insure this at one point two. Even with his bad press, it doesn't lower the value. In fact, it probably makes his work more desirable."

"Okay, so what do we do?"

"Well, do you have any coffee?"

"Yes! I'm so sorry. My brother's not feeling well, and my hospitality game is off."

Jane was in Brady's room with the door closed. I quickly whipped up some fancy cappuccinos on Brady's Italian espresso machine, and I served some almonds in a small bowl, which Electra didn't touch. We went over the paperwork, and after getting her Venmo handle, I sent her a down payment to insure the painting. Since Brady's loan was dwindling, I really had to start making my own money.

"So, Page, I'm curious. What do you plan to do with it?"

"Well, I want to start a gallery here, eventually. I actually talked to Rex about . . ."

"Oh yes, he told me. Please, take some of the art off our hands. We're drowning in it."

Must be tough, I thought, almost blinded by the flash from her diamond-studded bracelet.

As she was leaving, she turned to me with an old friend's smile, even though we'd just met.

"Listen, as it turns out, I have a lead on a space. It was a gallery at one point, but they turned it into a hair salon. Now it's belly-up, and I bet you could get a deal on the lease. Lovely space. On Church Street, near Fifteenth, know it? Great block."

"Wow, thanks. I'm not sure I can do anything right now, but maybe it wouldn't hurt to take a look at it?"

"Of course. Let me do a little legwork, and I'll set up a time for you to see it."

"Great. I have go to New York tomorrow, just for an errand, but generally I'm around here all the time with my brother."

"New York for an errand? Sounds scandalous."

"No, just a banking transaction," I said, but it came out shady. Was it? Would I be getting myself in trouble doing it?

"Ok, Page, so nice to meet you. Rex spoke very highly of you, and he doesn't do that often. And it's the right choice to insure the piece, it's absolutely stunning."

"Thanks, Electra."

"I hope your brother feels better. Be in touch."

Later that afternoon, I told Brady everything about Langhorne, except the kiss.

"I have to make a transaction in New York tomorrow. For him. I'm pretty sure it's legal."

"Pretty sure? Hmm."

"With Jane and Mom here, I thought it would be okay to go? Just a day trip."

"Yes, fine," Brady said. "Are you going to see Jack?"

"No!"

To change the subject, I filled him in on Rex and Electra, and the gallery lead.

"I work out at the gym across the street. That's a cool block," he said, as if both of us were in totally normal situations. As if all of it, our hopes and failures, weren't beginning to boil over and seep down the edges of our lives.

CHAPTER 44

PIPE DREAM

My New York trip went pretty smoothly, considering my errand was a little sketchy. I followed all Langhorne's instructions, hoping I wasn't too late. The worst of it was the BoltBus ride back, during which someone next to me decided to eat a questionable tuna sandwich. But still, how could I complain about anything, really?

When I got home, Jane, Brady, and my mother were all around the kitchen island. Brady looked weak but freshly showered, and Jane was separating his meds into the little plastic compartments with the days on them. Mom was stroking Brady's back, and everyone seemed content. But they were all staring at me.

"What?" I said, getting some water out of the fridge.

"We've been talking," my mother said.

"Yes," Jane added.

I felt like they were going to fire me from a job. I took a sip and braced myself.

"We know that some stuff is happening that you've been putting on hold," Brady said.

"What are you talking about?"

"Your gallery plans," Jane said.

"We all want you to be able to do it," Brady said.

"But I need to be here," I told them.

"You can still be here," my mother said, "but that doesn't mean you can't follow your passion."

"We can cover for you when you need it," Jane added.

All three of them had this look on their faces, and I couldn't describe it as anything but love and support. The opposite of being fired, as it turned out.

"Well, I'm not even sure . . ."

"Listen, honey, if you have momentum, just keep at it. We all know timing is everything in this life."

"Exactly. I'm not going to run off and open a gallery while my brother's . . ."

I couldn't finish the sentence.

"Look," said Jane. "I have commitments with my work, too, and now we have a larger support system. We're not saying for you to completely bail, just keep trying for that dream."

"More like a pipe dream."

"They all start out that way," Brady said. "My restaurant did . . ."

"Okay, okay. I'll see what I can do."

All three of them smiled, and it felt wrong, for this to be about me.

"By the way," Jane said, pointing at the sticky note on the fridge, "Kevin called our landline. I guess your phone was dead. You need to walk Sammy."

My mother didn't say anything, and it felt like something was released between us. How could we judge each other now?

Kevin seemed excited to see me when he answered the door. He asked where I'd been, and I told him I had to make a quick trip to New York. He looked different somehow. Had he lost weight in his face?

"I've seen the doctor," Kevin said.

"Great!"

"He has me on this Eastern medicine. It tastes horrible, but he swears it can help me. And it's dirt cheap. Actually, I think it *is* dirt."

"Ha. Excellent. Bring on the dirt."

"I will pay you back, for the consultation."

"Don't be ridiculous. Just get better."

Sammy looked tired and didn't seem up for going for a walk. I noticed Kevin's door slightly ajar.

"Kevin, I meant to ask, can I see the wall again?"

"Oh, sure," he said, like it really was nothing. But when he fully removed the tapestry, I still got that feeling, similar to the one I had when seeing Langhorne's work for the first time. It wasn't the same as looking at the picture on my phone. Standing in front of it was incredible. It was more than just doodling; it was like a city of pictures crammed together to make one extravagant story. There was so much there, it made me want to sit down and really take it in. If someone had it in their living room, years could go by and they'd still find things. The harsh profile of a woman, the elegant wing of a bird. When we were kids, Brady and I used to lie on the trampoline and find shapes in the clouds. It was similar to that, except Kevin's masterpiece was much more detailed and nuanced. And unlike the clouds, it wasn't temporary.

"You would be okay showing this?"

He tried to keep calm, but he stood a little straighter.

"Sure, why not."

"Well, I'm going to walk Sammy and think some more about it. Will you be here when I get back?"

"No. I have therapy."

"Well, I'll email you then, or see you when I come get Sammy next?"

"Okay."

As I walked out the door and onto the street, Sammy looked at me with a question in his eyes. He seemed to be asking, *do you really think Daddy is an artist?*

I didn't actually answer the question, but I stopped, took Sammy's head in my hands, and nodded.

The EDP was pretty empty, but I was happy to see Sumner in the corner, drinking from his little silver bowl of Pellegrino. Barkley kissed me on both cheeks, and Sumner looked up from his bowl as if to say, *oh, it's you again.*

"Darling, you look wonderful. Where have you been?"

"Well, there's kind of a lot going on," I said.

"Do tell," he prompted.

I looked at him, admiring all the effort that went into looking like he did. Although I was tempted, I couldn't start in about Brady. If I didn't talk about it, would he just get better and it would go away?

"I think my gallery idea is starting to look like a possibility." I told him about Langhorne's piece, and Kevin's doodle wall.

"That all sounds quite promising!"

Just then, as if I willed it to happen, my phone buzzed with a text from Electra.

1440 Church. Can you be there in twenty?

I texted Jane, who said Brady was all good and they were watching a movie. Then I texted Electra back.

Yes

"Barkley, would you want to look at another possible gallery space with me? I could use your expertise."

"Sure. Preston is at the gym, or should I say, in the steam room. He'll be hours."

We decided to take the dogs with us, and as we walked past a group of old ladies perched on benches outside the Jewish Community Center, I told him about the strange kiss from Langhorne.

"You act like that's a surprise! Of course the painter-slash-convict wants you. You have an allure. I'm gayer than Elton John, and I noticed it. You need to give yourself more credit."

"Well, credit is what I'm going to need to get a lease on this place," I said as we approached the space, which was perfect—right out of Tribeca, a converted garage that merged modern and industrial to form just plain cool.

"Barkley, are you seeing what I'm seeing?"

"It *screams* gallery," he said, and even Sumner barked appreciatively. Sammy was excited by the prospect as well, wagging his tail and doing a little head shake I'd never seen before.

The storefront was floor-to-ceiling glass, and there was even a built-in platform creating a little stage, the proportions matching Langhorne's painting exactly. An attractive young man in a suit opened the door and introduced himself as Kyle. He smiled at me, then gave Barkley the once-over. Was *everyone* gay in this city? If I didn't already have my sights on BR, I'd give up all hope of finding true love in DC.

Ken Doll Kyle took me around the space, shooting looks at Barkley the whole time. He explained how even though this was the "it" neighborhood, the salon had not done well because of competition across the street, so they needed to offload it quickly.

I broke off from the two of them, taking Sammy with me. I tried to imagine Kevin's wall, some of Rex's Impressionists, maybe a small local section. It really was the right space. I looked back to see Kyle waving hi to Sumner but not touching him.

When I asked what it was listing for, he got right down to business.

"Well, the landlord wants sixty-four hundred monthly, but there may be some wiggle room."

"Oh, I just love it when you say *wiggle*," Barkley said.

I knew my marriage money would be available, which was $10,000. I wasn't sure how I'd get the rest, but it felt so right that the words just tumbled out of my mouth.

"Six thousand and I'll take it," I said.

He smiled, like he was used to people lowballing him. Even so, it seemed like the only low balls he was interested in were Barkley's. He looked at him, flashing his pearly whites, then turned back to me.

"We can certainly try. How is your credit?"

Barkley and I looked at each other, and I almost laughed.

"I'll be honest with you. I don't have bad credit, but I don't have much credit either. I'm an old-school check-writer."

"Well, checks are money." He handed me an application, and I glanced at it, wondering what rabbit I was going to pull out of my ass to make this happen.

"Why don't you fill that out and scan it, then email it to me." He handed me his business card. "I'm actually late for another showing, but Electra is a great client, and you came highly recommended."

Even though I didn't really know Electra, I felt like I did, and I was warmed by her faith. Apparently she hadn't seen my checking account lately. The dog walker to gallery owner trajectory was not a fast track.

"Great. Thank you so much. I really appreciate it. The space is exactly what I need."

So Ken Doll Kyle left us standing on the curb looking at my future gallery, the two dogs at our feet.

"Do you believe in me? In this?"

"Absolutely," Barkley said, and he meant it.

"The space is perfect, but I'd need someone to cosign. I wonder how my mom's credit is . . ." I trailed off. "I have ten grand of 'marriage money,' but realistically I would need another ten to open it."

"That sounds like a doable number. I'll have my guy write some-thing up. We'll call it a starter loan. Sound good?"

"Wait, are you serious?"

I could feel a tingling in my fingers, like maybe this could actually happen.

Sumner barked twice in resistance, as if to say, *stop! don't give her your money!*

"What are you going to call it?" Barkley asked.

"Not sure," I said. "Let's just see if it happens."

"Oh, it's happening," Barkley said. "I can feel it."

CHAPTER 45

UNFOLDING

My mother had started drinking wine at night, only one or two glasses, but I think it helped. I often joined her, and she seemed to have a stronger appreciation of me, and vice versa. Deep down we knew that if Brady left us, all we'd have is each other, and that going through this alone would be worse than going through it together.

"You know," I told her that night as Brady dozed off, "I always resented the fact that you checked out when you met Charlie, but now I get it. You needed that."

"Well, that train has left the station," she said, downing her glass.

"There'll be other trains," I said.

"Well, let's just say my prospects are thinning every day."

"Mom! Sixty is the new forty."

"We'll go with that. So how'd it go? With the space you looked at?"

I filled her in, and she seemed genuinely happy for me, which made *me* happy, if that was even possible given what was going on.

I slept in the chair in Brady's room that night, which I was getting used to. Besides, no matter how much I pumped up the air mattress, I always ended up on the floor. It was inevitable and inexplicable, like losing socks in the dryer.

The next day, Jane came to take Brady to the park, and my mother went to a matinee. I was all alone in the apartment, my brain bubbling over with thoughts about the gallery, so I just started doing stuff.

First I called Liv, and she actually answered on the first ring.

"So it looks like I'm actually starting a gallery here, in DC."

I could hear the sound of her sipping. I waited for some snide comment, but she said, "Page, that's the best news I've heard all week."

"Thank you. It's come at a weird time, but I'm going with it."

"That's the spirit."

"Langhorne's 'Somewhere Else' is going to be the focus, and I've got some great Impressionists," I told her.

"Of course, of course."

I was dumbfounded. I thought the woman hated me, but it was most likely my previous lack of ambition she abhorred.

I could hear the other line beeping, and she said, "Just send me all the details when you have them. We'll put it in our email blast."

"Okay, thank you so much!"

I then called Michael of Austria, who said he would consign some of his skulls. I emailed Kevin again about the wall, and Barkley confirmed the "starter loan" and that he'd cosign the lease. Since the wire to Langhorne hadn't gone through yet, I could print out a decent bank statement.

When Mom got home, I asked her for the marriage money, and she said yes immediately (Brady must have prepped her for this). After Barkley's loan, that would buy me another month, and I'd have a reserve for utilities.

"I'm kind of getting married," I told her. "I'm actually getting a life. The man will come later. In fact, it may just come in the form of BR and his winery."

"What?" Mom asked.

"I'll get into it later."

I talked her through the wiring instructions online, reading her my routing number. I was surprised by her efficiency. There was a time when she couldn't even open an attachment. Thank God for Apple.

Groups of pigeons circled outside the giant windows of Brady's home office. The translucent shades were drawn, so the birds looked like fleeting shadows—the effect was magical. I closed my eyes and did my little prayer for Brady, which just consisted of the word *please* over and over again. I don't know who I was asking, but I was hoping the universe would hear it.

My mother went to make more coffee, and I started to draw up contracts based on the ones Liv emailed me. This was my specialty, having overseen so many deals at the gallery in New York. I could do it with my eyes closed. I planned out how many pieces I would start with and sketched their placement on a pad.

At my estimated price points, one or two sales within the first two months would pay back Barkley and Brady. The great thing was, I didn't have to do hardly anything to the space. I wrote at the bottom of my application that I needed the sinks to be removed, and the floors waxed, and then scanned and emailed it to Ken Doll Kyle.

That night, Brady looked better, like getting fresh air with Jane had done him good. But there was frailty in his voice, which I was having a hard time getting used to. He asked me about the gallery, and I gave him general answers, to play it down.

"How is Elbow going?"

"It's amazing what they're doing. They are all coming together and really showing up, and the numbers are getting better. The thing can run without me, apparently."

"Not really. But that's great. Hopefully it won't be long before you're back."

"I don't miss the work as much as the people. And it sucks to not be mobile."

"I know. When we were kids, you were always moving. You would even run in your sleep."

"Well, at least I didn't steal the covers."

I took his own covers and pulled them up to his neck.

"Hey, will you put this on?" He picked up an album from his bed and handed it to me.

It was Joni Mitchell, the one where she looks angelic on the cover, but also eerie, which kind of described the music, which we sat listening to for I don't know how long. I just know that at one point he reached out his arm, and I grabbed his hand and held it, saying my *please* prayer again.

Jane came in late, crawling next to Brady on the bed, and I gave her a nod, heading sleepily into the office. Even though it was pointless, I pumped up the air mattress again. Maybe this night would be different. Maybe miracles do happen. Maybe the lost socks resurface. Maybe after hearing my *please* so many times, the universe would answer with an *okay*.

CHAPTER 46

GALLERY GIRL

My phone buzzed at 7:00 a.m., and I sprang up for it, hoping it was Ken Doll Kyle saying my application was accepted. But the name on the screen was the last one I expected: Jack.

Miss u, how r u?

I made a deflating noise and lay back down on the air mattress, which also made a deflating noise. I turned the screen off and went back to sleep. An hour later, the phone woke me up again, but this time it actually *was* Ken Doll Kyle.

U got approved!

Meet me there @ 2pm

I got up and did a little dance around the room. Then I looked at myself in the mirror. My hair was a mess, but my face looked way younger than thirty-four. *Fuck it*, I thought. *Who cares? I am what I am. And I'm gonna start a gallery!*

But then the balloon of excitement popped, and my insides went cold. My brother was in the other room, possibly dying. What would a gallery mean to me then? *Goose egg*, my father would've said.

There was a note on the kitchen counter from Jane saying he was sleeping and that she was on her morning run. Then she wrote which meds he still needed to take with food. Mom was still asleep in the guest room, or what I still liked to think of as my room.

I made us both smoothies, and him a piece of the quiche Jane had cooked (for some reason, quiche was the one thing he'd usually eat). When I brought it into his room, he was already up, listening to music on his headphones. He took them off and asked me to stop the record spinning on the side table. It was the Indigo Girls.

"Hmm," I said. "Never thought you were a fan."

"You don't remember 'Closer to Fine'? I first heard it in a CVS and stayed in one place, listening, until it was over."

"Before Shazam, huh?"

He chuckled. "Yes, before we all began the slow descent into our screens."

I fed him a bite of his quiche, happy that he didn't resist.

"We find out later today if all of this is working," I said. "Dr. Bang Me is supposed to call."

He laughed again, this time without the cough.

"Page, you can't call her that to her face."

"Of course not!"

He took a huge sip of his smoothie. More color had returned to his face. I thought about all the things I had to do that day, but they all seemed petty, completely irrelevant. I told him just that.

"Page, this is your moment. It's your time. You can't let me stop you from any of that."

I gave him the little minibowl of pills and a glass of water. He downed them with aplomb, used to it by now.

Jane came in, sweaty from her run, and went into Brady's bathroom to shower. Listening to the water through the closed door, we sipped our smoothies. I tried to feed him another bite of the quiche, but he grabbed the plate and fork, saying, "I can do it."

His hands were a little shaky, but he was determined. Just as he almost got it in his mouth, the quiche crumbled onto the covers.

"Fuck!" he yelled so loud it startled me.

I tried to find the pieces of egg, but he pushed me away, facing toward the wall.

"It's fine, it's no big deal," I said.

Then he turned, his eyes glassy, looking so utterly desperate and out of control. "That's what I keep telling myself, but what if it is?"

I didn't have an answer. The only thing I could do was try not to cry myself, which turned out to be impossible.

When Jane came out of the bathroom, we were two messes, clutching each other on egg-mushed sheets.

Of course, Jane was the one who snapped us out of it. She just pulled the sheets off like it was normal routine, picked up the fork from the floor, and said, "How about something more simple, like toast?"

Brady looked at her as if maybe, just maybe, toast would solve everything. "Okay," he said.

I got him more sheets from the hallway closet and put them on the end of his bed for now. Then I went into the kitchen, where Jane was staring at the toaster, willing the bread to cook.

"It never cooks faster if you stare at it," I said.

"I know. I'm going to make some coffee, want some?"

"Yes."

She went about the process, her arm movements graceful as a ballerina.

"Jane, how do you do it?" I asked her.

"What do you mean?"

"You're always so together."

"Well, it helps to keep busy."

"That's the thing. I have all these things to do for my gallery today, but how can I do it when . . ."

"It's all the reason *to* do it, Page. You think Brady wants you sitting around with your finger in your nose? I'll be here, at least until three when I have a meeting I couldn't get out of. And your mom's here. Absolutely go do your stuff."

I thought about it. Maybe she was right.

We sipped our coffee, mine black, hers with almond milk. I wondered what we would do without her. Mom and I could've handled it, but nothing would've been going this smoothly.

"Jane, you know you're like, pretty much an angel, right?"

She rinsed her coffee cup at the sink, her upper body hunched over. She got quiet for a second, then swiveled around and looked at me with tears in her eyes.

"Don't tell him this, but I'm scared shitless."

I hugged her, and she moaned into my shoulder a little. When we separated, I grabbed a tissue (which we had all over the apartment now) and handed it to her.

"Gosh, you're even stunning when you cry."

"Stop."

"It's true. You guys are going to have incredible babies."

She laughed. "Let's get over this before thinking about a family."

"It's too late. You are family now."

She hugged me back, and this time it was me who couldn't help myself. Both of our shoulders were damp from each other's tears.

"Thanks, Page."

"No, thank you. You're totally inspiring."

"Really? Well, I don't know about that . . ."

"Absolutely."

I finished my coffee and rinsed my own cup in the sink, then grabbed my bag from the kitchen hooks.

"Will you text me when the doctor calls?"

"Of course. Go be Gallery Girl."

Gallery Girl. I had to admit, I liked the sound of that.

CHAPTER 47

PLAN B

I walked over to Barkley's to borrow his vintage red pickup truck. He wasn't there, but Mauricio had the key for me. First stop was Kevin's house, where I was to meet Jose-Luiz, the contractor whose number I got from Electra. He was standing outside in jeans and a flannel shirt, looking completely hot. I reminded myself there were actually straight guys in DC. At least two of them. "Thanks for meeting me on such short notice," I said.

"Of course," he replied, sneaking a glance at my legs. I checked him out too. He had that wonderful mix of a strong, muscled body and warm, light eyes. Not BR, but maybe Mr. BRB.

I led him inside and into Kevin's room. As he ran his hands over Kevin's wall, I couldn't stop staring at his tanned forearms. The good news, he explained to me in his sexy accent, was that the wall was originally wallpapered, then painted over, so all we would really need to remove it was a razor blade. He told me he'd do it for $125.

"A hundred cash and we have a deal," I said.

He smiled and then slowly nodded his head. While he went to work, I sat with Sammy, who whined a little as if to say, *does daddy know you're doing this?*

Jose-Luiz was right. It came off very easily. When he finished, he rolled it up carefully and sealed it with string at both ends. I tacked the tapestry back up. Amazingly, it hardly looked like anything had changed. Of course, we would have to rewallpaper the wall, but I would handle that. As we were leaving, Sammy barked at me, as if saying, *you're going to come to my house and steal a wall and not take me for a walk?*

"I'll be back, Sammy!"

Twenty minutes later I made it to the Navy Yard, which seemed like a whole different city. Everything was brand new, and the streets were lined with every trendy chain restaurant you could imagine. Rex's sprawling loft overlooked the Anacostia River where sailboats loafed and rowers darted.

He led me into the back where he had portioned part of the place off into a pseudo gallery space and showed me the five pieces he wanted me to represent. I chose three, giving the excuse of not having enough room. The two I rejected were large-form abstracts in odd colors, clearly impetuous purchases Rex was desperate to make good on (maybe at a garage sale). But the three we loaded into the truck were stellar, a Spanish painter à la Rothko with a bit more urgency. We signed the contracts Electra had drawn up, with the commission splits we had agreed on, and I thanked him profusely. He, too, seemed to be peering at my legs. Maybe it was Jane's pencil skirt I was wearing, the one she gave to me a few days ago when she was "purging" stuff. I could totally relate. I purged $500 skirts all the time.

Ten minutes later I was off, driving Barkley's vintage truck filled with art, and I hadn't even gotten the keys to the gallery yet.

I pulled down Church Street, the cutest little modern block with a few storefronts and chic apartment buildings. Ken Doll Kyle was waiting outside, this time dressed down in khakis and a pale-blue polo shirt. He noticed the paintings in the back and said, "I see we're not wasting time."

"Well, to be honest," I began, "and I know it sounds cliché, but it's my dream. I didn't know it until a few weeks ago, but this is the natural progression of where the trajectory of my life was supposed to go. I just got derailed. It took me forever to figure it out."

"Tell me about it. I have a dream, and it's not to be Realtor of the month," Kyle said.

He walked me around the place once more, we signed the lease, I gave him the check, and he gave me the keys. Five minutes later I was alone, in my own gallery, surrounded by four pieces of art, as yet unpacked or unrolled. I couldn't help myself. I squealed and spun around, yelling, "Oh my God!" But then I was brought back to the dark reality of my brother's situation. It was completely polarizing. I locked up the place and looked at the key in my hand. I could hardly believe it was actually happening.

As promised, I walked Sammy to the EDP. No one was there except the smiling woman with the Yorkie-poo and a hipster with a chocolate Lab. While Sammy tried with no luck to get close to the Yorkie-poo, I got a text from Jane.

Blood work came back better but not out of woods yet

After a few more minutes of furious texting, I learned that the cancer had been diminished, but he still needed the chemo for at least another three weeks. Jane was taking him in the morning.

I looked up at the sky and the tops of the buildings that surrounded the park. The world was alive, breathing. There was so much to do, so much that could happen. I pictured Brady and Jane in Montana, running a little place, both of them juggling work and kids with grace and composure. This couldn't be Brady's time to leave the earth. It just couldn't.

My phone dinged. It was an email from Rex's friend, the sign guy, who I had contacted earlier. I had decided to name the gallery Plan

B—after Brady, of course, with a little bit of my story in there too. He had included two sign mockups in the message. One was the name, over black, written in thin lights, but I thought it was too art deco looking. The other one was the winner: red lowercase letters on what looked like a piece of dark, lacquered wood:

PLAN (FINE) B (ART)

It fit the vibe of the neighborhood—understated. I looked toward the gate to see if April or BR might be coming with Pinot or Cab. No such luck.

But as I was leaving, Preston came in with Sumner.

"Girl, wait a second. I hear you like, already have a gallery now?"

"Yes! It came together really fast. The opening party is in three weeks."

"Oh my God, I'm so stoked for you. Barkley told me everything. He's bragging about it to everyone."

"Hey, would you want to help me out at first? I mean, I couldn't pay you much, but you don't have a full-time job right now, right?"

"No. Besides working on my line, I just babysit Barkley and Sumner."

"Right. So what do you think?"

"Sure. I'll come by tomorrow, and we can talk about it?"

"Great. Oh, and one more thing. I know you're going to attract all the rich gay men in the area to come in, but you can't wear sneakers. It's a gallery thing."

"Got it."

"Somehow I knew you'd understand."

We kissed on both cheeks, which seemed a little ridiculous, but that was my world now.

When I dropped Sammy off, there was still no sign of Kevin, so I left him a handwritten note.

K–

As you can see, it worked really well!

Thank you thank you thank you.

I'll email you the agreement to sign.

I hope I will make you a star☺

Oh, and I'll repaper your wall!

P

When I got home, the door to Brady's room was closed. It must have been Jane in there with him, as I heard muffled voices. Hopefully they were talking about the future.

I went into Brady's office and copied and pasted Rex's friend's design to make a PDF invite. After getting approval over text, at the bottom I added, *very special musical guest, April.*

I emailed it to Liv, and she wrote back saying she'd send the blast in the morning. I also emailed it to a FedEx Office so they could print out a master and make me a hundred copies. *Now,* I thought to myself, *I have three weeks to get everything together. But tonight, I'm going to drink some wine and hang out with my brother.*

CHAPTER 48

WE GOT YOUR BACK

The doorbell started ringing around six o'clock that evening. Brady had been to the restaurant on one of his good days, and most of his employees knew something was going on but didn't pry. But when Straight Jake let it slip to the hostess, the whole restaurant knew in a matter of minutes. The first visitor was Toby, an ex-dancer who had waited tables at Elbow the longest. He had a shock of prematurely gray hair and could totally pull off a mock turtleneck. I let him into Brady's room, and I could tell he was trying to act normal about his boss's appearance. Brady's face had sunken a little, despite the hopeful prognosis, and he hadn't been eating much since the last round of chemo.

"At least I have drugs," Brady said, and Toby laughed nervously. "Don't steal them."

"Me? Steal some Perc-me-ups? Not a chance. Maybe just one?"

"Shut up."

Toby was super tall, with a lithe dancer's body. As he approached Brady's bed, I kicked some of his dirty clothes under it.

"Do you want to hear about my waiter dream?"

"Bring it on," Brady said.

"Well, you gave me this really important table, but it was five blocks away, in an alley."

Brady started laughing, but then the coughing started. I wondered if this was the right time for his coworkers to see him. But what if something happened? He loved his crew.

"So," Toby went on, "the whole dream I was running back and forth. And every time I got to the table, the person would want something different. Like, I'd come with the coffee and the person would say, 'Um, I wanted decaf.'"

"I hate it when that happens," Brady said.

"Here's the worst part. Every time I asked you what I should do about it, you just laughed."

"How cruel of me to haunt your dreams like that."

"But then something switched. Instead of being annoyed, I just laughed with you, and it was our response to everything."

"As it should be."

"Anyway, I was thinking. We do laugh a lot at work, all of us. And that's largely because of the . . . culture you've created . . ."

Toby was starting to get emotional, so I suggested Brady get some rest. They went to shake hands, but Toby hugged him instead, and held on for quite a long time.

Most of the evening went like that, followed by me and my mother having a glass of wine in the kitchen with whomever had just visited. Angela, the barback with one too many tattoos, brought him "really good" cookies. She told us about the time she found Brady and John Cusack sitting on a crate of onions in the walk-in cooler, smoking a joint. "He was forever cool in my eyes after that," she said. Then there was Pete, the cook with the pockmarked face and the too-loud laugh. He was too late to see Brady, who was overstimulated at that point, but he took our offer of a glass of red. He told me that Brady once picked up his kid from school when he burned his hand badly on the line and had to go to the ER.

"That's my boy," my mother said, getting a little misty.

"You raised him right," Pete said.

"What about me?"

"We're still working on that one," my mother said. Normally I would have been offended, but she was obviously joking, and I realized then that my sense of humor may not be just from my dad.

Mom went to bed early, and when Jane arrived after having dinner at her parents' house, I filled her in on everything. I was a little sloshed at that point, so I made sure to eat one of her spinach lasagna squares. She poured herself a glass of wine and sighed.

"Did everything go okay with your space and everything?"

"Yes. It's happening. But like I said, it feels strange, even caring about myself right now. It doesn't matter, you know?"

"I know, but you have to remember that Brady wants it to."

"Yeah. But there's like, this cloud hanging over everything."

"Yes, but we got good news!"

"I guess. I didn't like the 'not out of the woods' part."

"Speaking of the woods, have you been to your French man's winery lately for crepes?"

I froze, midbite, remembering the BR lie at girls' night. From the look on her face, Jane already knew.

"Well, I did meet him, and I do want to date him, and we almost kissed, it just hasn't happened yet. And he's not French. That I know of."

"Your secret's safe with me."

"By the way, the skirt was a hit."

"Well, it must have been, you've got legs for days."

"Yeah. Let's just hope I have a brother for way more than days. Years and years. And you have a boyfriend . . ."

"How was he?"

"His total self, which is astonishing. Even being weak and on meds. It's like his smile overpowers everything."

"It always has," Jane said, swirling her glass of wine.

Before we both retired, I got out one of the old photo albums Brady had and showed Jane pictures of us together as toddlers. In one shot, it looked like I had knocked Brady's ice cream cone to the ground. He wasn't crying, but his face was in total shock, the look right before the tears. In another, we were both on a swing. He was looking at me, laughing, and I was looking away, like the people in Langhorne's piece. The last one was a picture of my father holding Brady, who was around four. Already you could see the resemblance. I only hoped, with every ounce of hope I had in me, that the resemblance was in spirit and looks only . . . that Brady wouldn't get dealt the same cards.

CHAPTER 49

CLOSE CALLS

The next two weeks were pretty insane. When I wasn't tending to Brady (the three of us had a schedule Jane wrote and printed out, always the efficient one), or at the EDP with Sammy, I was at the gallery space. Getting the phone installed, hiring people to wax the floors (Kyle's firm didn't agree to that), wash the windows, and install a special light for Langhorne's piece.

I found the perfect reception table at Design Within Reach, which I called Design Nowhere Within Reach after I realized it cost almost $2,000. But as Liv always said, never skimp on the non-art pieces in a gallery. You want the customers to feel like they are in the presence of an expert, and if that means a weekly manicure and an overpriced desk, then so be it. So I took out a business card with no annual fee for the first year. Jane helped me, explaining that it would actually improve my credit. And after the desk, all I'd need to spend was $500 more and I'd get sixty thousand miles. I could go to Hawaii! When I got the shiny card, it was like a key to the modern world (and maybe adulthood).

It was mid-May, and the city held an air of promise—or maybe it was just my wishful thinking. We still didn't know, but I had to believe that everything was going to work out. Brady had lost his hair really quickly, but he still looked handsome in the variety of hats that Jane, Straight Jake, and I bought him. Elbow got another write-up, which

I framed for Brady and hung in his room. He acted like it was no big deal, but one afternoon I found him looking at it with tears in his eyes.

"Brady," I said from the doorway.

"Thanks for that. It's nice to know I've made some kind of mark."

I led him back to his bed.

"You'll be making a lot more marks."

"I'm not so sure," he said.

It was very up and down, with the treatments and the meds. But Jane and I, and even my mother, were all being positive. We had to.

I had never forgotten overhearing someone in college refer to me as "Beige" instead of "Page." It didn't sink in until months later that the person was trying to be clever, insinuating I was boring. And come to think of it, I *was* boring in college. If only that person could see me now. Page, gallery owner extraordinaire. Move over Airport Bar, make room for a Bright Light. Brady had made another mark on me, and thanks to his belief and support, I was on my way to hopefully making one of my own.

There was one thing I hadn't fully realized about the neighborhood the gallery was in. It was a little gritty. It reminded me of New York, and Jack—who had since texted me three more times, asking if he could visit. Yeah, that wouldn't be weird at all! Let's do sushi!

A few days before the launch, Dr. Bang Me told Jane that the cancer had come back a little, but that she was still hopeful. The same day, Jose-Luiz came to fix the sink in the small bathroom, and he also cleaned the baseboards. When I went to pay him, he said, "How about instead you take me to lunch?"

There was a flash in his wheat-colored eyes, something that said he was hungry for more than lunch. I felt reckless, and disillusioned. I wanted the doctor to say the cancer was gone. I wasn't sure how much longer I could deal with the uncertainty of my brother's life. I took Jose-Luiz to Logan Tavern and watched him eat his burger while I sucked down two margaritas. After lunch, he took me to his apartment in

Columbia Heights, and we fucked desperately on his futon, underneath the glow of his fish tank. I didn't realize how long it had been. Yes, I had plenty of sex with Jack, but not this. This was train-whooshing, sky-opening, my-brother-might-be-dying-and-I'm-in-denial, I-don't-even-care-that-I-haven't-showered-or-shaved sex. It reminded me that I'm a sexual being, deep down, and that I had been deprived for so long. Afterward, we drank beers in our underwear, and he told me that he really wanted to be a cook, but being a contractor just happened.

"It's never too late," I said.

"Yes, I think so."

I knew he meant no, it's not too late, but I didn't correct him.

I talked about Brady, because I had to. I still hadn't told anyone, except Barkley, who caught me crying in the gallery after a particularly hard afternoon caring for him. Jose-Luiz looked at me deeply, like he knew all about pain, and death, and dying. Still, his eyes seemed to be saying, *Don't worry.* My heart was saying, *I will worry. I'll worry until the cancer is gone.*

"Page, how about I make you my mole sauce? Tomorrow night?"

What was I going to say? It was something out of a rom-com: the hot, straight, well-endowed man wants to make me his mother's chicken mole? Tough call.

"Sounds like a plan."

The next day, during my morning shift with Brady, we played cards and listened to music, and he showed me some properties in Montana he was looking at online. One had a tennis court.

"You thinking of taking up tennis again?"

"Why not?" Brady said. "Or I could make it a pool."

"Good idea."

When Jane took over the shift, I headed to the gallery, and it really felt good to concentrate on something, otherwise my brain went into a downward spiral. I texted April about what her setup would be at the launch, and she didn't mention anything about her father attending. But honestly, I wasn't as obsessed with BR at that moment. It may have been the Jose-Luiz distraction, but everything, including the gallery, seemed pointless compared to what Brady was going through.

Still, life brought small pleasures. Jose-Luiz's mole sauce was otherworldly. During dinner, he told me stories of his grandparents, who were apparently in the circus. He made me laugh and almost made me cry. Later, on the futon, I looked him in the eyes. He checked off the sexy Latin Lover stereotype, sure, but he was also smart, funny, and kind. Maybe it would become more than a fling.

Since Jane was on duty, I stayed the night, but when I woke up the next morning, Jose-Luiz was gone. As I was getting ready to leave, his landline phone rang. He had one of those archaic answering machines, and I could hear a woman, leaving a message in Spanish. She sounded rushed and slightly annoyed, like it definitely wasn't a "Hi, how are you, call me later" message. Far from it, actually. When I walked out into the courtyard of his building, two different neighbors were watching me intently. I waved to them and smiled. It was clearly a walk of shame, but I just smiled and *killed them with kindness*, like my dad taught me, though he probably wasn't envisioning this kind of situation when he shared that advice.

I walked to the Metro, wondering just who that woman was who left the message. His mother? Sister? I thought briefly about how weird it was being intimate with someone I barely knew. It was totally different than with Jack, but I wasn't sure that was a bad thing. On the train, I saw one of Brady's hostesses and gave her an invitation to the opening. When I got to the gallery, Preston was already there helping string the lights. He showed me a dress he had made for me, and I couldn't believe it. It was a perfectly tailored, midthigh length, gunmetal gray tube dress with a slight sheen.

"It's beautiful," I said. "Thank you!"

"I would say it would get you laid, but clearly that's already happening." He ruffled up my already ruffled hair.

"Oh, is it ever," I told him.

I turned to look out the window and immediately dropped the bag of candles I was holding. It was BR, crossing the street. I jumped behind the desk and crouched at Preston's feet, completely hidden. Okay, maybe I *was* still a little obsessed with him.

"What are you doing?"

"It's BR. I don't want him to see me like this! I'm not here!"

Preston shushed me as the gallery door opened.

"Hi there," Preston said, a little too cheerfully.

"Hi . . ." BR sounded confused. "Wait, didn't I see you out in . . ."

"Virginia! Yes. Love that winery. Your winery."

"Did you realize you left the wines you bought?"

I was sweating now, staring at Preston's Cole Haan shoes and trying not to breathe.

"Oh, I know. Page, she was . . ."

"Indigestion, was it? Is she around, by chance?"

Luckily Preston was all business, talking up the opening and handing him an invite.

"She'll be at the opening, obviously. You'll have to come."

"Yes, my daughter told me about this. I will try to make that happen," BR said, and I could almost feel him winking. After he was out the door, Preston said, "Coast is clear."

I got up, trying to dekink my neck from crouching in a ball under the desk. "He is so on to us. Thank you, though, Preston. I owe you one. Do you think he knew something was up?"

"Yes, but it will endear you to him when you tell him your dorky stories of how you were crushing on him. Trust me, I can tell he's super chill."

Just then a text came in from Jose-Luiz. Preston rolled his eyes.

"Someone's super popular," he said.

He'd texted a few times, but I was too preoccupied to respond. Tomorrow was the gallery opening, so I went to the EDP in the afternoon to decompress. I gave the Sad Poodle Lady an invitation, as well as Umbrella Woman, who looked at it like it was going to blow up in her delicate hand. Her greyhound seemed equally freaked out. On my way out, I ran into Nadine, the little white head of Beanu peeking out of her bag. I said hi and petted her dog's tiny head.

"I don't know why I bring her here. She doesn't even move."

"Maybe she likes to see the other dogs?"

"That's what I'm thinking."

Nadine looked tired, and she didn't have her bracelets on. I asked her how everything was going.

"Mean Face is completely out of the picture. But I have my sights on a country boy," she said. "Like, a real country boy. He actually has cattle!" She took out a flask that had a picture of the Eiffel Tower on it.

She handed it to me, and I took a swig, the warm liquid burning my throat.

"Whiskey?"

"Bourbon," she said. "I'm celebrating. No more horrible guys in my life."

"Yes! I'm celebrating too," I said, handing her a flyer for my opening.

"Holy shit. You did it!"

"Yes."

"Girl Power."

"Something like that."

Beanu licked Nadine's face, like she was proud too.

"Well, I want to meet him."

"Country Boy? Absolutely. He says 'y'all' and plays the ukulele!"

"Wow. Where'd you find him?"

She took another swig from the flask.

"Bumble! A friend of his made an account for him. He's kind of tech-challenged, but who cares? He's definitely not sex challenged."

"Ha."

"What's up with Banana Republic?"

"Well, I haven't seen him much 'cause I've been so busy, but I did have a tryst with this contractor guy."

"Ooh la la."

"I can't really be attached right now."

"I know, but that's when it usually happens, doesn't it?"

"I guess."

Beanu started licking Nadine's face again, with more gusto than before, which meant she wanted to go.

We hugged, and she promised to come and bring her new guy.

"What's his name?" I asked.

"You're not going to believe it."

"What?"

"Rusty! It's short for Russell, though, so it's all good."

"Russell for the parents, Rusty in the bedroom."

"Oh my God, you're so naughty! Love!"

I laughed, then kissed Beanu on her tiny white head, and they were off.

CHAPTER 50

SECRET WISHES

I got back to Brady's to find Jane crying on the doorstep. I sat down next to her as she tried to compose herself.

"I've kept it together," she said. "But tonight, he just . . . I don't know . . . he's so out of it."

I held her, and she rested her head on my shoulder. I knew what she was feeling. Sometimes he seemed completely normal, and sometimes it felt like death was lurking right outside his door.

"I know, I know," I said. "But none of us could be doing this without you. In the beginning, my judgment was wrong. I thought you were . . . well, maybe a little shallow. But you have so much depth, Jane, much more than I'll ever have. You're not just one of the Sweater Set."

"The what?"

"Forget it. What I'm saying is, you're what, twenty-six?"

"Seven."

"Wow, the world has no idea . . . you've got a huge future."

"I know, I just want it to be with your brother."

Jane started to sob. I hugged her as hard as I could without breaking her. After a minute, she calmed down.

"I'm still coming tomorrow," she said.

"Oh God, this is terrible timing. What about Brady?"

"It's all set. We've got a cane, or a wheelchair if he needs it, and Dr. Langley is going to give him steroids, so he'll be energized."

I shook my head in disbelief. She really had everything covered. I looked at her, and she smiled a little, a spark flashing through her dewy eyes. It was another moment of "everything's going to be okay," even though we had no clue.

I sent Jane home to get some real rest, and then I went to check on Brady, who was fast asleep. I reached out and touched his bald scalp. He was very warm. I noticed the drawer of his nightstand was open, and underneath a few prescription bottles were some loose pieces of lined paper. On one, he had doodled a picture of a house with mountains behind it, his version of Montana I guessed. On another, there were a bunch of tic tac toe boxes where no one had won. Who even wins that game unless you're playing with a two-year-old? The one on the bottom was a handwritten list, and my heart flipped over itself when I saw it:

WHAT NOT TO DO AT MY FUNERAL

1. *I know it's cliché, but I still love the song Hallelujah. But please, only Leonard Cohen's version—definitely not Rufus Wainwright's version (too nasal).*

2. *Don't serve anything nonalcoholic. Drink tequila or wine and tell stories. They don't have to be about me. Or if they are, don't make them embarrassing. Actually, I don't care. Just don't sit around being sad.*

3. *Don't be quiet. Sing something. Even if you suck. Even if it's some one-hit wonder from an '80s hair band.*

4. *Don't say that I was too young, or taken too soon. It may be true, but it just makes it worse.*

5. *Don't worry. Go on with your life. Once in a while, light a candle, and think about how life was with me around.*

Drops of tears fell out of my eyes and splattered on the wood floor. I tucked the note back where it was, like a child who knows she saw something she shouldn't. He was thinking about this? Should I be thinking about this? Were we all still in some sort of major denial?

My brain was racing, but I tried to calm down, settling into the chair next to his bed in case he woke up in the middle of the night. I listened to him, breathing steadily now. The breath of someone with a fully functioning heart.

In the early morning, I woke to the sound of Brady clearing his throat. The first rays of sun pierced through the window, giving the room a sobering clarity.

Brady looked hopeful for a moment, but then his face collapsed.

"Every time I wake up," he said, "for a split second it feels like everything's normal, that this isn't happening. Then it kicks in."

"Yeah, same here, and it's not even happening to me. But it feels like it is. Like you're an extension of me. You always have been."

"Don't worry, Page, I'll save you a space up there," he said.

"*Shh.*"

He was well enough to shower on his own. Mom had already made us coffee and eggs, and when I came back with some, he was sitting in the chair with his headphones on, listening to Brandi Carlile. I handed him his coffee, and he nodded. Except for the hair being gone, he looked good. Better than yesterday for sure. I looked at my watch. Jane would be here in twenty minutes.

I took a shower and changed, then cleaned up the kitchen as best I could. When Jane arrived, she switched out Brady's eggs, which he hadn't touched, to one of her quiche slices, which he devoured. She definitely had more of the right touch in that department.

My phone buzzed, and my mother, not one to ever miss a beat, said, "Who is Jose-Luiz, and why is he sending you hearts?"

"Oh, he's just a friend. My handyman."

"Super handy," Jane added, coming up behind her. They hugged, and I snuck out.

The sky was clear, the air was clean, and everyone seemed to be smiling. I tried to smile back, but it wasn't really working. I kept thinking of Brady's list. One that I hopefully would never need.

CHAPTER 51

THE BIG NIGHT

It was a mild and breezy Thursday evening. As Preston lit the candles, April's boyfriend, Jorie, brought in a small sound system they set up in the corner, and Straight Jake arrived with champagne and trays of apps from Elbow. I looked around the space. With the candles and the strung-up lights, everything seemed to glow. The collection of art wasn't exactly thematic, but I tried to separate them in sections. Rex's Impressionists on the back wall; Kevin's huge doodle along the side, lit by blue halogen; Michael of Austria's skulls on little platforms dead center, lit from beneath; and of course, Langhorne's masterpiece, "Somewhere Else," in the window.

I decided to walk around the block for some fresh air, and when I arrived back fifteen minutes before the scheduled start time, there were already about thirty people there, one of whom was from the *Washington Post*. He recorded a short interview with me on his phone and asked me what the inspiration behind the gallery was.

"Well it's all been unexpected . . ." I paused, realizing I should have been prepared for this. The reporter gestured for me to go on.

"What I meant to say is that to get here, to stand here with you, it's all come from putting myself in unexpected situations. It's a hundred small sparks that merge together to shine a light. That's what I hope the artwork does for people. Makes them blinded. Makes them . . . awash in brilliance."

I really didn't know what I was talking about, but it seemed to be working. Someone handed me a glass of bubbly, and I downed half of it.

"I noticed there was a Langhorne Rey piece in the window. What's your connection to him?"

"I discovered him, in New York. Accidentally."

The reporter smiled. I knew he wanted dirt on Langhorne, but I diverted those questions until he was done.

By seven thirty, the place had completely filled up. When Jane and Brady arrived, everyone clapped. She looked radiant in a white dress, next to Brady in his blue suit and skull cap, only needing a cane. As usual, his smile was shining across the room. My mother took pictures (or at least tried to) of everything with her phone. Jane ran over to air-kiss the Sweater Set, who accessorized with pearls and their Ivy League-turned-banker fiancés. I told myself that tonight I was going to learn their names. I'm sure, like Jane, they had substance, and I really needed to stop being so quick to judge people.

Michael of Austria and his posse of international movers and shakers perused the room, carrying with them the scent of cigar mixed with Vetiver cologne. He told me I looked "stunning" and asked what I planned to do after.

"I just need to get through this!" I said.

"Yes yes yes," he said. "Your big night!"

Barkley was in a three-piece vintage suit, of course, and he brought Mauricio, after I insisted.

"Sumner couldn't make it, but he gives you his best wishes," Barkley said.

I pulled him aside and told him, "You know, I couldn't have done this without you."

He blushed, dabbing at his forehead with his monogrammed handkerchief.

"What was it that you saw in me?" I asked him.

"To be honest," Barkley said, making sure no one could hear him, "I saw a little bit of myself. The fact that you were there, at the dog park without a dog. It took guts. And you wanted to belong to something. It's the same with me. My whole life I've tried to belong to something. In fact, I'm still trying."

"But you have Preston, and Sumner, and . . ."

"Yes, well, we create our own little islands of misfit toys, don't we? But all this"—he gestured around the packed gallery—"this is your island. And it's only the beginning, trust me."

"Well, thanks for talking to me that day. And more importantly, looking at me like I was someone . . . I don't know, worthy."

"Beyond, my dear. I'm so proud of you."

Kyle and a group of equally attractive young guys walked past us.

"Just keep Preston away from that one," Barkley said.

"Who, Ken Doll Kyle? He's got nothing on you."

Felicia and Greg walked up to me as Barkley and Mauricio made their way into the crowd.

"Congratulations!" Felicia said. "It all happened so quickly!"

"Wow, thanks, you guys, for coming all the way down here. It means a lot."

The following silence was a little strained. Greg's suit was too tight, and he tugged at it while Felicia kept glancing around the room. She spoke about their upcoming wedding, but something in her face was different. Her happiness seemed painted on, like a kid who's not happy smiling for a picture. I hoped I was wrong. She was a good person, and she deserved true love.

"I hope we can stay in touch, Page. And that you'll come to our wedding, of course."

"Absolutely."

"Is everything okay with Brady?" she stage-whispered.

"Oh, yeah," I lied. "Just a bump in the road. He's fine."

She hugged me, then turned and walked away, and somehow I knew that I wouldn't attend the wedding. It felt like Felicia and I had grown apart. Still, given where I was standing right then, anything was possible.

My mom came over and arranged my hair a little. I didn't squirm away. "You know," she said, "this is incredible. What you've done. I'm bragging to everyone that I'm your mother. Is that okay?"

I laughed. "Go for it. I'm glad I finally gave you something to brag about."

"Honey, I've always bragged about the both of you."

Then she was off to refill her wineglass.

The rest of the attendees were all the real art people, in cuff links and shiny shoes, some in casual attire, a lot of them gathered on the curb, unable to take their eyes off Langhorne's piece. It figured, the one piece I wasn't selling. But it definitely gave the gallery a certain panache.

Kevin, who had lost a lot of weight and now swore by the doctor we sent him to, arrived looking scrubbed and handsome, and I made a point of introducing him to Rex and Electra.

"I can't believe I'm here, seeing my work on display."

"It's beautiful, Kevin. You deserve it."

We looked at some of the guests staring at the "uber-doodle," as I'd named it. Some were pointing out certain areas, and some had their heads tilted and their mouths open in awe.

"You know what I also deserve?" Kevin asked.

"What?"

"Someone who loves me back. I stopped following Penelope weeks ago, but I just recently threw out all the tapes."

"That's the best news ever," I said, hugging him.

Liv, overly Botoxed but looking chic, pulled me aside and gave me the lowdown on some of the people who had come in from New York. She said a few of them had very deep pockets. Before she went back to mingle, I thanked her again.

"I knew you had it in you, Page," she said. "I think you'll do well with the oils—might want to rethink the skulls, they're reading a bit morbid."

Maybe she was right. But it was what I had to work with, and though some people avoided them, others seemed intrigued. Especially Greg, who was currently standing next to them, talking to Michael of Austria.

Preston was cool and collected, schmoozing the art people, and I realized he was exactly the right person to hire. He quieted the crowd before April played, and when she started to sing, you could hear a pin drop. It was astounding that someone so young could make it seem so effortless. Her voice was ethereal but also grounded, a blend of sandpaper and honey, and the songs were unassuming—simple but powerful. After she was done, I pulled her aside and told her she was incredible.

"Thanks, Page. It was technically my first live show."

"You'd never know it!"

Before I had a chance to ask about her father, Jose-Luiz showed up, in a red checkered sport coat that somehow worked. He picked me up and swung me around a little, and the jaws of the Sweater Set dropped in unison. I noticed my mother whispering something to Brady, who was standing with Straight Jake.

"I have something for you," Jose-Luiz said.

"I'll bet you do. But right now I need to mingle a little, okay?"

He smiled, but then his face contorted as he looked beyond me. In walked a short woman with wavy hair and piercing black eyes. She stood there and stared at us like she was a firecracker about to go off, then turned around and walked out. Jose-Luiz followed, and I tried to act like what had just happened was completely normal.

As I met all these new people, I had one eye on the sidewalk, where Jose-Luiz was obviously getting chewed out by the short woman. Must have been the same person who left the answering machine message. An ex, maybe?

I spoke to each member of the Sweater Set, whom I would now refer to only as Emily, Madison, and Serena. I found out that Emily was a triathlete, Madison was a midwife, and Serena had worked for Obama. Everyone was interesting, it seemed, if you dug deeper and looked past the surface.

Aside from the Jose-Luiz wrinkle, it felt like the wedding I would never have—even the Sad Poodle Lady showed up, with an awkward dress and makeup that looked like it was applied by a five-year-old. I was touched.

Since everyone insisted, I gave a small speech.

"I just want to say thank you for being here and celebrating this milestone with me. And how about April?"

The crowd whistled and clapped.

"I am still pinching myself that all this is happening. Some of you have asked if the B in Plan B stands for anything, and it does. It stands for Brady, the name of my big brother right here."

Everyone hollered and clapped, and Brady did a little bow. My mother was crying, of course, and Jane handed her tissues.

"Brady has always been my right-hand man, and I love him more than anything in the world . . ."

I could've gone on, but it felt like it was enough. Inside, I knew it wasn't enough. I needed him back. I needed him healthy.

"How about the dog park contingent?" someone yelled.

About ten people hooted and whistled.

"You're all the best, especially Barkley, Preston, Nadine, and Kevin. You know, it may be a coincidence, but when I started going to the S Street Dog Park, everything changed for me. Maybe now I should actually get a dog."

The crowd laughed.

"Also, thank you to my mother, for teaching me how to drink . . ."

More laughter.

"No, really, for never giving up on me. Some of us blossom after the rain. Cheers."

During the uproar of applause, I noticed a lot of misty eyes. Even Michael of Austria looked choked up. Barkley had his arm around Preston, smiling ear to ear. Nadine and her "country boy" Rusty, who completely pulled off his cowboy hat, clinked their glasses. Kevin gave me a thumbs-up. Jane blew me a kiss. Brady gave me a bear hug.

"I love you, Peanut Butter," I said.

"I love you more, Jelly."

Over by the uber-doodle, I noticed a young woman in an elegant dress who, after finding out that Kevin was the artist, clearly started flirting with him. It was unbearably sweet.

The rest of the night was kind of a blur. I remember Preston telling me that two people were interested in one of Rex's oils, a random guy dropping a champagne glass, and a lot of praise and congratulations.

By the time it was all over and Straight Jake had cleared all the platters, I was absolutely exhausted. Jane and my mother were taking Brady back home, and the only people left were April and Jorie, who were loading their stuff into his van in the alley. I helped them carry the microphone stand, and when I stepped outside, there he was.

Banana Republic.

"I missed it!" he said to April.

"It's cool, Dad. Jorie got it on video. You're probably sick of my songs anyway. We're going to run to CVS. Can you watch Jorie's van for a sec?"

"Sure."

BR turned to me and said, "So is she a star or what?"

"She brought the house down."

"That's my girl. I had to deal with Cab. My dog sitter was late, and I couldn't leave him alone."

"Of course!" I felt like I was in a dream state, that I might collapse right there. I straightened my dress and hugged him, because it was the only thing I could do.

When we released, I could see that he'd been crying.

"I might have to put him down. I don't know. I don't know if I can . . ."

I hugged him again, and he started laughing nervously.

"What am I doing? This is about you. This is your night. You look amazing," he said, like it was an undeniable truth. I couldn't see myself, but my face was probably purple.

"You're not too shabby yourself," I said. I touched the lapel of his coat. "Is this Banana Republic?"

"As a matter of fact, it is," he said suavely.

This was where everything became even more fuzzy. I thought he was going to kiss me—it certainly felt like he was—until I heard a familiar voice say, "Page," and I turned to see Jack getting out of a cab, walking toward us with a giant bouquet of flowers.

"Did I miss it? Shit," he said.

"Jack. What are you doing here?"

"Well, I heard you were . . . I . . ."

He was speechless, and so was I. April and Jorie came back, got in the van, and asked BR if he wanted a ride.

"Well, this is where we part, I guess. Page, congratulations. It was great seeing you."

BR got in the car and they pulled away, leaving me alone with Jack. I closed my eyes, then opened them wider to make sure what had just happened was real.

Jack just cockblocked BR? No. Fucking. Way.

I turned around and walked into the gallery, shut off all the lights, and locked the doors, and when I came back out, Jack was standing underneath the streetlight like a scolded puppy.

"Jack, I'm going to ask you once again. What are you doing here?"

"I wanted to support you on your big night."

He handed me the bouquet.

"Jack, you're a little late for support. You and I, we were comfortable. I know it's scary, but we both have to let go, so we can be there for someone new. Do you get it?"

He just stood there, shaking his head.

"I just took you for granted, I guess. Then Mimi died, and you started doing really well, and I don't know, I screwed up, Page. I screwed up."

He was starting to get emotional, and I just couldn't get drawn into it.

"Just go, Jack. Go back to New York, or go to a hotel. I need to have my own moment here."

I started to walk away, and luckily he didn't follow.

As I walked home, I saw a woman wearing a beret, smoking on her stoop. I handed her the bouquet of flowers, and she smiled.

I did it, I thought. *I freaking did it.*

CHAPTER 52

No Mo Drama

The next day, I woke up happy about the success of the opening, swiping through the memories in my mind. All amazing, except for the one at the end of the night. The missed chance with BR.

After having breakfast with Brady and Jane, and helping my mother (reluctantly) get on Match.com, I impulsively went over to Jose-Luiz's house to break it off with him instead of answering his multiple texts. I needed to keep myself open for BR.

But then he answered the door in a ripped T-shirt and boxers, and I could barely contain myself. I peeled off my jacket, and we started going to town on each other. I wanted sexual satisfaction, and he was a nice guy, so why not? I had just opened a gallery, so clearly I could make my own adult sexual choices.

Just as he got my bra open and was working on my jeans, the phone rang. It was the same woman on the answering machine, sounding even more perturbed.

I stopped him and said, "Is that the woman from last night?"

"Yes," he said. "Forget about it."

"But what's the deal? Is she your ex or something?"

At that point, I was so ready for him, it didn't seem to matter when he didn't answer. I leaned my head back, and a few seconds later, we were in full sex mode. But I couldn't get the voice out of my head.

"Who is she?" I whispered again.

He stopped, looked me right in the eyes, and said, "My wife."

I pushed him over so I was on top.

"What?"

One would think that this information would be a jaw dropper, but our jaws were occupied. We continued kissing and then it hit me, like getting a joke too late.

"Your wife?"

I jumped off him and started gathering my clothes.

"Your *wife*?"

"She lives in Colombia. She is not, we are not together."

"But you're married."

"Only by the book, Page . . ."

I put up my hand, even though I loved how he said my name, with a soft *g*. "Stop," I said.

After I got completely dressed, I stood at the foot of his bed.

"Jose-Luiz, listen to me. This has been fun, but you obviously have issues, and I have a gallery to start. So let's just call it a day."

"Call it a what?"

He looked like I'd just slapped him in the face. What was it with men? They think they should just be able to have it all?

I walked out of there half expecting the wife to ambush me from behind a tree. Thankfully, I made it to the gallery without a hitch, and I immediately got Preston up to date. First, he wanted to know about Brady (the secret was out, obviously) and told me he'd do anything to help. Then I told him about Jose-Luiz and the wife.

"The one from the opening? Oh, you definitely don't need that drama."

"Exactly."

"Okay, but I have news too."

"What?"

"April came by 'cause she left her scarf, and guess what? BR was with her! And he asked where you were!"

"No."

"I said you were under the handyman."

"Stop!"

"No, I said you were meeting with collectors."

"Perfect."

"And . . . are you ready? He left this for you!"

On the back of one of my cards he had written his name and number.

"Oh my God, he has a name!" I said.

"Mark," Preston said. "He's a total Mark."

I let out a whimper, staring in awe at the digits before me.

"Let's celebrate . . . happy hour at Annie's?"

"Preston, I'm just overwhelmed. I think the only thing I can do right now is check on Brady, then hopefully sleep."

He started fixing my hair a little. "I hear you. It's a lot."

"Brady . . . he wrote this list of things not to do at his funeral. It killed me. He doesn't know I saw it."

"That's deep."

"Yeah."

"Well, you just go make sure he's okay, and let us know if you need anything at all."

We hugged right in the center of the gallery, my gallery.

When I got back to Brady's, Mom was reading an article to him, and it was so sweet, I let them be.

In bed, I entered Mark's number into my contacts, then put the phone under my pillow.

CHAPTER 53

LIFE AND DEATH

Preston took care of the gallery as I became consumed with helping Brady through his next two chemo rounds, and even though I came close a few times, I just wasn't in the right frame of mind to call BR.

When I finally did call him a couple weeks later, it was too late. He was now casually dating someone, which he told me nicely through text. Still, I looked out for him every time I took Sammy to the EDP (Kevin was still in therapy, but doing great). It was April I ran into first. She seemed tired, her shoulders slumped. Pinot also looked tired, not his usual bouncy self. I knew it without her having to say it.

"Cab died."

She nodded sadly, then took out her phone to play some game that made strange noises.

I held Pinot's face and looked into his eyes, which seemed to say, *they took him, they took away my best friend.*

I started bawling, because of Cab but also because of Brady, and April tried to comfort me, but I couldn't stop.

"I'm sorry, April, it's my brother . . ."

"I know."

I took several deep breaths and tried to calm myself down.

"It's like I've always seen the brightness of the world, but this is different. I went through it once, with my father, and it broke me a little. I don't think . . ."

I started to lose it again, and April hugged me, and I instantly felt embarrassed, crying in a teenager's arms! She didn't seem to judge me, though, which was amazing.

"What about you? How are you doing with the whole Cab thing?"

"It sucks. Cab was wicked cool."

"He was the best."

"My dad hasn't left the house in a couple days, ever since they put him down."

"Oh." I took out a tissue and cleaned up my face. "I'll have to reach out to him."

"Cool."

April started playing with Pinot, who was dangling some used rope he'd found in front of her. She laughed, and it sounded like hope. Even in the darkest times, you had to laugh.

Jane was on a work trip, Mom was sick herself, and Preston was on deadline for some fashion reality show audition, so I closed the gallery for the rest of the week and stayed with Brady, who was still very up and down. One night he asked me to take him to Elbow, and even though it probably wasn't a good idea, I could see how much he needed it. We ate at the bar, and he seemed so in his element, even looking the way he did. It was clear he just wanted to be out in the world. Who wanted to sit in a bed all day?

When we got home, Brady asked if I'd stay with him until he fell asleep. We listened to some obscure indie band, and I ended up falling asleep next to him in his bed.

That Friday, Mark showed up at the EDP. He looked like he had showered for the occasion, and I could smell that simple Irish soap on him. Even through his loss, which you could see on his face, he looked as handsome as ever. And Pinot seemed a little more energetic. *Look, he was saying, Daddy came with me!*

I waved him over, and he sat right down next to me.

"Nice to see you out here," I said. "Did you get my texts?"

"Yes, thank you. Sorry, I've been . . ."

"It's cool. April said there was a little seclusion going on. I get it."

Mark smiled, then his face got serious. He took Cab's avocado toy out of his pocket. It had been mangled, but he held it like it was something precious.

"It was brutal, Page. He was looking me right in the eye when he died. The same look from when he was a puppy. I just told him over and over that he was a good dog. That he just needed to go to sleep."

Mark's eyes watered, along with mine, and I felt a flush in my cheeks.

"Then he just . . . he just closed his eyes."

I thought of Brady, probably still sleeping off the latest round of healing poison at home.

Pinot came and put his face in between Mark's left thigh and my right. The dog was so pure in his attention, looking right at Mark, rigid in his devotion. *You still have me*, he was saying. *You still have me.*

Mark put the avocado toy back into his pocket for safekeeping, then turned to me.

"So is your brother going to kick it?"

"The bucket or the cancer?"

Mark laughed and put his hand on my arm.

"The cancer."

"I hope so. Sometimes hope is all you really have."

"Yeah."

"That April, though, she's something else."

"Yeah, she's basically smarter than me at this point."

Sammy brought me a super gross tennis ball that had been licked and chewed by a hundred dogs. Still, I grabbed it and threw it, because that's what you do as a dog person.

"So I never got to ask you, why did you give me your number? For the back burner?" I asked him as I wiped my hands on my jeans.

He laughed. "Actually, at the time I was free game."

"I know, I lost my window of opportunity."

"I guess."

Despite Mark not being single, we definitely had a connection. The next few times I saw him at the EDP, our arms would brush against each other while petting the dogs, or I'd catch his eyes lingering on me a little longer than usual. But as I learned more about his current squeeze, Marissa—fitness guru, thirty-one, wrote a bestselling diet book—I started to think I was nowhere near his wheelhouse. Still, when he talked about her, his eyes didn't light up like they did when he talked about April, or Cab when he was a puppy.

The gallery only had one sale in its first month (Rex's Impressionist) but a lot of traffic. Preston was on me about "BR" as he still called him, and I told him it didn't look promising.

But then, one bright morning at the EDP, Mark put his arm on my shoulder and asked me how Brady was.

Right exactly then, I got a text from Jane:

REMISSION!

Balloon emojis flew up my screen. I showed Mark the text.

"That's fantastic," he said.

I burst out into tears and squeezed his arm, which was still around my shoulder. His grip was strong.

"Oh my God. Remission." I had to say it out loud. "Remission. I have to go see him. We have to celebrate."

"Absolutely!"

Even though the EDP was packed, right then it felt like we were the only people on earth, like our usual I'm-flirting-with-you-but-not-really thing had played itself out, and the train we were on was about to enter uncharted territory.

"Are you still dating the contractor?"

"Wait, how did you know about that?"

"I have my sources."

"No. He had some issues. He was a really good person, though. Mostly. What about you? Still dating Miss Diet Book?"

"Wait . . . how . . ."

"The internet," I said.

"Well, I'm done with Marissa. It didn't work out."

I tried my best not to scream with joy or break into some kind of improvisational dance. First remission and now this? Surely I was going to get hit by a bus within the next twenty minutes. But I didn't, making sure to look both ways and being extra cautious. There was a small, bright flower blooming inside of my heart. Brady was going to get better, and maybe Mark and I were possible. Maybe love was possible.

CHAPTER 54

FINDING HAPPY

When I got in the door, Jane grabbed my hand and led me to Brady's bedroom. He was sitting on his bed next to my mother, both of them beaming.

"You did it!" I said.

He nodded. "Looks like you're stuck with me."

I hugged him, and when I stood back up, I heard a scratching noise from behind his closet door. I looked at Jane, and my mother, and Brady. They all seemed to know something I didn't.

"There's a present for you in there," Brady said.

"Go ahead, see what's inside," Jane said, looking like she might burst.

I opened the door, and out came a vizsla puppy, who proceeded to lick my face. I saw the small scar below his eye . . . it was Happy, the dog I'd been wanting to adopt!

"Wait a second . . . how did you . . ."

"The computer," Jane said. "You left the browser up with the profile like, a hundred times."

I felt like I might explode with happiness.

"I wanted to wait until I, you know . . ." Brady trailed off, his eyes watering.

"Aside from you being healthy, this is the best, most amazing gift I've ever gotten," I said.

If there was such a thing as love at first sight, I was experiencing it. Happy sniffed my ears and turned around in circles. He was truly a happy dog. I could barely see through the tears in my eyes. My own pup!

"He's . . . oh my God, he's so beautiful!"

"There's a crate and toys and everything in the office."

"Brady was obsessed with getting the one you wanted," Jane said. "He's been planning this for weeks."

"It was a little selfish too," Brady said. "Because I thought if I worked on this thing, then the other thing would work out."

I hugged him again and looked back at Happy, who was jumping at my legs.

"You always loved your dogs," my mother said. "Now you've got your own. Just make sure you train him."

"The agency said he was good to go," Jane said. "Brady's technically Happy's guardian, but we can change the paperwork to your name. But they said he was potty-trained."

"Well," my mother said, "there can be accidents with new environments."

As far as I was concerned, the dog could pee on my legs right now and I wouldn't care. I was ecstatic.

"I can't wait to take him to the dog park!" I said.

"Yeah, that's a concept," Brady said. "Going there with an actual dog."

Jane laughed, and we all looked at Happy, who was doing another spin around. It was the cutest thing ever.

That night we had a little party. Brady's crew, the ones who weren't working, came over, as well as Barkley, who brought over a magnum of champagne.

Watching Happy jump all over Sumner while he scoffed at his affections was hilarious. But in general, Happy was adjusting so well. He didn't even bark!

Jane made chili, my mother made sangria, and Brady brought his record player into the kitchen. I closed my eyes and said to whoever was listening before, *Thank you.*

At one point, I was talking to Barkley and looked over at Jane half dancing with her arm around Brady, who was writing something on a Post-it notepad. He showed her what he had written, peeling off two in succession. Her face went through a dozen emotions, starting with shock and ending in joy.

Jane held the notes to her chest, and they danced some more, the notes falling on the ground. They were in this bubble of bliss, the two of them, like no one else was there. I walked over and picked up the two notes from the floor.

The first one read:

I want to give you all of me

The second one read:

Will you marry me?

"Oh my God!" I yelled, but no one heard me over the music. Jane and Brady had danced into Brady's room. I went over to his doorway and saw them, beaming at each other, sitting on the end of his bed. I opened the door a little farther. He was sliding a ring onto her finger.

"Wait a second, can someone tell me what's going on?"

"She said yes!" Brady sang out, like a boy who just won a game.

"Wow, congratulations!"

I hugged the both of them, then said to Jane, "My brother's a lucky guy."

"I'm the lucky one," Jane said.

"We all are. I'm so proud of both of you! Can we tell Mom?"

"Not yet. It'll be our secret, just tonight."

"You guys, I love you so much."

I felt my face heat up. It was overwhelming, all this love and hope around me. And my brother was going to be okay. I could say it and really mean it. Everything was going to be okay.

I let them be alone, but I was giddy with the secret I now shared. Later in the evening, Brady brought out one of his medical marijuana joints, and we all smoked some of it, even Barkley. Straight Jake had brought homemade ice cream from the restaurant, and my mother kept saying, "Oh my Goodness, what is this flavor again?" Everyone just laughed.

I remember thinking, *I'm getting high with my mother, and Brady is in remission. And he's getting married. And I have a dog!*

At that moment, life was more than good. It was great. Spectacular even.

CHAPTER 55

DREAM DATE

A week later, on the same day that I sold my second piece at the gallery, I got a text from Mark, asking to meet him at his place in Georgetown and to wear something sporty, but bring a nicer change of clothes.

"Sporty?" Brady said when I told him I was finally going on the date of my dreams. "Are you going rafting or something?"

"Let's hope not. Listen, Brady, I'm trying to be chill about this, but it's kind of hard. It just feels so *right*."

Brady, whose hair was starting to grow back, was looking at properties in Montana on his laptop. "You can live like a king there for nothing," he said.

"What does Jane think of moving to Montana?"

"She's kind of obsessed with the wedding planning right now, but I'm slowly getting her on board."

"Well, we all know everyone gives in to your charm. By the way, make sure you throw that list out—the one in your nightstand."

Brady's face flushed.

"You won't be needing that for a long, long time."

I hugged him, then pointed at his screen. "Make sure there's a guest room."

"There'll be room for a whole soccer team!"

As I started to leave, he said, "Page, just be yourself. But like, tone it down a bit."

I smiled and looked at myself once in the hallway mirror. I was sporty but chic, my outfit approved by Preston over text and pic sharing. My bangs had finally grown out. I had really good hair that could've been advertising shampoo.

Tone it down? Don't think so.

In the Uber on my way to his house, I thought of all the events that had led me to this moment. I was going on a date with BR! My brother was fine! My driver, a round-faced woman with Mardi Gras beads hanging from her rearview, said, "You seem really happy."

"Yes, I am," I said, and it was the first time in a long time that I really was. I was obviously excited about the date, but it wasn't about Mark. I would no longer rely on men for my happiness. I had found it in my gallery, in my friends, in my family. I had carved a place for myself in the DC world.

Mark's row house was painted yellow, and he came to the door smiling but didn't let me inside. "You ready?" he asked, leading me to his car. "C'mon."

"As long as we're not skydiving," I said, then added, "Well, maybe if it's tandem."

He chuckled as we got into his Land Rover.

Mark was wearing a gray pullover and blue sweats that were so thin I could see the muscles on his quads. We drove past Dupont toward the Penn Quarter, then into a lot near three huge dumpsters overflowing with wood scraps and rotted appliances.

"Okay," he said, "this may be weird, but our job here is to demolish a wall. My buddy's running this construction site."

Five minutes later, we were handed massive sledgehammers, and Mark told me to start. *What the hell*, I thought, and took a huge piece out of the wall between two conference rooms in the already half-gutted office building.

"That's what I'm talking about!" Mark said.

I kept going, and I never wanted it to end. I imagined the wall was Jack, and the cancer that killed my father and plagued my brother. I imagined the wall was all my insecurities, being annihilated. He kept looking over at me like he was impressed. It made me demolish even harder.

When we took a break, both of us sweating, he kissed me under an open doorway while a neighbor boy watched from the sidewalk. My whole body was swooning. I finally understood the expression "weak knees."

"I've wanted to do that for a long time," he said.

"You have no idea," I replied.

We went back to work, destroying the rest of the wall as dusk approached. The glass building across the street reflected the burning orange sun, making everything glow. As it turns out, glow was an understatement. I truly felt like a Bright Light.

After we finished, we got into the car and he said, "You were great in there."

"Ah, that was nothing," I said. "You should see me with a chainsaw."

He laughed and said, "We'll stick with sledgehammers."

As we pulled back onto Connecticut Avenue, I asked him why he took me there, to do that, of all things.

"Well," he said, wiping his brow with a black bandanna, "I recently asked these friends of mine, who've been married awhile, what their first date was, and they couldn't remember."

"What?"

We waited for an old couple to pass at the end of the block, the man leaning into the woman as they crossed the intersection.

"Page, it was the saddest thing. They didn't know! So I wanted to make sure, you know, if this . . . you and I, go further, that we'd always remember this date."

I looked out the window to hide my face, which I'm pretty sure was bright red.

Later that night, after I'd showered in his marble shower and put on the same little black dress that had started it all, Mark's neighbor, who was a Peruvian chef, cooked us paella, which we took up to his candlelit rooftop. I told him about my sale, and he told me about April, who was writing all these songs for a new showcase in New York.

"You must be so proud," I said.

"Yes, but also a little scared. I don't want her to get eaten up, you know?"

"She's too strong for that."

"She gets that from her mother."

Mark made a regretful noise, like he shouldn't have mentioned his ex, but we were beyond that. We had already talked about our exes in the park. Still, it felt different. We were officially on a date.

To show him I really didn't care, I kissed him. It felt so natural, and it was that moment when you realize the other person is a good kisser, a complete make or break in the book of Page.

Naturally, we started with a pinot and ended with a cab, both small-batch reserves from his vineyard. I was smiling so much I thought my face was going to fall off.

As our glasses clinked, and I said, "To your Cab."

"To my Cab," he repeated.

"May there be avocados in the sky."

He smiled, his eyes a little watery. The wine was bursting with flavor. Dark fruits with a hint of spice.

"So how did you get into winemaking?"

"I was a kid, really, traveling through Spain with a backpack, in this small, crumbling town. I had dinner at this hole-in-the-wall restaurant where the menu just said, 'red' or 'white.' In Spanish, of course. Anyway, I ordered the rioja and . . . what can I say? It just sang to me. It was both smooth and complex, with jammy fruits but also a hint of black pepper. I closed my eyes every time I tasted it."

I did the same thing as I sipped and listened.

"So anyway, I thought to myself, how am I going to get this? The bottle had no label. Like the olive oil and the tomatoes and pretty much everything else, it was made in the owner's backyard. After some insistence, they let me buy a bottle to take with me. I saved it for years, finally opening it by the river in Brooklyn with one of my oldest friends, who'd just had a baby against many odds. I thought about that bottle without a label, or more specifically, how wine can mark time and connect us in our own history. For me, it's not so much about the grape as the person who's tasting it. In other words, who you share it with is just as important as what the label reads. Every bottle has a story."

We clinked glasses.

"What's the story of this bottle?" I asked.

"Still unfolding," he said.

It was all I could do not to unfold myself right there on top of the paella.

An hour later I was in Mark's bedroom, and he was carefully unzipping my dress.

"This is happening?" I asked.

"Oh, it's happening," he replied.

He spun me around and kissed me hungrily. Lips, cheek, neck, collarbone, breast, and finally, nipple. I secretly thanked myself for going to Nadine's class regularly in the last few weeks. I needed to keep up with Mark, who had pecs that could've been sculpted by Michelangelo.

He took his time with me, like no one ever had before. I wanted to live in that moment forever, on his four-poster bed, with pictures of his vineyard on the walls, perfect lines of grapes rising and falling with the hills.

They say women like men to be endowed, but it's not so much the size as the shape and how they use it. Mark checked all the boxes in that department.

I sang to the sky and to art and to everything under the sun. I let myself fall into the night. There were no other thoughts, just pure connection.

He fell asleep first, making tiny, adorable noises that I wouldn't even classify as snoring. I curled into him, breathing in that woodsy scent, and thought, *Don't let this one get away.*

CHAPTER 56

MOVING ON

As promised, I met Langhorne in Washington Square Park, NYC, a year to the day after seeing him in Boston. He had done some jail time, and though he looked older, he seemed grounded. As we walked toward the Hudson River from the West Village, I filled him in on my life, which was working out pretty nicely.

"I'm so happy for you, Page. It's all as it should be."

"Well, there were some bumps."

"There always are, don't I know," Langhorne said.

I remembered the time I was ready to give up, crying in my brother's arms at three in the morning, and then that very same day someone bought one of Michael of Austria's skulls. A few days later, someone else bought Kevin's uber-doodle. It was the girl in the elegant dress who was flirting with him at the opening, and from what I could tell from his texts, they were now officially dating.

After that, it really started taking off. I met a student artist at Nadine's yoga class whose work I absolutely loved. They were photographs of children, painted over with washes, so that you had to really look at them to notice what it was. The price point was reasonable, and because she was unknown, she gave me 30 percent commission. They started moving out of the gallery pretty fast, and then someone put a deposit down on one of the Impressionist pieces.

"And your masterpiece is still in the window. You'll have to come see it sometime."

"I will. But I want you to know something . . ."

We stopped at a corner, waiting for the light to change, and he put his hand on my shoulder. "It's yours now."

"What? Don't be ridiculous."

"I'm serious. I want you to have it."

I didn't know what to say. The walk sign came on, and he had to push me as I had just frozen in place.

"Are you sure?"

"Absolutely. You deserve it."

I was starting to think maybe he was right, but I was definitely in shock. No one had ever gifted me anything of that value before. I couldn't stop smiling.

When we got to the park that jutted out into the river, we sat on a bench and watched people jogging, cycling, and walking their dogs. A dirty-looking kid with a guitar sang a lullaby while a businessman shuffled by him, frowning.

"Also, I want to apologize, Page, for, you know . . ."

"Kissing me in a weird moment? It happens."

"I thought . . . I was just lost."

"Lang, you always looked better with a model type on your arm, anyway."

"What makes you think you're not a model type?"

"I get cute a lot, not beautiful."

"That's the thing, Page. You never knew how beautiful you were. But you carry yourself differently now. Like maybe you are starting to."

I let my hair fall down so he couldn't see my face, because I knew I was blushing.

He took me to dinner at the Little Owl, where we drank a nice white burgundy and got caught up. He mentioned Liv, who he was working with again, and how he taught art in jail. Then he got me up to speed on the whole drama with his uncle and how he was supposedly getting some of his money returned. I told him about Brady and Jane planning their wedding and subsequent move to Montana, and my mother online dating. When he put me back on a train to DC, he promised to visit, and asked me if I would represent some of his new work.

"Duh," I said.

He smiled, kissed me (on the cheek, thankfully), and said, "I'll be in touch, Page."

A couple weeks later, I had some of Langhorne's new work in the gallery. They were large-form portraits, as if seen through glass. The price point was super high, but it did great things for my foot traffic. People were impressed. And to be honest, so was I.

One day, as I was closing the space, Felicia showed up out of the blue. She looked like she needed a drink, so we went to Logan Tavern, and over dirty martinis she told me that she and Greg never went through with the wedding.

"What happened?" I asked, acting more surprised than I was.

"He had been video chatting with this girl in Indonesia for like, two years," Felicia said, as if it really wasn't that strange.

"Wow."

"There was other stuff too. He had a whole hard drive of porn, not kiddie but some weird stuff."

"Ugh. I'm so sorry," I said, even though I was kind of happy for her. I knew that she and Greg weren't meant to be.

"It's fine. I actually ended up going to Julia Hurst's house, and we drank whiskey and ate popcorn and ended up kissing. So we're kind of seeing each other now. I really think it was fate. Did you know that I wasn't even going to invite Julia, until after my aunt ran into you here in DC? It's all connected!"

"Wait, you're a lesbian?" I asked.

"Yes. Well, I did always wonder about it, but never acted on it. When it finally happened, it felt right. Besides, fuck men."

"That's exactly what you will inevitably miss, though, fucking men."

She laughed. "Maybe you're right. Or maybe I won't. We'll see."

"So you came all the way down here to tell me this?"

"I'm actually on my way to a wedding, of all things, in Virginia, tomorrow."

"Ah."

"I won't be trying to catch the bouquet."

"Yeah, maybe run in the other direction."

Two martinis later, I dropped her off at her hotel and gave her a long hug. I didn't know what would become of her, but why did we have to figure everything out? No one's path was clearly marked. There were holes, slippery corners, and roadblocks. But for me, it had finally happened. I came of age somewhere around the middle.

EPILOGUE

A Few Days Later

Mark and I are walking along the Potomac River at the peak of the cherry blossom season. It looks like some kind of magical rose-tinted snow has fallen on the trees only. They look so delicate, as if you could blow on them and the petals would fly away, like a late-stage dandelion. I look over at him, and he gives me the smile that I like to think was created only for me. If it's even possible, he's more handsome than when I'd first seen him at the EDP. He has some unruly nose hairs, and he leaves his coffee cups everywhere, but he loves me unconditionally, which is the most important thing. Besides, I'm not exactly perfect. Who is?

Pinot runs ahead of us, chasing a squirrel. He misses Cab, as we all do, but he adores Happy, who circles us in a state of frantic delight.

Preston is at the gallery, over the moon, having just been selected for the next season of *Project Runway*.

As we make our way along the river, I think about how silly I was, pretending I was going to have the life I actually have now.

"Did you know that I used to call you BR?"

"No," Mark says. "What does that stand for?"

"Banana Republic. When I first met you, you looked like you had just stepped out of a Banana Republic ad."

He blushes, and it makes me do the same.

"Stop," he says.

Happy runs over, and I try to sneak him a treat without Pinot seeing, but it doesn't work. Pinot tries to take it out of his mouth, but Happy stands his ground, my canine True Love. I'm starting to think I have a human True Love as well. Right next to me.

"Did you know that I listened to the iPod you gave April?"

"What? When?"

Pinot barks a little, as if asking the same question. Happy whines a little too.

"It was before I knew you. She left it at the dog park, and I couldn't resist."

He blushes again, and I make a note to myself to try and make him blush as much as possible. He has that boyish quality that comes through often, but blushing is like a direct conduit—cuteness on tap.

I think, like I do a lot these days, of how lucky I am.

Mark stops and kisses me on my bare shoulder, and I feel a quick flourish in my heart, like I actually am worthy of someone like him, someone who will always have my back, in every way. Is it too good to be true?

As if some higher power answers my fears, when I get home that night I become sick—very sick. I wake up to go to the bathroom yet again, looking in the mirror, thinking, *Sickness, morning, morning, sickness, no . . . really?* I count back, and it hits me. *Yep, I'm very late.*

I text Brady, who is out to dinner with Jane.

He texts back immediately: Uncle Brady, I like the sound of that.

I smile at my reflection.

Maybe second chances do exist.

ACKNOWLEDGMENTS

THANK YOU

To my "girls" who are very much woven into the fabric of this story: Hilary Old, Jennifer Phelps-Montgomery, Flavia Stanley, Susie Holland, Lisa Rowe-Beddoe, Heather Cathcart, Alida Kinnie Starr, Nadia Saghafi, Amy Chamberlain, Katrina Van Pelt.

To Mike Boone, who opened me up to a world I knew would someday end up in a book.

To my wonderful agent, Christopher Schelling, for believing in me, and for having the best dogs ever (besides mine).

To my swift and clever editor, Alicia Clancy, who is full of killer ideas and a joy to work with.

To my lovely daughter, Rowan: I hope you read this one day and think I'm cool.

To my kind and loyal husband, Steve: you make everything better.

Lastly, to my readers. You held this book in your hand, you carried it around, in your bags, on your devices. You make it all possible.

ABOUT THE AUTHOR

Photo © 2019 Kate Drew Miller

Stewart Lewis is the author of six previous novels, including *You Have Seven Messages*, which has been translated into five languages. He is also an acclaimed singer-songwriter who has opened for such artists as Shawn Colvin, Graham Nash, Better Than Ezra, and others. He lives in Nashville, Tennessee, and Nantucket, Massachusetts. For more information, visit www.stewartlewis.com.